ALSO BY

AUDREY SCHULMAN

Theory of Bastards
Three Weeks in December
Swimming with Jonah
A House Named Brazil
The Cage

THE DOLPHIN
HOUSE

Audrey Schulman

THE DOLPHIN HOUSE

Europa
editions

Europa Editions
8 Blackstock Mews
London N4 2BT
www.europaeditions.co.uk

A catalogue record for this title is available from the British Library
ISBN 978-1-78770-395-7

Schulman, Audrey
The Dolphin House

Art direction by Emanuele Ragnisco
instagram.com/emanueleragnisco

Cover design by Ginevra Rapisardi

Cover illustration © Xuan Loc Xuan

Grey letters throughout the text are intentional.

Prepress by Grafica Punto Print – Rome

Printed and bound in Great Britain by Clays Ltd, Elcograf S.p.A.

CONTENTS

This is a work of fiction based on an experiment that happened in the summer of 1965 at a research facility in St. Thomas.

Although some of the events occurred, the characters are the product of my imagination and not based on real people, living or dead.

THE DOLPHIN
HOUSE

ONE
Tampa, Florida
Feb. 1965

At the age of 21, Cora got a job as a waitress in a club in Tampa.

It seemed right that the costume was difficult to pull on. She had to wiggle in and tug it on, then lie down to zip it up. The management required all the suits be cut one size too small. The outfit had ribs that pressed tight against her skin and pushed her breasts up. The result transformed her. Standing up, she was sleek and curved, had a rabbit's ears and a tail. She did not recognize herself in the mirror.

The things the men said, the things they did, she tried to consider as intended for the rabbit.

The work shifts were long. She developed welts along her sides from the costume's ribs. Her arms, strong from mucking out her dad's pigs, trembled by the end of the night from carrying the trays of drinks and dishes.

One plus was, in this echoing hard-surfaced club with the loud music, everyone was partly deaf and had ringing in their ears. Here, she had the advantage of knowing how to lipread. And, since her shift didn't start until five in the afternoon, she had the whole day to be outside.

She worked here for three months. Rented a room nearby and bit by bit finished paying off her new hearing aids, the ones that masqueraded as cat-eye glasses, no bulky transistor hidden in her clothing. Instead, everything was built into the thick arms of the glasses, a miracle of miniaturization. She was so grateful. Wearing these eyeglasses outside, under the right circumstances, she heard things she hadn't heard since she was eight. Paper crinkling, a bird chirping, her own gut rumbling. The first time she heard a child laughing, she jerked around from surprise. The toddler, some blond tourist kid, walked by, staring.

Of course, she didn't wear the glasses in the club. Management didn't allow that.

That final night at the club, she wasn't sure what set her off, what made this interaction different from the others. Perhaps it was something about the way the stranger did it, reaching out with no notice, cupping her left breast like his hand was a scale. She had always considered touch as another language, more honest than speech. It expressed what the person would never say.

The stranger didn't look at her face, had no interest in her reaction. The way a butcher would heft a lamb, thinking of the meal, not the animal.

Nice piece of tail—he said, pretending to refer to the tail pinned to the back of her costume.

Lipreading, she would have thought he had said *nice piece of hail,* but she glimpsed his tongue tap the roof of his mouth to make the *T* sound. Most times she could lipread men more accurately than women, their mouths closer to the level of her eyes, easier to spot the movements of the tongue.

With this man, from the way his head was angled, she knew he wasn't addressing her, but was talking to his friends, two executives in suits standing next to him. He was trying to impress them with his membership key to this club, the young women in their costumes, his action of grabbing her breast.

His hand squeezed. He didn't squeeze to the point of pain like some of the men did, but this was one touch too many. Her vision tunnelling in, a staticky sound rising in her ears.

(Her dad's nickname for her was Scrawny, after a terrier

who was an escape artist, would nearly kill herself to get free at least once a week).

She reached between the man's legs, to cup what her grand-dad called the tackle. She lowered her voice as though from desire and said her shift ended in an hour, which was his car?

There was a pause. He was looking at her now, focused. When he spoke this time, it was to her, not his friends.

She strode off to the changing room, switched into her real clothes and collected her hearing glasses. Exiting the building through the kitchen, she picked up a sugar pourer. In the parking lot, she poured the contents into his gas tank.

She never went back.

Walking home that night through downtown, she passed the Tampa Theatre. A brightly lit marquee for the musical *South Pacific* caught her eye. The posters by the door showed a beach and the sea, a woman leaning against a palm tree, all alone and staring out at the waves. What kept Cora's attention was the woman.

To the men back in the club, this poster would be inviting, each imagining himself approaching, the woman turning, her need.

Cora saw the poster differently. She thought the woman looked happy staring out at the water all alone.

So she went to the travel agent's the next day, leafed through some brochures and ended up buying a one-way ticket to St. Thomas, an island not that far away, less expensive, more tropical. She hoped there, she wouldn't have to dress like an animal to get a job.

Reaching the top of the dune, Blum saw the crowd standing on the beach. Off to the side was the policeman assigned to protect the body for him and Tibbet. The policeman and a few others had handkerchiefs pressed to their faces like mourners. All of them stared about 30 feet away at what appeared to be a dark ledge of rock lying half in the water.

When a wave hit the rock, its tail undulated.

A pilot whale, the smooth curves, the gleaming oneness. A body so simple in form, a backbone sheathed in muscle and fat.

Blum shifted the bag of surgical instruments to his other hand and strode forward.

With the first incision, the smell was released. Blum and Tibbet began to cough. Insulated by blubber, the internal warmth had cooked the body.

Behind them, the policeman and crowd backed up, pressing the handkerchiefs closer.

The scalpel, intended for human bodies, was too small. Blum switched to the carving knife. Once he'd reached the skull, he picked up the hatchet. He and Tibbet took turns, stopping every few hits to see if there was any sign of breaking through the bone.

The next time Blum looked over his shoulder, the crowd was gone.

He chain-smoked to reduce the stench. Each time he needed

a cigarette, he'd tap one partway out, then tug it out the rest of the way with his lips so his hands in the surgical gloves never fouled it.

So far as he knew, they were the first scientists to do this, to harvest a whale's brain and bring it back for study. A decade ago, Blum had been the first to publish on the brains of the chimpanzee and gorilla. Even though the weight of the apes' brains was less than half of that of a human's, he'd found strong similarities in the convoluted furrows, in the shape and size of the frontal lobe. He'd concluded there were likely implications in terms of intelligence and abilities. Quickly a scrum of other researchers had followed him, all competitively trying to define their specialty in the new field of great-ape neuroscience. In response he'd decided, as soon as his current research was published, to switch to a different species. He was considering elephants, had heard their brains were huge. The problem was that elephants were so far away, expensive to ship and feed.

Then yesterday he'd spotted an article about this stranding. Modern science knew so little about cetaceans. It was possible they were smart. And there was the added benefit that in New England, they lived just off the coast, so the subjects could be easily replenished.

When he spoke at public events, the audience tended to assume that Blum was an infallible expert, capable in every field of science. Although he would never admit this in public, he'd nearly failed statistics in college, as well as organic chemistry. Even now he relied on his postdocs for these parts of the work.

No, his greatest strength was curiosity. An interesting research question caught him, wouldn't let him go. He'd started with gorillas because, after paging through a *National Geographic* article, he'd had a dream that night about one of them shaving. Handling the shaver adeptly, stretching the mouth to the side to get the cheeks, eyeing the progress in the mirror, the ape had removed the hair bit by bit, looking more and more human. In the morning, Blum had woken, wondering just how smart they were under all that fur.

Several times so far, once he'd started investigating a subject, other researchers would follow, the topic becoming trendy. By then he would already have established himself, made a few big discoveries, and he could move on to some new subject.

His second strength was being able to convey the importance of the work with a single well-chosen analogy—essential to securing funding. Other neuroscientists might be as good or better with the science, but they didn't comprehend the funders' desire to be associated with an analogy like that, to buy it with money and mention it at parties.

When he started his research on gorillas, the newspapers had been filled with stories about computers and their many potential applications. The word, "computers," no longer referred to women in the back office hunched over adding machines, but instead to huge cabinets of humming machinery capable of adding up a thousand numbers in a second. This new type of mechanical computer was associated with everything futuristic and impressive.

And so, with his research into gorilla brains, he'd associated the work with computers. He told the funders that brains were like *biological computers* and he would unlock the secrets to the gorillas' foreign circuitry, capabilities and speed.

Blum and Tibbet had opened a crack in the whale's skull with the hatchet. Blum was Tibbet's department head. When Blum asked him for help, he'd said yes.

They used a hammer and wood shims to widen the crack systematically. They worked carefully, so they wouldn't harm the brain or its protective bag of meninges. When the crack was wide enough, running three quarters of the way around the skull, Tibbet got his fingers into the crack and leaned back, pulling. Blum sat on the animal's forehead and applied the crowbar. Working together, rocking with their bodies, the gap widened. There was a sudden crack and the top of the skull opened.

Blum fell forward onto the side of the animal. His eyes at the level of the brain, he stared across its surface like an astronaut on the moon.

Even through the thin cloth of meninges, the organ was clearly convoluted and dense with power.

Jesus—said Blum and sat up.

Gently he slid his hands in, between the meninges and the skull, to heft the bag of brains up—the contents a trifle soupy from decomposition. Tibbet cut the bag free at the base and Blum pulled it out.

He held the organ in his arms, a father cradling a newborn. Or a miner with a bag of gold.

But Tibbet must have nicked the meninges, for the fabric began to sag at the base, then simply to rip, the contents dribbling out. Within a moment, no matter how he grasped and hugged the organ, he ended up holding just the wet and empty bag.

Not that it really mattered.

For from the moment he cupped the weight of that brain—easily twice as much as a human's—he knew his life's direction had been changed.

O n St. Thomas, Cora got a position at the Cantab, a bar on a dock in the harbor. When the boats landed, the Cantab was the first place the tourists saw. It was always crowded.

There was a Help Wanted sign in the window, so she'd stepped inside to ask about it. When she said she had experience, the manager hired her.

Dishwasher?—she asked, hoping for a job with minimal conversation.

He blew air out of his mouth, amused. He looked her over and said—Waitress.

It was a noisy restaurant, the clatter of silverware and plates, the blender in the kitchen and the background chatter. With the customers sitting down, facing their menus, it was hard to see their tongues. Even with her hearing glasses, she frequently had to ask people to repeat.

The men would smile and lean toward her, wanting a reason to get closer. Staring at their mouths, she'd try to figure out if they were saying *Some fries* or *Beers, guys*? They liked her looking. On the other hand, when she asked the women to repeat, their eyes got hard and they tightened their mouths, making it harder to see what they were saying.

(Most of us understand so little about sound. Having always had good hearing, we take it for granted, never analyzing it.

So much of what we experience as sound is not the original sound, but its reflection off nearby objects.

Say the word *Hello* in a large auditorium with hard surfaces. The word ricochets around, tiny and lost.

Now say *Hello* at the same volume in a living room full of furniture. It bounces once off the walls and is caught in the soft cushions. The sound is clear and solid.

Finally say *Hello* on a lake, in the fog. The word flies away and is gone without a ripple.

As a child, her favorite place was the pig barn, the hay and the dirt floor, the wood walls and the backs of the pigs. Sound reflected just enough. Her second favorite place was the mudroom at home, a contained area with raincoats, shoes, bags of laundry and a carpet. The sound gentle and warm. If she wanted to talk to anyone in her family, if it was going to be a conversation longer than a sentence or two, she would time for this moment as they stood in this room, pulling on or off their shoes.)

The restaurant had three distinct sections.

- The main seating area was long and narrow, with a wood floor and old rafters. It functioned as an echo chamber that two or three tables of customers could fill, every sound multiplied. A single laugh barked back and forth, harsh, hurting the ears.
- Sound at the tables on the pier outback was muffled by the background slur of surf and wind. With the waves, the sound was not reflected at all, but fractured it in all directions. On the back deck, a customer's words disappeared as if they had never been.
- The kitchen itself was all hard wood and metal, the water in the sinks running and the clang of a pan on the stove, the chopping of a knife. Here at least it was easier to read the

situation, people's body language, complete with props. She could make a good guess at what had been said.

Over the years, she'd learned to prefer being on her own. Alone, she didn't worry she'd misheard (handing someone the check when they'd asked to move to the deck). The way she got stared at when she made a mistake made her feel so much more lonely.

So, she took long walks on the island, exploring. Away from town, the dirt roads moved from patches of jungle to bright clearings with small cabins, goats and red dirt.

Aside from a few beaches near town, the shoreline was deserted. Mile after mile of boulders and sand and lizards, donkeys blinking in the shade of the palm trees. She'd walk until she found a quiet cove, then she'd place her hearing glasses on her folded towel and wade into the waves to snorkel. The water was clear, and fish flitted about, whimsical and shimmering. What she enjoyed the most however was that, with her head underwater, she could truly hear again.

Most of her hearing had disappeared overnight when she was eight. She'd had a bad ear infection (she used to get them a lot), went to bed feverish and aching. She woke the next morning, a Tuesday in May, to a pillow wet with pus and a world eerily quiet except for a small hissing noise like a deflating tire in her right ear (what would later turn out to be her good ear).

Since that day, the only place she could hear well without gadgets was in the dense medium of water. There, sound somehow bypassed her middle ear. Perhaps it was because the human body, after all, was mostly water. Any sound down here just continued unimpeded through her body to vibrate deep in her skull, reaching whatever was left of her hearing.

In the sea, sound had clarity and complexity and range. The

susurrus of the waves, the hiss of tiny creatures, the tumbling of pebbles, it was all crisp and immediate, no static from the hearing aids. Since the sickness took her hearing, she thought of the sea as Oz or Narnia, some vivid world where strange creatures glittered and floated and magical powers were granted for a limited time. She thought of herself as the little mermaid, who suffered on land and felt at home in the sea.

The only negative part of swimming was that when she had to step out onto dry land, she returned to something worse than before, because, wading back onto the beach, she couldn't put her glasses on until her hair dried. Seawater could short-circuit the electronics.

So she toweled and toweled her hair, but it was thick and, even in the Caribbean sun, took an hour to dry. With her hair turned to the sun, she sat there waiting, mostly deaf, occasionally turning to check behind her.

FOUR
March 1958
Orlando, Florida

O f course, there were dangers associated with anesthesia, the art of bringing a living being halfway to death.
Those dangers increased when working with a new
species, one with unknown sensitivities.

Thus, when it came to the second dolphin, Blum switched
to Diazepam and injected only a third of the previous amount.

This smaller amount of Diazepam took longer to work. The
animal shivered and struggled, but once it went to sleep, it also
stopped inhaling. They stood over it, listening to its heart and
waiting, Tibbet staring at his wristwatch.

After five minutes they tried intubating it, but the muscles
around the blowhole were strong, meant to hold back the pressure of the sea. The flesh inside so delicate.

As Blum explained later to the director, these animals did
not die in vain. The information from these deaths would
result in a peer-reviewed paper explaining this discovery: that
dolphins were the first species known to have voluntary, rather
than involuntary, respiration. In the sea, they had to control
when to breathe, to ensure they did not inhale water while
sleeping or unconscious. His published paper ended up rec-
ommending any operation on dolphins (and potentially all
cetaceans) use only a local analgesic and strong restraints.
Published in *Neuroscience*, a well-read periodical, the paper probably saved dozens of animals from a similar fate. He felt
proud of that achievement.

Of course, to ensure publication, to feel confident that the first two results weren't just an artifact of sample size, they had to use a small amount of anesthesia on a third.

They injected barely enough ketamine to put a five-year-old child to sleep. The dolphin, weighing over 300 pounds, must have been extremely sensitive. Or maybe the vein into which Blum injected the anesthesia had somehow disproportionately affected the blowhole. There was so much to learn.

The animal continued to breathe, but only through the left side of its blowhole, jerking convulsively with each inhale. It vocalized also, a high sort of squeaking noise, the sound of balloons rubbed together. The noise ascending higher and higher, echoing in the narrow restraint tank, until the humans could no longer hear it.

At this point, the woman who cared for the dolphins came sprinting back around the corner, returning from the office where she'd phoned the favorite lunch place of the director of Marine World, asking the cashier to tell him there was an emergency, come back now. She was sobbing and incoherent. Blum never understood the logic of this type of female reaction (his wife Babs sometimes got like this when the children were hurt). Crying reduced a woman's ability to communicate just when she needed it most.

The woman's breath was labored, reminiscent of the dolphin. She called it Nellie and pleaded with the men to bring this dolphin back to the tank, to see if it could recover there.

Tibbet spoke up, agreeing with the woman, his voice tight. Throughout the morning, his reluctance to continue the procedures had increased. The intention had been some exploration of the brain's anatomy, to try stimulating a few different areas. The subjects were not supposed to die.

So Blum nodded, and the dolphin's restraint tank was wheeled back to the pool and the dolphin released.

As the animal slid into the pool, she (Nellie) gave a loud crescendo/decrescendo squeak. At the sound, the two dolphins remaining in the tank instantly banked and shot over, like this was a trick they'd been training for years to do. Stopping under her, one on either side, they shouldered her weight to bring her to the surface, so her blowhole was above the waves. An adept fireman's carry, performed without hands. Underneath her, the two dolphins basically trod water, pushing upward. Holding her up this way, it took work to get their own blowholes high enough to breathe. Still, they didn't move from their positions, both of them keeping her there for over twenty minutes—long after it was clear Nellie was dead.

Blum watched all this. He pulled a chair over to sit by the side of the pool and absorb every detail. Once the dolphins finally let go of the body, it bobbed and rolled in the water. It was difficult to see exactly what the other two were doing, but he could hear a fast clicking as they rubbed themselves against the body.

Blum sat back now, thinking about that strange crescendo/decrescendo sound the dying dolphin had made and the dolphins' reaction to it.

There was a bird feeder in his backyard, which his home-office window faced. Each morning he saw his wife, Babs, fill the feeder while the birds flocked to it. He referred to it as a "hawk-feeder," since it congregated fluffy snacks for the local redtail which every few days would dive from above, hitting one of the birds like a fist. Occasionally the predator was the neighbor's cat instead, pouncing from behind a bush.

Just before either type of predator struck, the blue jays would scream a warning, a specific type of piercing cry, at which the other birds scattered in every direction, most heading for cover in the nearest bush (the correct action to get away from a hawk), while a few flapped for the sky (the appropriate action in the case of a cat).

Clearly the blue jays' scream communicated a warning that the other birds understood. However, from the difference in their reactions, it appeared the warning did not convey any specifics about the type of danger.

The sound Nellie made must have related more information than just a bellow for help. It appeared to have conveyed the type of the help she needed because both dolphins had instantly banked at the right angle to end up just beneath her, one on either side, the perfect cooperative action for her situation.

In front of Blum, one of the remaining dolphins came to the surface, not to breathe, but to stick its head out of the water, 10 feet away, bobbing there. It seemed to be looking at the humans, looking specifically at Blum. Staring at him with its dark eyes. From its size, it was probably a male, perhaps the offspring or mate of Nellie.

Last night, Blum's son had been watching *War of the Worlds*. The boy was fascinated by the concept of extraterrestrials, as so many kids were these days. Both Sputnik 1 and 2 had launched last fall, a Russian dog in orbit, the attention of the world on outer space, the possibility of life on other planets. Passing through the TV room at about eight P.M., Blum had paused, watching the scene where the alien's bulbous three-fingered hand had reached out to tap the woman's shoulder from behind.

This morning since there'd been an op-ed in *The Globe* suggesting that, now humans had shown themselves capable of entering space, contact with extraterrestrials might occur soon. If aliens were out there, they'd probably been watching for a signal like this for years, a signal that intelligent life existed on Earth. The editorial asked what would happen if they arrived here tomorrow—if say some large gleaming saucer landed on the White House lawn and a ramp was lowered, how would we know if they came in peace? How would we communicate with beings with whom we shared nothing? How would we even recognize what was communication?

Americans had been so surprised by the success of the Soviet Sputniks, the government caught off guard. In response, Congress had allocated immense funding, NASA now actively searching for projects, throwing money at anything related.

The dolphin was staring directly at Blum. It didn't blink. In the background was the glug-glug of the pool's drain. The animal's gaze so intent.

And this moment, here, was when the idea hit Blum. Clearly intelligent, the creature bobbed there, limbless, breathing through the back of its skull, its heavy body designed for no gravity.

The director hurried in, returning from lunch, yelling, forbidding Blum from ever touching one of his dolphins again, from ever setting foot in Marine World.

Blum turned to him, grinning. For it didn't matter. He knew now his exact research question, the one he would work on, the analogy he would use to get funding.

For this analogy, this idea, he would get a lot. He would demand his own research center.

ARRIVAL

FIVE
June 4, 1965

One morning, walking along the beach on the more deserted end of the island, Cora came upon a concrete chute set into the rocks next to the sea.

This sluice angled down, away from the sea, a narrow corridor cut through the rocks, the seawater pouring in along it. She hadn't seen a home or dock or human for at least half a mile, but here was this cement chute, as engineered as a sidewalk and clearly new, not a speck of moss growing on it. She looked for a moment, then stepped into the water, splashing her way along it, between the boulders, curious about what the water was used for.

After a dozen yards, she reached the other side, the boulders opening to a wide vista.

The sluice poured water into a lagoon, sheltered from the waves and wind. On the dock, a man was sleeping. On the far side were stairs leading to a stone veranda and a gleaming house built 50 feet up the hill, palm trees all around.

Then something big broke the surface of the water, a grey back rolling forward, the spray of its exhale, a dorsal fin and it was gone, just the ripple spreading out from where the animal had been.

Such surprise, that the lagoon had anything that size in it.

A moment later, a second dolphin surfaced on the far side: the exhale, the fin, then gone.

She understood the water in the chute was too shallow for them to escape. For a swimming pool, this lagoon was huge, but as a sea, it was miniscule. Like having several cougars penned in the backyard.

She was still staring at the water, when an alarm rang. A metallic clanging loud enough for her to hear from a distance. The man on the dock jerked up, slapped the alarm off on the timer next to him, stared at the empty waves and scribbled something in a notebook. He appeared dazed, somewhere in his mid-twenties, a few years older than her, athletic and wearing a polo shirt, his blond hair disheveled.

She approached, and he blinked at her. He smelled of stale cigarettes and beer.

She asked—Dolphins?

This wasn't a serious question, more a conversational opening.

He struggled to his feet, his face pale, his attention internal. Sheltered from the wind and surf, it was quiet and he was facing her, so she could watch his lips.—When the buzzer goes, take notes, will you?

She understood his sentence was not a question, but more of a command. She knew this not just because of his stance and tone, but because he handed her the notebook and pen and was already moving toward the building, speeding up from a walk to a trot.

He added over his shoulder something more, but she couldn't hear it. Then he disappeared inside.

She was left standing there. Opening the notebook, she scanned a few entries. Written words were so easy to understand.

7:55 ———
8:00 dolphin surfaces, blows
8:05 ———
8:10 dolphin jumps
8:15 ———
8:20 ———
8:25 dolphin surfaces, blows

*

Page after page of this.

She stepped onto the dock, near the timer. When the buzzer went off, the water was quiet, no dolphin visible. So she wrote *8:30* and drew a line after it.

For a while she sat on the dock, watching and making these notes, feeling the morning slowly warm. She did not have to be at work until just before lunch. The place was peaceful. She'd never seen dolphins up close before. Occasionally one of them exhaled, or a flipper appeared, or a body shot by under the water. Other than that, she had no idea what the animals were doing, didn't even know how many there were.

The man didn't come back outside.

Gradually she got curious. So she put the notebook down on the dock, placed her hearing glasses on top and stripped down to her bathing suit. She pulled on her mask and snorkel and lay down in the shallow of the lagoon, just deep enough to get her head under the water. She wanted to hear the dolphins.

(She would always remember her last evening of normal hearing, that night sitting at the kitchen table, aching and feverish with the flu. Her mother was washing the dishes, singing to herself, 'When You Wish upon a Star.' Everything Cora looked at seemed a little too bright and shimmery, so she closed her eyes, rested her head on the table and drifted. Her mother's breathy voice, the squeak of the cloth, the clatter of plates. Occasionally her mother switched to humming, throaty and relaxed. Outside were the Florida night sounds: cicadas, crickets, tree frogs and a whippoorwill.

The thing that had amazed Cora afterward was she hadn't known enough in that moment to feel gratitude.)

As soon as her head was under the surface, the dolphins' noises filled her. Sound, bright as light, hard as touch.

Ping-pong balls bouncing down metal stairs.

Dolphins are constant vocal innovators, playful geniuses with unspeakable power, the Maria Callases of the sea, their sounds unworldly and pure.

A gospel group on helium, hitting the high notes.

She found herself wiggling a little deeper into the water. Two feet deep, two and a half. She saw white sand, a crab scuttling sideways and the pilings of the dock.

A tired mouse crying.

She barely paid attention to her surroundings, her entire being focused on the sounds. She inhaled through the snorkel and felt the sounds in her lungs.

Styrofoam squeaking.

The noises were vibrating in her bones, she tasted them on her tongue, saw them between her ears. So clear and crisp and three-dimensional.

Martians arguing, metallic and intent.

Just beyond, a dolphin flashed by, big and gleaming. Surprised, it spotted her and, with a flick of its tail, was gone.

Now the sounds got louder. Excited. The crying, the clicking. She eased forward deeper, floating now, balanced on just her fingertips, breathing through the snorkel, the waves sloshing across the top of her head.

Around the corner of the dock, the dolphins were revealed.

Clustered on the far side of the lagoon, maybe 60 feet away, they stared at her. Their presence, their sheer size. The largest one (at least 11 feet long, must be over 450 pounds) floated in front, the three others behind. The positions a family would take if she walked in with a gun.

They geigered and squealed in her direction. A crinkling sensation like plastic wrap twisting in her gut. The sound exploring her insides.

The big one opened its mouth and clapped its teeth. Agitated. It had a red mark across its chest, maybe a rope burn.

It held its flippers out to the sides and arched its back, trying to look even bigger than it was.

The two medium-sized ones stayed just behind, one to either side. One of them had a gash along its right flank, probably 6 inches long. These two kept their bodies between her and the fourth dolphin who was almost the same size, probably an adolescent. The adolescent peered around them, shifting from side to side, trying to see, clicking at Cora.

Scared. Not used to humans. Perhaps their injuries were from being captured.

From twelve years old on, she'd worked part-time at the horse stable next door, Beach Ride Bobby's. There, she could muck out stables, groom and saddle the horses, with hardly a person speaking to her all day. With the dolphins, she acted the way she would when the horses were jumpy. She didn't freeze motionless, staring the way a predator would. She turned away and acted busy.

She'd always felt relief being with the horses, perhaps because they talked with their bodies, with their stance and ears and tails, stepping forward or away. This type of language was so easy to read. Over time she learned to speak back. She moved confident and relaxed, approaching always from the left, clucking to give them warning. Touching the fetlock meant pick up your foot, her hand on the ear meant lower your head, her posture leaning back in the saddle meant stop. She spoke with her body. Go left. Faster. Canter.

The horses told her with their ears and posture and stride if they wanted to run, where they wanted to go, if they trusted her. Riding a horse was a dialogue that could range from a choppy argument to a joyful conversation.

Floating in the shallows, she rummaged in the sandy floor of the lagoon, searching for mussels. She was someone going about her day, uninterested and occupied. She relaxed her body, breathed slowly through the snorkel, and listened to the dolphins' sounds gradually calm down. The noises washing through her.

A squeaky floor.

Castanets clicking.

Occasionally, at the purity of the sounds, her eyes fluttered closed.

Stars sizzling in space.

By the time she'd found the tenth mussel, the dolphins were surfacing regularly to breathe. Each exhale sounded like a soda can opening, the *pssh* of pressure releasing. They'd begun to drift closer, curious about her.

Abruptly their sounds shifted, an intense clicking. She turned to look. A school of silvery fish, each the size of her hand, scooting in from the sluice, flitting here and there, exploring.

The dolphins pumped forward and scooped the fish up with fast claps of the mouth. In a single moment, the school was gone.

The dolphins geigered about, searching for any missed fish, then they jerked in her direction. Something was splashing through the water behind her.

They fled, even further than before, to the very corner of the lagoon.

Turning, she saw two pale human legs in the water behind her.

She rose from the lagoon, standing up. Leaving sound behind. Returning to muffled air.

A man was standing there, in his late forties, skinny, with very bright eyes, the strong sense of someone in there, peering out.

He spoke. He had a cigarette in his mouth, distorting his lip movements. His eyebrows were high; probably it was a question. Her hearing glasses were on the dock and with her hair wet, she couldn't put them on.

She tugged off her swim mask.—Hi. I'm Cora. I . . . Some

guy asked me to keep notes on the dolphins. He looked sick and went inside.

Without her glasses, her voice boomed inside her quiet head. Without the hearing aids, she tended to speak too softly for others to hear.

The one word he said was easy to lipread—What?

She repeated her words, pushing the words out with her gut, trying to feel for the right level of sound in her mouth. Perhaps she was too loud now.

He said—I'll talk to him. Did you keep the notes?

Vowels were always easier to hear than consonants, formed in the gut and not the mouth. Consonants were made in the front of the mouth and pushed out with a puff of air were the hardest: *ch, sh, th, f, s, h*. The lips partially closed while making the sounds, so it was hard to see what the tongue was doing.

And when she wasn't wearing her hearing glasses like now, she missed more consonants. Language became a fast-moving crossword puzzle, with her guessing at the full word from just a letter or two.—What?

He looked at the notebook on the dock and spoke again. With his face away, she couldn't hear any of it or lipread.

She guessed.—The notes? Yes, I kept them for a while, then got in the water instead.

He turned back, looked her over in the bathing suit.

(This was what men did. They chain-smoked and cradled mixed drinks while they eyed young women like they looked at brand-new Cadillacs, the mens' expressions both appraising and hungry.)

He said a complex sentence. His chin was up, his attitude offended. The only words she was fairly sure of were *notes* and *research*.

She looked up at the building and veranda, with its beach umbrellas and patio furniture, bathing suits and towels draped everywhere. She asked—Research?

He flicked ash off the cigarette into the water. With it out of his mouth, the words were easier to understand.—We study dolphins.

—You're scientists?

He nodded, irritated. He rarely seemed to blink.

She jerked her chin toward the notebook—That doesn't contain a lot of information.

He cocked his head and waded over to the notebook. From the way he scanned the first page, it was clear he hadn't read it before.

He flipped the page and muttered something. He didn't look happy.

He turned back to her, gesturing at the lagoon. His eyebrows high, asking a question.

She took a guess—I couldn't see them from above, so I got in the water.

He considered that, then turned back to the notebook and said something else.

She said—Excuse me?

He faced her, angry now. His cigarette still in his hand. She could see his tongue.—Am I not speaking clearly?

—I'm partly deaf.

Those bright eyes focused. A pause. No sympathy, but at least he was interested now. He spoke more deliberately.—Both ears?

—Left ear entirely. Right one partly. I have hearing aids, but I can't wear them with wet hair. Your cigarette makes it harder for me to lipread.

He tilted his head, considering this, then ground the cigarette out on the dock. Now, he remained facing her when he spoke, left more space between the words. She could lipread more of what he said.

—What did the dolphins do when you were in the water?

—They got scared.

—How do you know?

She answered—They bunched in. The big one in front.

—How close?

She raised her eyebrows, confused.

He held his hands close to each other, then far away, his brows raised.

She said—Within 10 feet of each other. They stared at me, made a lot of high-pitched noises.

She imitated the squeaking sounds as best she could.

He pointed at his ear.—I thought you were deaf.

—Partly deaf. In the water I can hear.

He cocked his head.

She said—In the water, the sounds bypass my ears. I think they vibrate through my bones.

He sucked on his teeth, as though this information had a taste he might like.—What else happened?

She added a rapid clicking sound.—They made these noises too. Especially at the fish just before they ate them.

His eyes lost interest.—There are no fish in there.

—There are no what?

He made a motion with his hand of a fish swimming.

—Ahh, fish. Yes, they came down the chute.

His eyes narrowed.—And the dolphins ate them?

She nodded.

—Wow. First time.

She asked—First time? First time what? That they've eaten?

He nodded.

She stared at the water, surprised.—Since they were caught? How many days?

He held up six fingers.—Why were you in the water?

—I couldn't see the dolphins from up here.

He eyed the surface of the lagoon. There was no ripple or sign the dolphins existed.

He paused, then came to a conclusion.—Can you find some?

—Find dolphins?

His hand wove forward again through the air like a fish swimming.—No, the fish they ate.

—The fish? I'm sure you can find that kind at the fisherman's dock in town.

He said—Buy 20 pounds.

She paused.—Excuse me?

He flashed all his fingers at her twice, twenty.—Buy 20 pounds. I'll give you the money.

Her eyebrows stayed up.

He pointed at the ground.—You live here?

—Yes, in town.

He eyed her.—You have a job? Waitress?

—At a restaurant.

He rubbed his index finger and thumb together in the gesture of money.—How much do you make a week?

She stared at him. He was not someone who worried about social niceties.

He asked—Under 200?

She earned significantly less. This was probably obvious in her expression.

And this next moment was when she understood how his brain worked differently than others.

He hit each consonant. He used gestures, some of them unclear but at least he was trying. He wanted her to understand. He tapped his chest.—I'm Dr. Blum.

He pointed to her and then at his eyes.—You know how to observe.

He pointed at her and then the ground.—Work here.

He held up three fingers, then rubbed index finger and thumb together again.—I'll pay 300 a week.

He tapped his watch.—You start now, today.

He pointed at the dolphins, then slapped his palm against his chest in the beat of a heart, then rubbed his fingers together again.—Alive. Keep them alive. So long as you do that, you have a job.

A t the fisherman's wharf in town, Cora found the type of fish the dolphins had eaten. The label on the crate said butterfish. She bought 20 pounds with Blum's money, then returned to the research center.

The building was clearly a home retrofitted to function as a research center, the outside a wide expanse of pink stucco, an empty stone fountain by the circular driveway, the flower beds and lawn neglected. Inside, the open dining room/kitchen had been converted into a workspace, shelves filled with thick science journals, a long worktable covered with files, typewriters and a reel-to-reel tape recorder. An empty 12-foot-long glass tank on wheels was shoved against one wall. On the far side were large windows and a screen door looking onto the veranda and the lagoon, the sea beyond.

She called out hello.

She heard something in reply and followed the sound through a door into the TV room. She adjusted her hearing glasses, pressing the earpieces a little tighter to her head.

A red-haired man in his late thirties lay on the couch watching TV. Badly sunburned, his skin was red and hot, his limbs arranged so they didn't touch each other. The pink of the burn gleamed through the thin hair on top of his head.

(Most of the people in Cora's family had dark hair and eyes and their skin had an olive tone. During the summer they could darken to café au lait. When she was a child, her dad used to say it was because the family had been living in Florida for enough generations that the blond relatives had died off. Her mom was the one to explain there was Seminole blood on both sides. The closest Cora had ever gotten to a sunburn was, after a full day in the sun, a pleasurable warmth in the skin.)

The color of this man's skin, at the moment, was closer to a piglet's than a human's.

She stepped over to the TV and turned the sound all the way down, so she'd be able to hear. She said—I'm Cora.

To make sure she'd said it loud enough, she repeated—Cora.

Just his eyes moved, probably he was scared of adjusting his head against the rough couch material. His eyes blinked watery and embattled.—What are you doing here?

In the quiet room, no background sound, she could hear relatively well.—I just got hired.

He was sucking on something, making it harder to read his words.—By Blum? About time. Can you get the signal better?

—What?

His eyes flicked to the TV.—The antenna.

The television's black and white scene was fuzzy, the sound filled with static. The moment she touched the rabbit-eared antennas the image cleared. *Gunsmoke*. The sheriff swung down from his horse, the flash of spurs, the sense of leather. A big man, he landed, adjusted his pants and the weight of his gun.

She twisted the antenna from left to right, trying to find the best reception, then let go. The scene disappeared into snow.

He said something, irritated and too fast for her to understand.

She didn't touch the antenna.—What's your name?

He answered Jim Tibbett (or maybe Tibbets). He asked a question. The only word she heard was *laundry*.

She looked from him to the bathroom door and then around the room. It was covered in dirty dishes and clothes.—I'm not the maid.

The next sentence contained the word *cook*.

—I'm not the cook either. Blum wants me to take care of the dolphins.

His eyebrows went up.—Really?

She said—I have to keep them alive. What kind of fish have you tried feeding them?

He said *Whatever* and then several words and then *freezer*.

To reward him, she touched the antenna. The screen showed a closeup of the sheriff's fingers on the handle of his gun.—Pieces of fish or the whole thing?

—Pieces. We throw them in the water. They won't get near them.

—The pieces were still frozen?

He said something that she couldn't hear, but he also nodded. She let go of the antennae.—Thanks.

—Hey!

She left the room.

* * *

Back at the lagoon, she picked out a butterfish that looked very fresh, the scales still shiny. She waded into the shallow end, ignoring the dolphins, just dragging the fish's body through the water with kitchen tongs, spreading its smell and taste, washing the human scent off it, making the body twinkle and twirl where the dolphins could see it. She waited until they calmed down about her being in the water again. After six days, they had to be hungry. Then she threw the fish into the center of the lagoon.

The body splashed into the water and floated there. She waited.

Nothing happened. It just floated. Untouched.

She pulled on her mask and snorkel and got down on her hands and knees so she could duck her head under the water.

The dolphins were spread out, looking at the fish bobbing above them. They glanced at her, dumbfounded. As if she'd just thrown them a hairbrush for dinner.

So she grabbed another butterfish with the tongs and waded again into the lagoon deep enough to float. She watched the dolphins' reactions through her mask while she rolled the fish through the water.

The dolphins eyed her and the fish. When she felt their interest was high enough and the fish no longer smelled of anything but the salty water, she used the tongs to lob the fish through the air, into the center of the lagoon. From under the water, she could see the body splash, then drift down a few inches, swaying lazily with the water, its mouth open.

The dolphins inspected it with clicks, turning from her to the fish and back. They didn't move toward the food.

She got another fish and tried cutting it up. The dolphins again watched her actions with interest, as though she were the afternoon entertainment. In the water, she squeezed the pieces until blood oozed out. This would work with a shark. They opened their beaks and sampled the water. Perhaps they were like snakes and ate only every few days. She tossed these chunks in also. The chunks floated. The dolphins looked at them, then back to her, curious about what she'd do next.

So she just floated in the water, studying them, searching for clues of what she was doing wrong. Gradually they began to get used to her, moving around more. The water was dappled and columned, the animals sliding through it.

They cut through the water with little effort, their tails barely pumping. They spun, twisting and gliding. Even at the speed with which they moved, they didn't collide. They were like professional dancers performing complex routines, sliding smoothly around each other.

Occasionally she threw a fish into the water, but she never saw the dolphins eat anything she threw. The dolphins didn't look weak or emaciated, but she wasn't sure she'd recognized the signs. They examined her with each circuit, creaking their noises in her direction, no longer startling each time she moved. She didn't know if they were a family, caught together, or strangers to one another, each caught separately.

Around three that afternoon, a school of butterfish entered the lagoon along the chute, scooting around, looking for food. The dolphins shot forward and snapped them up, their hunger apparent in their bolt of speed.

Perhaps they wanted prey that moved.

She waded out of the water and searched through the building until she found a fishing rod in a closet. She cut off some fishing line, thin and transparent. Tying one end around a whole fish, she walked up the sluice about 10 feet, then dropped the body into the water. It tumbled down the sluice toward the lagoon. She jerked the string every second or so. She'd jigged for fish this way before with her granddad, was competent at it, letting the body roll with the current, then jerking it up in a way that made it appear alive, at least to simple predators.

None of the dolphins even approached it.

The dolphin with the cut on its side stuck its head out of the water and stared, not at the jerked corpse, but at her holding the string.

* * *

At the end of the day, as the sun went down, Tibbet stepped on the veranda above, his skin appearing to glow red in the sunset. His defenseless watery eyes. He called out—Did they eat anything?

Blum had clearly told him she was hard of hearing because he half yelled these words while pointing to the dolphins and then his mouth.

She was out of the water, sitting on the dock, watching the lagoon and thinking. Her hair dry and her glasses on.—No.

He grunted, exchanging glances with someone inside and turned away, already considering her gone.

The Cantab, the restaurant she had worked at, was built on a wharf extending out into the water, popular not so much for its food as for the view and location. About two weeks into working here, there'd been an accident. At the point it happened, the men at the table in the far corner of the deck, the table with the best view, were telling her the story of having killed a shark.

Four feet long—said one man, his hands held out to show the size.

Another said—You kidding? Five feet at least.

She just wanted to find out if the third guy wanted another margarita, but they kept her there instead, describing how hard the shark fought as they dragged it still thrashing onto the boat, how close they had gotten to being bit. She was concentrating on their lips, each word a struggle. The background noise of some engine interfering, so she lost more and more of the words. Meanwhile they lounged in their chairs, young and sunburned and muscled, while they looked her over.

Then their eyes jerked up and froze, something behind her.

Partly deaf, she had gotten used to the concept of sudden. The honk she didn't hear, the *heads-up!* she'd missed. Warning sounds were a luxury she didn't have. She'd gotten trained to just react.

A shadow rising over her.

She turned, glimpsing the yacht backing up, too close, too

fast, wrong angle. The white perfection of its stern. The start of the slow-motion impact, the crunch of wood and weight.

So she vaulted the table, the heel of her hand square in the men's fries, her legs tucked up and over, her feet landing in the small space between the chairs, the men still staring, mouths open, their nice meal in front of them, as she sprinted away.

One of them ended up in the hospital, while she continued her shift without injury.

* * *

The next morning, she arrived at the research center at dawn. She hadn't called the restaurant yesterday to say she quit. It was possible she'd already lost her job. She didn't care: all those people, the garbled words, her confusion.

At the lagoon, she used the pool skimmer to clean up all the floating uneaten fish leftover feeding from yesterday. It looked like the dolphins hadn't eaten one piece, not even after she'd left. She stripped down to her bathing suit, dropping her clothes on one of the chairs, waded in and began to snorkel slowly through the shallows.

Alarmed, the dolphins huddled together on the far side of the lagoon like yesterday. She puttered about ignoring them, searching for mussels, glancing at the dolphins only every once in a while. She didn't approach them. Their sounds bounced around in her gut and bones.

A ray gun shooting bursts.

She could taste them in her mouth, feel them in her teeth, hear them in her sinuses.

Marbles dropped one by one into a can.

Gradually, the dolphins got less scared. They eased closer, 40 feet, 30 feet, examining her from the left, then the right eye. They rotated upside down to look at her that way. Their sounds changed.

The roar of a gorilla sped up so fast it sounded like a chick-adee.

Even in the periphery of her mask, their sheer size was apparent, weighing three to five times as much as she did.

One by one, over the next hour, they reached the same conclusion and twisted away, accepting her in their lagoon.

That morning she studied the dolphins with short glances. In order to feed them, she had to understand them, to sense what was the problem.

To her, at this point, their smooth seamless bodies appeared as similar as mass-produced toys. All of them had brown eyes and pink mouths, their skin an identical battleship grey. There was no visible sign of gender, just an indented slit along the underbelly. Their bodies were different sizes, but it was hard to see the difference unless they were lined up next to each other and motionless, which hardly ever happened.

The easiest way to distinguish them was their injuries. The biggest dolphin had the rope burn across its chest, just in front of its flippers. She called this one *Burn*. Burn spent time that morning clicking at the sandy bottom of the lagoon and then digging its beak through the sand. Occasionally it ate something it found. Some small burrowed fish? Some type of worm?

The medium-sized one with the cut on its side, she named *Cut*. The smaller one, the adolescent, was *Junior*. And the fourth one, the one with no marks or differences, the same size as Cut, was *Other*. At times, since Junior and Other didn't have distinguishing marks, she got them confused, but she worked at learning which was which, testing herself, trying to see at a glance the difference in size and style of movements, the way Junior's face was a little rounder and Other's eyes deeper set.

Partway through the morning, the surface of the lagoon began to ripple with the wind. A storm blowing in. A short time later, something blew into the water 20 feet to her right. Fabric. She recognized the sleeves of her shirt, but before she could kick toward it to retrieve it, a dolphin streaked in to grab the shirt in its mouth. The dolphin (she guessed Junior from the size and playfulness) zipped away, delighted, the arms of the shirt waving bye-bye.

Junior did several circuits of the lagoon, turned slightly sideways to watch the fabric rippling through the water. Then it dropped the clothing beside Cut, who, without missing a beat, grabbed a sleeve in its mouth while corkscrewing forward so the shirt twisted around its body like a maypole. Once it let go, the shirt swirled off in a watery striptease, landing next to Burn, who snagged it neatly on its tail and drove toward the surface, jumping repeatedly, a needle sewing in and out of the water. Burn dropped the shirt beside Other, who deftly swirled it round its head and, using the shirt as a blindfold, chased the others in a squealing game of Marco Polo.

The dolphins never tugged the shirt from each other or fought for it. Instead they passed it, letting it go precisely in front of the next dolphin, clean as soccer players. Polite as Canadians.

After ten minutes, when they finally got bored with the shirt, she fished it out with a pool skimmer and looked around for another toy. There was a football and a frisbee on one of the tables. The dolphins had their heads out of the water, watching her. She threw the frisbee in first. They tracked it through the air with interest, watching it skip across a wave and tumble in. When it landed, they looked back at her. Not one of them swam toward it. So she fished it out and tossed the shirt back in, figuring that was what they liked. Burn, with its head out of the water, watched her. The shirt fluttered down into the water and Burn looked back at her with sadness. None of them moved toward it.

She tried throwing in different things for a while, assuming she had to find the right toy, a new one that would interest them. A plastic cup, a stick, one of the men's bathing suits. The dolphins just watched her throw in object after object, curious to see what she would do next. They didn't move toward any of the objects.

Then a towel, hanging on the railing, was blown into the water by a wind gust. This, they bolted for, sprinting around with it, passing it back and forth, playing.

Perhaps the wind was the secret.

She placed the football on the dock, next to the water's edge and sat down to wait.

When the wind nudged it forward into the water, they bolted for it. Cut got to it first, grabbing it with its mouth to dash forward, faster than any running back, then flicking it with its nose sideways to Other (or maybe Junior, hard to tell from above). This dolphin bopped the ball into the air with its tail, passing it to Cut.

When they finally stopped playing with the football, she repeated the experiment with the frisbee and then a towel. If the wind blew the object in, they would play with it. If she threw it in, they wouldn't touch it. She didn't know if this was distaste for her or some type of dolphin etiquette.

It was at this point, sitting by the lagoon, watching them play with the towel, that the idea hit her. She coughed with surprise. This was why they wouldn't eat the fish. She was throwing it to them.

So she lugged the basket of fish 30 feet up the chute, walking up the cement ramp between the boulders to the beach, where the dolphins couldn't see her. She left the basket weighed down with rocks in the water of the sluice, the fish inside being washed clean, while the dolphins could taste them in the water pouring into the lagoon. She ate her lunch nearby on the beach, watching the clouds roll by.

After twenty minutes, she returned to the basket, picked up a fish with tongs so it wouldn't smell of her and lobbed it high into the air over the boulders. She was out of sight of the dolphins and had been for a while, so they didn't know where she was. The tossed fish landed in the water of the lagoon like a gift from God.

She waited a few minutes, then wandered around, carefully approaching the lagoon from a different direction. She couldn't see the fish floating anywhere. She put on her mask to look under the water and still didn't see the body. Burn had his head up out of the lagoon, looking in the direction of the chute.

So she went back to the basket of fish and over the next few minutes, from different places on the beach, well out of sight, tossed ten more fish high into the air so they dropped from the sky into the lagoon.

When she returned to the lagoon, there were no fish on the surface. All the dolphins now had their heads out of the water, watching the sky with attention.

She returned to the basket of butterfish. Over the next half an hour, she lobbed fish after fish into the sky. When all 20 pounds of fish were gone, she walked around again to the lagoon, coming in from the side, and saw the three men standing on the veranda, staring, having spent the last few minutes watching the fish rain down and the dolphins snapping them up out of the air, famished.

Blum turned to her, his bright eyes impressed.

Sunburned Tibbet and the young guy (the one who'd originally asked her to take the notes) looked at her in a different way, sizing her up, as though she'd just stepped into the room.

EIGHT
June 6–10, 1965

She fed the dolphins frequently over the next few days, trying to make up for their time without food. Five or six times a day, she walked down to the beach where they couldn't see her and threw 20 pounds of fish, one body at a time up into the sky, so each splashed down into the lagoon.

Feeding the dolphins, however, didn't take much time. So she relaxed snorkeling in the shallows, observing them with sideways glances, never approaching the dolphins but letting them approach her. She needed to learn about them, to know them intimately the way she knew her dad's pigs, or the horses at Beach Ride Bobby's, so she could figure it out if they needed something or were getting sick.

In and out of the water all the time, her hair got in the way. Under the water, a curtain of it would roll in front of her face, obscuring her view. Out of the water, it was wet most of the day. At night, she shampooed the sticky salt away and fell asleep with it in a damp lump on the pillow beside her. With her hair almost always soaking, she could not wear her hearing glasses. Instead, she moved back and forth, from the air (where noise was muffled and confusing), to the water (where the dolphins filled her skull and chest with sounds of surreal clarity).

Tibbet and the third man, the younger one who had told her to take notes the first day, seldom talked to her. They sat on the veranda, taking notes, or they bustled about, carrying equipment and tools and notebooks, watching her from the side. The younger man always seemed to have a cigarette hanging from his mouth.

She noticed that when she prepared to get into the lagoon, the men turned to look directly. She wasn't sure if they turned because she was a young woman stripping down to a bathing suit or if they were worried about her getting in the water with the animals. They themselves stayed back from the water and the dolphins.

At the end of that first week, seeing her lug a basket of fish down toward the lagoon, Tibbet said to her—You're like their maid.

In terms of lip reading, it took her a few weeks to learn how each new person chewed through the motions of speech, the subtle individual differences between *All set* and *Not yet*. She had a particularly hard time with Tibbet. He tended to purse his mouth a little, even when speaking. This made it hard to see what sounds he was making. He carried a rolled package of Tums with him all the time and, when thinking, would shake one out and pop it into his mouth like a breath mint. Rather than chewing on it, he'd suck on it until it dissolved, warping his mouth movements.

—What?

—You're their maid.

She wasn't sure if he meant *maid* or *made*. She asked again—What?

She had told the men she was partly deaf. She'd asked them to face her when they talked, to enunciate and not cover their mouths. However frequently, working on something else, they forgot, speaking muffled and angled away or scratching their noses, until they'd finally turn frustrated and half-bellow the words.

Maid—Tibbet yelled—You're the dolphin *maid*.

Within a day, the third man, the younger one, was also referring to her as the dolphin maid. He appeared to be some kind of assistant. Blum or Tibbet would speak and point, and he would move in that direction to lug bags or repair a machine or file papers.

She was surprised because lugging, repairing and filing were the sort of tasks her family did, and this man didn't move or talk like them. With her relatives, she could read with a glance from 20 feet away what they were feeling. They telegraphed emotion with posture and gesture and expression, as subtle as Buster Keaton. Greeting each other, they would clap backs and hug repeatedly, the tone of their voices loud and high. Arguing, they leaned in, their faces inches apart, spitting out the words. Amused, they threw back their heads to laugh, surrendering to the joke so loudly that nearby people startled.

The third man wasn't like this. He acted like he was playing bridge and had a good hand. His face didn't move much. His voice was controlled, his posture correct. He hardly ever gestured except to knock the ash off his cigarette. Emotion was betrayed in the stillness of his gaze or in his nostrils flaring. He had straight blond hair and white teeth, the good looks of Barbie's Ken. He had an endless number of polo shirts and madras shorts.

She knew his family was not like hers. His family was the kind to vacation on the island, not live here. It seemed likely he was working as an assistant for a short time, as a way up the ladder.

She kept trying to figure out his name, but it started and ended with hard-to-hear consonants, the ones formed in the front of the mouth and pushed out with the smallest puff of air. Steff? Jeff? Shep? Since she was only sure of the vowel in his name, she thought of him as *Eh*.

In general, she preferred being underwater. There, she could see what was going on. The dolphins accepted her without comment, examining her with curiosity. They were muscular and sleek birds swooping and twisting through the brilliant water. She marveled at the fact that they existed on the same planet as the dingy bathroom she and her roommates had shared in Tampa.

The dolphins' sounds echoed in her bones. The sounds were not like a bird's song, the same pre-programmed snippet of a tune repeated endlessly. Nor did they sound like a dog's bark or whine, raw emotion made audible. The dolphins' vocalizations instead varied constantly, changing pitch, volume and style, like a toddler burbling to itself.

The clacking of a typewriter.

They directed their sounds at whatever they were interested in, a rock, the sand floor, some seaweed, beaming vocals at the object as though wondering why it didn't reply.

A bat squeaking.

The volume varied from a background hum to a blast that vibrated through her bones.

Pulses of a jet engine, trying to start.

She began to suspect there were many more noises than these, noises she couldn't hear, since at times the trills went up and up until she couldn't hear anything, but still the dolphins were angled toward one another, attentive. From humans she knew well what a conversation looked like that she couldn't hear.

With each day, they got more used to her, approaching closer, staring. They studied her as much as she studied them.

When they surfaced, there was a fast hydraulic exhale, quick as a machine's breath. Unless a dolphin was busy playing or fighting or examining some object, it would rise to the surface to breathe every few seconds. The four of them exhaling this way created an irregular beat, a steam engine of life.

They were not always calm. Sometimes they raced and shoved each other, sideswiping and ramming, screaming and popping and wagging their open mouths. Their speed and strength were such that she couldn't tell how much of this was good-natured playing and how much was true aggression. Perhaps being creatures used to having a whole sea to roam in, this small lagoon increased tensions, prisoners jousting for space in the exercise yard.

If the roughhousing got too intense, she waded out of the water. She was a puny slow-moving land creature who could get in the way, hurt unintentionally.

* * *

The fourth day when she pulled herself out, Tibbet was there. She tugged off her mask and mopped water from her face.

Turning to him, she realized he was speaking.—Sorry, say again?

Why do you get in the water?—He gestured with his chin to the lagoon. In his cheek was the lump of a Tums he was sucking on. She wasn't sure why he sucked on the Tums rather than chewed them. Perhaps he thought they would last longer. The Tums constricted his lips. At least he did not also smoke.

She made an educated guess.—Get in the water?

He nodded.

—So I can see them.

The only word she recognized in his response was *bad*.

She asked—Why is it bad?

He spoke, irritated, moving the Tums from one side of his mouth to the other.

She waited, her brows raised.

He inhaled and said in an exaggerated fashion using loud Tarzan English—We want wild dolphins. Want to learn about wild dolphins.

She asked—Wild dolphins?

He nodded.

—Then why keep them caged?

Tibbet blinked.

(Decades later, when Cora thought back to the way people moved and talked during this era, she realized it was as though everyone doubted their own gender. In reaction, they over-compensated in a thousand small ways.

Men tended to speak in a deep voice with little emotion. They made statements, Joe Friday from *Dragnet* just stating the facts. They talked at length, assuming all were interested. They didn't ask questions. Their hair was flattened with grease. They sat with their legs spread as though something in their pants needed the room; perhaps it was all the keys in their pockets, to their homes, their cars, their offices.

On the other hand, women had no keys in their pockets, for mostly they had no pockets at all but only purses that they clutched in their hands. Wearing dresses or skirts, they turned their faces to the men, giggling and nodding and exclaiming, their voices pitched high, so much harder for Cora to hear. In general, they acted like nervous guests, perched uncomfortably on a chair, their thighs crossed, trying to deny there was anything there at all.

Cora wore the appropriate female clothing, but she could not do a lot of the other behavior. She didn't giggle at the men's jokes because she tended to miss the punchline. She didn't utter constant affirmations because she wasn't sure what specifically needed supporting. She did however lean forward into a conversation, staring at the mouth.

The way men reacted to her depended a lot on if they were happy in their relationship or not.

Tibbet, it appeared, loved his wife a lot.)

He said—*What*?

She was pretty sure he'd heard, but was making her repeat her question.

She said—Then why do you keep them caged?

Tibbet snorted as though in disgust and walked away.

* * *

That afternoon, when she waded out of the water, Blum was sitting on the dock watching her. He had no weight on him, a bony man, something inside burning all his energy, a small hamster in his head or chest running and running.

The air was quiet, no wind, and he tended to be easier to lipread: his mouth opened wide, his tongue moved crisply. (With him, she only had real difficulty when he had a cigarette clamped in the corner of his mouth.)

At the moment, watching the neat gymnastics of his mouth, she thought he enjoyed his body. She had an image of him standing up from the toilet and looking back in the bowl with pride.

He said, his eyes moving lazily over her bathing suit, pausing on her left breast—Why do you spend so much time in the water?

Having recently answered Tibbet's question about this, she was able to respond faster.—So I can watch the dolphins.

Unlike Tibbet, he seemed to approve. His eyes were still focused on her breast. She wondered if the bathing suit was stained there.

He asked—What do they do?

—Them? They dance. They fight. They play. They make the most beautiful sounds.

Blum considered this, then stepped into the house and brought out a lab book, a bound notebook with a speckled cover and a label on the front. This was the type of book that Tibbet and Eh kept their notes in. He handed it to her along with a Bic pen. The lab book was untouched and had a weight to it, each blank page waiting for words.

—Put the date and your name on the label.

She checked his face to make sure he was serious, examined the pen, then wrote lightly on the label so it could be scratched out later if necessary.

He said—Every twenty minutes get out of the water and take some notes. Write down whatever you notice.

He walked away.

In a way he scared her. She knew what to expect from the other men, what the limits and expectations were, but not from him. As soon as he was gone, she glanced at her left breast, but could see nothing different.

For the next few days, she worried about when Blum would ask for her notes and if he would approve. Underwater, she didn't know when twenty minutes had passed. So she simply waded out whenever she felt enough time had passed and dried her hands carefully, thinking about what she'd seen. At the top of each page, she wrote down the date. With each new entry, she noted the time. After that, she'd pause, uncertain.

She didn't have any love of words. People with good hearing, they blathered all day long, saying whatever occurred to them, the speaking and hearing so effortless they didn't bother to enunciate or think through the meaning or syntax or their emotions. Meanwhile she had to concentrate to know what they were saying, staring at the mouth, piecing the sounds together to deduce the most basic content. Hearing took her work. At times it felt like she had laboriously translated an ancient scrap of Sanskrit, only to find a grocery list.

Complicating this was the fact that what people said with their mouths didn't always agree with what they said with their bodies. She figured this fact out in middle school when one day she happened to be close enough and the room quiet enough to hear the two girls in her class talk about their roles in the school play. The shorter one with the dark hair said it's not that she was jealous. She said this with her arms crossed over her chest, her body hunched and furious.

Over time, Cora learned to focus on the language of the

body first, then secondly to listen to what their mouths were saying.

Perhaps because of this, she didn't have as strong a faith in words as most people did. Faced with this notebook, instead of writing down words, she started off with sketching the dolphins. She needed to learn how they moved normally and how to read their emotions. She used to draw the pigs in her dad's barn as they rubbed against a barn pole, or the horses at Beach Ride Bobby's as they plodded off to the evening beach ride with a tourist sitting on top. Drawing was how she'd learned an animal's body and posture and typical movements. Drawing was how she learned how to read an animal's moods and health and interactions. Sometimes while she sketched and erased, sketched and erased, trying to get the line of a rump or jowl right, a sow would amble up to the fence to watch, its nostrils blowing heat into her hair.

Underwater, she would observe one of the dolphins for a while, then wade out, dry her hands and start to sketch, using a pencil so she could erase what looked wrong and try again.

The curves took the longest time to get right. She'd drawn fish before, the ones her family were about to eat for dinner, but fish had flat bodies with surprised eyes as though they'd been squished between two books. At first her drawings of the dolphins looked like fish with dolphin beaks and tails grafted on.

So she tried again and again, sketching and erasing, trying to figure out how to show the muscled curves, the placement of fins and flippers. Her drawings got better when she began to think of them as misplaced mammals, as piglets that had wandered into the water, losing limbs and ears, growing fins and flippers and a streamlined form. An underwater pig that had traded its snout for a beak and a toddler's playful eyes.

Once she could draw a recognizable dolphin, she sketched each of the four dolphins individually, noting down the distinguishing marks, writing their names below the sketches. Physically sketching the differences between them helped her know what to look for: the notch in Burns' fin, Cut's missing tooth, the scratches from old wounds on Other's fin and the rounder unscratched Junior.

Once she was able to draw them, she started writing actual notes. She wrote down only what she was sure of and what seemed important. She described specific actions, using the fewest words she could. Unlike the men, she wrote in pencil, never assuming that what she'd written was right or couldn't be improved later.

No matter how she dried herself off, the paper got a bit wet at the edges, like the dolphins themselves were keeping the notes.

* * *

One day while the dolphins were roughhousing, she noticed Burn had what looked like a thumb sticking out from below as it chased Cut around and around.

Oh, she thought.

She began watching the others for this same protruding thumb during the chasing. The penis emerged from the slit at the base of the belly. Evidently Burn and Junior were males, Cut and Other were females. The coupling was fast and performed stomach to stomach. Once she comprehended this action, she saw they did it many times a day. Perhaps they did it just as frequently in the wild, or maybe, in the lagoon, they were bored.

The activity (first sonaring the other's genitals and chasing each other for a while, then coupling stomach to stomach) appeared to happen just as often between different genders as between the same gender. She wondered if this also was because they had nothing else to do.

Considering their genders, she renamed them. Burn became Bernie. Junior stayed Junior.

Cut and Other became Kat and Mother.

She wrote down their genders on the pages with their sketches. She did not write down how she knew. She wrote down that they roughhoused, but not about the coupling. She didn't want the men to imagine her watching this. Her notes so much less than what she'd seen.

9:55 A.M.: Bernie chased Kat @ 10 minutes, squeaking. Junior and Mother watched.

Each morning on the way to the research center, she stopped by the fishermen's dock and picked up a crate of butterfish, the bodies still shiny from the sea. When she arrived at the center, she stood on the beach, on the far side of the boulders, out of sight, lobbing fish into the lagoon. Once the first fish hit the lagoon, the dolphins would swim to the surface, watching for more. If her hearing glasses were adjusted right, she could hear the clap of a dolphin's beak catching a fish in midair.

Every day, she stepped a few inches closer to the lagoon to throw the fish. After a few days, she sometimes spotted a dolphin's tail or fin as it jumped for the fish. She didn't know how good their vision was, if they could glimpse her standing there watching.

After she'd thrown the last fish, she'd wait twenty minutes, then circle around the lagoon and walk in, coming from a different direction each time. She wanted them gradually to wonder if she might have something to do with the fish raining down from the sky, to get used to the idea bit by bit, and adjust to it. Once they accepted it, assuming they did, she would be able to get close enough to make sure all of them were eating, to watch for any changes in diet that could signal health problems.

For now, each day, she wrote down how many total fish they ate.

June 16: 193 butterfish, 42 lbs. eaten.

* * *

For her, the slow part of the day was during the noonday heat, because this was when the dolphins didn't move much.

They lay close together under the dock, the only part of the lagoon that remained shaded when the sun was high overhead. They rested against the sand, in the deepest part of the water in that shade. They didn't seem to be sleeping, since their eyes were open.

(The first time she saw them sleeping was when she'd slipped into the water earlier than normal one morning. They were in a circle at the far end of the lagoon floating near the surface and at first she hadn't understood what they were doing. Every few seconds, each of them would surface, a deep slow exhale, and then submerge, sewing their way through the surface. As she swam slowly closer, none of them looked at her. At first she felt slighted. Gradually she became alarmed; it was like they were hypnotized, or turned into robots. Surface, breathe, submerge. Surface, breathe, submerge. She noticed each of them had one eye closed and one open, the gaze of the open eye motionless and staring. With each of them, the open eye was the one facing out toward possible danger.

As Cora got closer, Mother's eye blinked. She startled back from Cora and focused, all of them shuddering awake.)

At noon, she lay on the dock, looking down through the slats. She could see that sleep was not what they were doing. Both their eyes were open and aware. However, they moved as little as possible, just coming to the surface to breathe. Through the slats, their exhales were slow and deep.

She lay on the dock just above them, staring down through the boards at the shaded dolphins. When they exhaled, she could smell their breath, an unflattering combination of brine, fish and rotting egg.

12 P.M.: All dolphins floating in the shade of the dock, eyes open. They do this at noon each day.

* * *

She sometimes sat at the top of the staircase to the veranda to observe the dolphins. From here she could look down through the metal railing to watch them in the water, moving about, interacting. From the stairs, she couldn't hear all their sounds or catch the nuances of their play, but she could see more of the action and could take the notes continuously, her hands dry.

The men watched the dolphins and took notes also. They didn't sit on the stairs even though it had the best view, but instead on cushioned chairs on the veranda, with a notebook. On the table beside them was a drink and snacks and an ashtray.

Since she was there taking notes now, they'd cut their hours down. Tibbet watched in the morning from ten to noon and Eh from two to four in the afternoon. If the animals did anything of interest outside of those hours, the men were not there to witness it. They also seemed to take different kinds of notes than she did, for they used their pen to make only small ticks on the paper every once in a while, pausing occasionally to take a long drink from their glass full of clinking ice.

One morning she waded out of the lagoon to find Tibbet sitting in a chair on the dock. He'd recovered from his sunburn, but now wore big hats and long-sleeved shirts and looked sweaty and hunched in the sun.

He had her notepad in his lap and was reading it. He didn't put down the book once he saw her. Instead he looked at her, over her notes, like a teacher grading her quiz.—What's Bernie?

The dolphin with the rope burn.—She ran her fingers across her collarbone to show the location of the burn.

He seemed a polite man struggling with his disappointment in the state of the world. At times when he watched her work or when Blum was talking, he'd pinch his lips between his teeth as though scared of all he wanted to say. He looked back down at the notebook. With his face turned partly away, it was harder to read his lips.—Blum asked you to take notes?

—Yes.

He gestured to the page, speaking. She heard a few of his words: *anecdote, can't* and *data.*

For most people, spoken language was such a powerful method of communication, an audio code that given enough time and skill and mutual trust, could briefly bridge the gap between two minds, allowing people something close to the same image or emotion or understanding. For her, speech worked in reverse. The more words used, the greater distance and confusion.

Her hair being wet most of the day here meant she couldn't

wear her hearing glasses. Constantly making guesses at what the others had said, she was feeling a little like she had as a child, isolated in a bubble.

He sucked on the Tums, moving it about. Of the men at the center, he was the hardest to lipread. He picked up a pen and started showing her the proper way to take notes.

At the top of the leftmost column on the page, he wrote $\male_1$.

He said—Bernie.

At the head of the next column, he wrote $\male_2$ and then looked at her with his eyebrows raised.

Junior—she said, supplying the name.

At the top of the next two columns, he wrote $\female_1$ and then $\female_2$.

Kat—she said—and Mother.

He made no comment on the names. He looked down and said a complicated sentence she couldn't hear, the last word of which was *communication*.

Communication?—she asked.

—Yes.

She looked left and right, trying to imagine what the sentence might have been. When in doubt, she asked questions.—What kind?

She didn't catch his words, but he wrote at the top of her notepad, *Touch*.

He watched the dolphins from his chair. Each time one of the dolphins touched another, he put a tick down on the notepad in that dolphin's column. When Mother brushed her flipper against Kat's as she swam by, he made a tick in Mother's column. He did not note who it was that Mother touched or with what body part or whether it was a bite or caress. When Junior chased Mother, half riding on top of her for a full circuit of the lagoon so she could not surface to breath, Tibbet made just a simple tick in Junior's column, no more information.

After a few minutes, he handed her notebook back to her,

clearly expecting her to continue to keep tallying these touches. He tapped the cover of it with his fingers and said in a loud voice—Data.

So she tried out his method. In a way it was a relief to know what kind of notes she was supposed to take. For that whole day she counted touches between the dolphins. However, when she added the tallies up, she saw how much was missing. Yes, she now knew that Junior touched the others 10 percent more than the rest, but there was nothing in the numbers about *how* he touched others. It didn't describe how he followed behind and to the side of Bernie like a fighter plane in formation, mimicking the bigger male's movements and posture, turning when he turned, breathing when he breathed, so close that his beak sometimes touched Bernie's flipper.

And there was also nothing in those rows of ticks that explained how he slept. He dozed like they all did, one eye closed, the other eye unfocused but open, surfacing regularly to breathe. The difference with Junior was that, while sleeping, he liked to hold Mother's flipper in his mouth, rising in sync with her to breathe at the surface as one. He was long past the age of nursing from her, but he still retained this habit of holding onto her while sleeping (whether she was his mother or just a mother figure while in the lagoon).

And there was nothing in the tallied numbers to show how Junior sometimes beamed noise at Kat's genital slit and then chased her, bumping her, his belly to hers, upside down, until she complied and angled her belly to his. An adolescent, he was old enough to be interested in, and apparently capable of, this action.

Each of these types of touches were simplified down to a simple tick mark. The more she counted different actions (how frequently they breathed, how often they chased each other), the less she found she liked the tallying. Simply counting actions missed too much information. It erased the dolphins themselves, their wants and personalities.

So after a day of counting, she returned mostly to keeping records the way she had before, sketching and writing notes. The only things she continued to count were activities that gave her an idea of their health. How many hours they slept during the day and how many pounds of fish the group was eating.

By now, when she fed the dolphins, she was only 20 feet up the chute away from the lagoon, close enough to see occasionally which dolphin jumped to catch which fish. She tallied the results. She let them at the apex of their jump glimpse her standing there, in the direction of where the fish came from. She didn't think any of them had yet seen her in mid-throw. She wanted them to come to the conclusion slowly. So far, no matter what their suspicions were, they still caught the fish and ate them.

After another week or two, once they were certain that the fish came from her, she would step entirely into view to feed them.

> *6/19: Butterfish eaten:*
> *Kat* 卌 卌 卌 卌 卌 卌 卌 卌 卌 |
> *Mother* 卌 卌 卌 卌 卌 卌 卌
> *Junior* 卌 卌 卌 卌 卌 卌 卌 |||
> *Bernie* 卌 卌 卌 卌 ||

In this way, she learned how little Bernie was eating.

* * *

Most times when the dolphins mated, it was fast and sensuous and mutual, the females as likely to start the behavior as the males, with much nipping and caressing and sonaring of genitals beforehand, the act itself fast. However it wasn't always this way. One morning when Cora was in the water, Bernie sonared Mother's genital slit until she bit at him and swam away. He chased her, his penis apparent now. He kept his body between Mother and the surface so she could not rise to breath. At high speed, they circled the lagoon, squealing and creaking at each other.

Growing up on a farm, Cora had seen the act of sex many times. Her introduction to sex had been when she was six. While she was in the barn filling the water trough for the pigs, her dad sat down on the shoulders of a sow that was in season, jouncing up and down and kicking her ribs to get her in the mood, before reaching behind to insert the turkey baster of boar sperm. The radio was on playing the news, his expression bored. When she'd asked what he was doing, he said this was how you made baby pigs. It was two years before she was sure the piglets were not related to her in some way.

On a farm there is no secrecy around sex, no romance, no taboos. It was just what happened. The dogs on the front porch, the chickens in the yard. The cows in the field mounting each other, no bull in sight. Once she started working at Beach Ride Bobby's, she would tether the mare to the rail while Mr. Pebbles, the stallion, was led closer, wrinkling his upper lip and drooling.

Bernie and Mother circled the lagoon at high speed, dancing and screaming, fighting. Mother had not been able to get to the surface to breathe for at least three minutes now. Underwater, the noise was overwhelming, vibrating in Cora's fingers and face and skull.

Her mom's responsibilities were the kids, the kitchen and the woodpile. She could be found most days, standing by the stove, stirring food and reading a romance book with a title like *Summer Love* or *Double Wedding*. Cora tried not to imagine her parents mating. Her mom tethered to a fence and reading *The Preacher's Son*, her dad drooling, white in his eyes, approaching from behind.

At eighteen, Cora had experimented with sex herself, first with the son of a neighbor. She wasn't sure what to expect, but had not been impressed. The three times she'd let him, the boy had not touched her with emotion, or humor, or even respect. More he'd acted like this was something that needed to be accomplished quickly and in secret, a little like he was going to the bathroom. So she experimented instead with the town pharmacist; an older man whom she figured might know more. With him, there were some plusses. She could lie down in a bed, instead of in a backseat, and he seemed so grateful. Still the act itself took under ten minutes. Around the time she was beginning to get interested, he was done.

One time when he was lying on top of her, just afterward, breathing heavily, she asked him if he could continue for a while with his hand. He'd drawn back from her, looking shocked.

In the two years since then, she'd tried two other men and had fairly similar experiences. Perhaps she'd chosen the wrong men. Or perhaps, in the same way that different eras engendered different types of dancing (slower or faster; rules and roles changing), sex also had styles. Perhaps at the moment, sex tended to take less time and involve more pumping. She didn't know. She assumed she could just be built wrong. Given her hearing, she was used to feeling defective.

Worried that she'd get hit unintentionally by the wild screaming dolphins chasing each other, she crept out of the lagoon. Within another few minutes Mother gave up and turned her belly to Bernie. After that, they settled down.

Cora didn't take notes on this part. She didn't want Blum or the other men to know she'd seen this and to think about her watching it. She noticed the way they watched her, especially Blum and Eh.

7 A.M.: Roughhousing, Bernie chased Mother.

* * *

One morning she pulled herself out of the pool and Blum was reading her notebook. Skinny man, legs spread, bright bird eyes. As soon as she saw the notebook in his hands, she realized even with the drawings and the tallies, there weren't more than fifteen pages of notes.

He looked up at her and ground his cigarette out on the dock. He asked her, his face puzzled.—Bernie?

Since she'd told Blum about being partially deaf, he always turned his face to her when talking so she could read her lips. He put his cigarette down and used fewer words. Most people would forget to do this at times. He didn't. She could see no condescension or irritation in his action, nor empathy. He just did it every time, a little like a machine. She missed fewer words with him than with the others and was grateful.

She said—He's the biggest dolphin.

He jerked his chin at the notebook.—Tibbet told you to tally things?

—Yes.

He said—Ignore him.

He turned to the page where she'd tallied the fish they ate.—Bernie isn't eating a lot?

—Yes.

He turned toward the lagoon, looking at the dolphin who happened to surface at that moment. She wondered if he knew this was Mother, not Bernie.

He returned to reading the notes. Flipping to a different page, he asked—They lie under the dock?

She saw which page he was reading.—Yes. They rest under the dock every day, when the sun is most direct.

—Why is that important?

She said—I'm not sure. They are at the bottom in the shade, where the water is coolest. They don't move much. It's possible the lagoon is too hot for them.

He looked at the dolphins, considering that thought.— Write more.

* * *

Around noon that same day, she saw Blum step out onto the balcony to watch the dolphins. The sun was high overhead. Standing on the balcony, he touched the metal railing, then jerked his fingers back from its heat.

Below, all the dolphins were under the dock, in that small patch of shade. Blum strode down the steps to where he could see them through the slats in the dock, watch them floating in the shade listlessly.

He went into the house and came out with a thermometer, a small skillet and some string. He tied the skillet and thermometer to one end of the string and threw the skillet into the lagoon. It hit the water with a splash and sank, dragging the thermometer down to the bottom of the lagoon. He tied the other end of the string onto a dock piling, and after half an hour came back to pull it and the skillet out and look at the temperature. Then he threw the skillet back in, tying the rope off so only a few feet of it was in the water, the thermometer closer to the surface. Half an hour later, he came back to see that temperature.

Afterward, he carried the skillet, thermometer and rope up the sluice to check the temperature of the sea.

The next day he had the men stretch two large canvas sails across the lagoon, tethering them on one side to several palm trees and on the other side to the railings of the balcony. The result shaded probably half of the lagoon. He lowered the ramp at the end of the sluice, so more seawater poured in.

Blum took the lagoon's temperature at different levels again that day, then opened the gate further. By the end of the week, when he pulled the thermometer from the lagoon he seemed to approve.

After that, the dolphins played more, sometimes even at noon.

* * *

An important man visited the research center. She knew this man was important because, an hour before he arrived, Eh started picking up all the bathing suits and towels on the balcony, and, through the window, she could see Tibbet inside washing the dishes. She jumped into the lagoon and snorkeled around, making sure not to look in the direction of the building. She knew if she were pulled into cleaning up even once, the men would expect her to do it always.

Once the cleaning had stopped, she waded out, and soon after that, Blum appeared with the man. Blum's voice was louder than normal, his gestures bigger. On display like this, he gleamed with the man's attention, puffing up like a bird, his bony body, his shiny eyes. He had begun to remind her of a crow, cocking his head at the world, his feathers shimmering, hungry and canny, observing everything.

He gestured to the sails stretched over the water and pulled the thermometer out of the water. While he talked to the important man, Blum didn't gesture to her. She didn't know if he mentioned her name.

Here on the island, little rain fell except at night. Every morning dawned sparkling and clear, t-shirt weather, 75 to 85 degrees, the sea always warm. Everything was brightly colored: fuchsia, cyan and lime. The birds, the water, the fleshy tropical flowers, the buildings.

She was in the water each day, watching the dolphins.

Her skin was sticky with dried salt. She wore her bathing suit all day. Each time she pulled herself out of the water, the men would turn to look, and she'd tug on a pair of shorts and a shirt over the suit. These clothes would get soaked, especially at the crotch and breasts, an outline of her erogenous zones.

* * *

She'd been here over three weeks and by this point was throwing fish to the dolphins while she stood only 15 feet back from the lagoon, partly hidden by the boulders. From here, she could see most times which dolphin caught the fish. Although by now at least one of the dolphins (while jumping from the water to catch a fish) must have spotted her holding the next fish, they continued to catch and eat what she threw. Maybe, when she first arrived here, they'd been suspicious of taking food from a stranger, or thought since she threw the fish, it was her fish and not to be touched. Whatever the reason had been, now every time they caught a fish (a hungry clap and a fast swallow), she felt a flash of joy at this, the purest kind of communication.

Gift, she asked.

Yes, they said.

Occasionally she threw other types of fish to the dolphins, not just butterfish. She'd toss in a snapper, squid, mackerel or tarpon, experimenting to see what they'd eat. She wanted to expand their diet, give them more nutrients. In general, the higher the fat content, the faster they jumped for it.

She varied the mixture daily. If they seemed less interested in any type of fish, she wouldn't offer that kind for a few days.

The dolphins clearly had individual tastes. Junior seemed to crave mackerel. He closed his eyes as he swallowed it, like a child eating candy. Mother, on the other hand, whistled in excitement (loud enough even for Cora to hear) at the sight of a tarpon.

It was Kat though who loved the squid. At the sight of a squid flying through the air, she'd jump high into the air, her mouth open, ready to catch it. Her eagerness was so large that Cora would throw the squid in her direction.

However Kat wouldn't eat the squid. She'd hide the squid instead at the bottom of the lagoon until feeding time was over. Then she'd pull the body out. It was such a different shape from the solid biscuit of a butterfish or mackerel. Kat would explore the tentacles for the longest time, nosing them and clicking, fascinated. She'd shoulder her way into the body, then swim forward trying to balance it in place, wearing the squid on her fin as an epaulet. Or she'd grab it in her mouth and torpedo fast around the lagoon, a frenzied beard of legs.

Kat would play and play with each squid until it was shredded and in pieces. Only then did she abandon it.

In the mornings Cora would take the pool skimmer and scoop bits of squid legs off the surface of the lagoon.

* * *

Each day the dolphins swam a little closer to Cora while she was snorkeling. They clicked and stared at her. Their brown eyes focused and curious.

Returning their gaze reminded her of a neighbor's baby she'd babysat as a child. The 11-month-old baby had stared at her solemnly, an old soul, considering each of her actions, not yet ready to speak.

* * *

One morning, she decided to breathe only when Bernie breathed. She wanted to find out how long she could breathe as infrequently as a dolphin. She picked Bernie because he was the biggest and she hoped he needed more air than the others.

So the next time he surfaced and inhaled, she sucked in air through the snorkel and then held her breath, floating there motionless, watching him. She counted off seconds in her head: one Mississippi, two Mississippi. Meanwhile he dove under the water and swam around, investigating the bottom of the lagoon, clicking down at it, turning rocks over with his beak, hoping to scare out something edible. The seconds ticked by, his actions relaxed and leisurely.

Within twenty seconds, the air in her lungs had expanded, the pressure in her throat. At twenty-six seconds, he rose to the surface and exhaled. The air burst from her mouth, loud in the snorkel. All the dolphins turned to look at her.

While Bernie had to inhale only one breath before sinking back down, she had to gasp several times before she could hold her breath again.

Meanwhile Bernie descended, trailing Junior in a sponta-neous game of follow the leader, investigating whatever Junior investigated, turning when Junior turned. Fifteen seconds, twenty seconds, twenty-five.

The moment Bernie finally exhaled at twenty-nine seconds, the air burst from her snorkel, even louder than the last time. The dolphins looked at her, Bernie with the most interest, surprised she was breathing when he did. He sank back under the water and nosed his way over to her, as she huffed in and out through her snorkel trying to catch her breath.

As soon as she felt able to, she sucked her breath in again and held it.

However, within a few seconds, her lungs began to hurt. Her body needed to breathe. Bernie cocked his head, clicking at her from a few feet away. The clicking vibrated in her tight lungs. He rotated 90 degrees to look at her sideways, while her heart thumped hard in her ears. Was it possible through the water he could hear her heart?

Although only ten seconds had passed since the last time he'd breathed, he looked her in the eyes and rose purposefully to the surface.

This time, she stood up and yanked the mask and snorkel off to gasp at the air. Bernie stuck his head out of the water also, much closer than he normally would have; she could have reached out and touched him. However she didn't really focus on that as she was rocking with the effort of breathing.

As her breathing slowed, she turned to Bernie. His head the size of her torso. His fixed grin and brown eyes. This close she could see his pupil was a strange horseshoe shape, different from a human's. Looking her in the eye, he began deliberately to make loud rasping gasps. His breathing, along with the raspy noises, emerged from the blowhole on the top of his head. This was how dolphins breathed. However, the strange thing was, while he made these noises, he kept his mouth open and rocked in time with the gasps.

Imitating her.

He stopped and examined her, then rolled beneath the water and was gone.

She wrote up what she'd seen, then looked it over.

In general she liked the written word so much more than the spoken word, for her hearing didn't get in the way of reading. Still, writing down her own thoughts was intimidating. It was difficult to think of all the ways the words might be interpreted. She had to imagine herself into the reader's mind, for the meaning of the words was in the intersection between the writer and reader. Both sides had to be willing to work hard, to try to imagine all that the other might be thinking.

Tibbet would read these notes in disbelief. He would say she needed data not stories. She did not know what Blum would think. How much observation did he really want?

She struggled to convey what she'd seen in a way that both Blum and Tibbet would understand and believe. Uncertain, she erased a little more and a little more, until she'd edited down the words to what she knew they could accept. Deafness can take many forms.

6/28—Bernie can breathe only twice a minute for several minutes without apparent difficulty.

* * *

So much hearing happens not in the ear, but in the brain. Like a partially blind person, Cora's brain struggled to make sense of the few clues it was given, to interpolate between distant points. At times, it made guesses and filled in the information it lacked. Hearing thunder (muffled and indistinct), her brain turned the sound into a large dog growling just behind her. She could hear the raspy breathing mixed into the growl. The clap of a book shutting was turned into a gunshot outside, complete with its after-echo off the nearby buildings.

At times her brain got more imaginative.

Like a bird's body is designed for flight, whole sections of the human brain are devoted to language. Back when she was eight, a few months after the flu took most of her hearing, her brain ached so much for spoken language that, out of sheer desire, it occasionally transformed noise into words.

The first time this happened was one morning when she cranked on the water in the sink. Instead of hearing the squeak of the fixture followed by the rush of water, she heard a voice. The voice was clear and vivid in a way she hadn't heard in months. The consonants, the emotion, the slight sibilance of dentures. An older woman's voice said with surprise and interest—*She should suggest it.*

The words originating from the mouth of the faucet. Cora stood there, staring.

A few days later, walking back from school, alone in her staticky silence, a cocker spaniel barked repeatedly at her from behind a fence, in a sarcastic teenage voice—*Right, right, oh right.*

Two days after that, the school flag snapping in the wind over the playground called out in a precise BBC accent—*Flip it far. Far.*

These voices cracked open a profound fear inside of her. So she began to plead with her parents for hearing aids. Although the devices were very expensive, in the face of her desperation, they conceded within weeks. As soon as she started wearing the aids, the voices went away.

But her memory of them didn't fade. She could recall them perfectly, each of their inexplicable phrases, could replay the tone of each voice in her head at any moment with unnerving clarity. She struggled even years later to make sense of them: why those words, why those voices?

Then in ninth-grade English class, she read the story of Moses hearing a voice from a burning bush, and she understood immediately. She wondered how long he'd been going deaf, if he'd been hearing different voices for years, from the goats and the wind and his own sandals scuffing the ground. She knew this bush had the first voice that said more than a phrase and where the words actually made sense. Perhaps all prophets were hard of hearing. This lack could make them listen with enough attention to hear what others were too busy to attend to. The lack opened up their minds.

If, for a week or so, she didn't wear the hearing aids, her brain got lonely, hungry for language, and the voices returned.

* * *

Blum's wife tended to visit the research center in the morning when her kids weren't napping. The first time she appeared, stepping out onto the veranda, it was about 10 A.M. Cora was sitting by the pool in her bathing suit, taking notes. Simply from the way the wife's attention locked on her and then her posture straightened, Cora knew Blum had had affairs.

The wife walked over, her two toddlers following. She was a thin precise blond, in her early thirties, a decade older than Cora. Although she held her face in a fixed smile, her tongue moved sharply, filled with long-term fury. She said her name was Babs. Her eyes missed no detail.

Cora told her she was hard of hearing and asked her to speak slower. She answered whatever questions she could hear, her name and her work here. She pulled on some clothes, slouched and tried to appear harmless.

When Babs left, her kids trailed along behind, the oldest sucking her thumb, watching her mom with a worried look.

Tibbet's wife, on the other hand, didn't have kids. She tended to drop by the research center more frequently, every few days. She'd appear around noon to have lunch with the men, drinking a gimlet or martini the way they did. She was maybe twenty-five, her hair red and her body ample. She laughed easily, giving into the motion, her whole body swaying, one hand against her chest.

The first time she appeared, she walked over to Cora to introduce herself. Her mouth opened wide while she talked, a generous spirit, her tongue unhurried and large.

She said her name. It might have been Terry or maybe Carrie.

Terry/Carrie asked if she was Eh's girlfriend.

Cora said—No, I work here.

Terry/Carrie cocked her head. Something about the way she did this reminded Cora of Bernie studying her with his dark eyes.

Cora said—I feed the dolphins. Make sure they're healthy.

Terry/Carrie still looked at her.

Cora added—Your husband calls me the dolphin maid.

Terry/Carrie nodded. She wore a t-shirt that said *Smith Lacrosse Team*.

Wanting to change the subject, Cora asked—What's Smith?

Terry/Carrie paused at this question, seemed surprised.

With a long neck and black hair, Cora had been told she looked a little like Audrey Hepburn. However the last few weeks in the sun had darkened her skin to a shade that Hepburn could have never achieved.

Ahh—said Terry/Carrie.

From being around the dolphins, Cora was more aware of breath, her own and others, the frequency of it, the speed and depth. Terry/Carrie exhaled that *ahh* with a movement of her stomach, her head nodded and her curiosity about Cora left her. She said—It's a college, dear.

Still she invited Cora up to have lunch and drinks with the men on the veranda. Cora replied she couldn't; she was work-ing. Terry/Carrie walked up there and sat down, tucking her skirt under her legs. The men watched her do so.

When either of the wives was around, the men acted differ-ently. They were careful not to look at Cora in her bathing suit. If they needed to address her, they talked with their faces flat and bland.

Cora wore a black bathing suit, one that covered her from the collar bone down to the top of the thighs. She kept her hair drawn back in a ponytail, wore no makeup and worked to be ignored. She wanted to stay here, watching the dolphins. She wanted no trouble.

Cora watched while the men and Terry/Carrie ate lunch on the veranda. At one point Blum leaned in and touched Terry/Carrie's shoulder, saying something. A few seconds later, Tibbet put his hand on his wife's hand, leaving it there for Blum to see.

For a moment, Cora considered taking out her notebook to tally these touches.

* * *

About 9 A.M., Tibbet and Eh came out of the tool shed car-rying a large fishing net. They unrolled it, 50 feet long, and dropped it into the water across the far end of the lagoon. The net had weights along the bottom. With Tibbet on one side and Eh on the other, they began to drag the net through the water toward the shallow end.

As soon as the dolphins saw the net, they began to panic, darting around the lagoon, looking for escape. Clearly, they'd experienced this before. They jumped, vocalizing, high squeals of fear. Blum stood on the veranda, watching and drinking his coffee.

Bernie tried to protect the other dolphins, keeping his body between the approaching net and them. He stuck his head out of the water and clapped his mouth open and shut, a warning to the humans. The claps were loud, and his sharp teeth shimmered in the sunlight. Then he charged the net, stopped just short of it and slammed his tail down against the water with all his power. The sound boomed, loud as a gunshot.

He did this over and over again, but the men paid no attention, chatting across the lagoon, continuing to drag the net toward the shallows. The fleeing dolphins had less and less room.

Cora was surprised the animals didn't jump over the net. They could easily escape to the other side; they jumped that high all the time. However, with the net, they didn't do so. They looked like they wanted to, for they repeatedly charged toward it, but then would turn away at the last second before jumping. Perhaps the netting confused their senses, leaving them unsure water remained on the other side for them to land in.

Using the net, the men herded the dolphins into the shallow end, then continued to heave in the net, dragging the dolphins bit by bit up the slope until they lay in an inch of water. The animals gasped there, pressed down by their own weight. Built for water, all of them (perhaps especially powerful Bernie) were transformed into fleshy paraplegics.

While Tibbet and Eh rolled up the net and put it away, Blum walked down to the lagoon, his coffee mug in one hand, stepping barefoot into the water and walking from dolphin to dolphin, considering each. He stopped beside Mother and jerked his chin at her. Tibbet and Eh shoved the other dolphins back into the water. Only Mother remained beached, watching the men. Each time she breathed, Cora could see the effort it took, the unaccustomed weight of gravity on her ribs. The men brought over a canvas stretcher and placed it on the ground next to her, then heaved her onto it. From the lagoon, the other dolphins squealed and stared.

Tibbet and Blum grabbed one end of the stretcher, Eh got the other end and they lugged Mother up the stairs. The men grunted with each step, moving slowly and red-faced, easing her into the house like an oversized couch. She disappeared.

The dolphins whipped around the lagoon, looking for a way to get to Mother, to help. At the surface, their fins cut through the water. They jumped into the air, hoping to catch a glimpse.

Cora wrapped her wet hair tightly in a towel and risked putting on her hearing glasses. She walked up the stairs until she could hear what was going on inside the house. The noises were not quiet; they echoed out the window. Mother was squealing, sometimes very loudly. There was a rhythmic metal banging. Instruments clattered. Occasionally a machine beeped. The men called out information or commands to each other.

She backed away slowly, unable to will herself inside to look through the windows or door to see what was happening. She took off her glasses, walked back to the lagoon and sat there on the ground, hugging her knees to her chest, looking only at the dolphins in the lagoon.

After an hour, the men carried Mother back out of the house and back down to the pool. She was alive. She had three incisions, each about an inch long, on the top of her head. It was unclear how deep the cuts were. The men tilted the end of the stretcher up to slide her into the lagoon. Mother tucked her head down, dove in and swam fast to the far end, the other dolphins rushing to her. The blood on her skin was washed away. She seemed to be moving well. The four of them clustered together, circling, rubbing against each other.

Within a few hours, Mother was eating normally. She swam and breathed and looked healthy. The incisions weren't bleeding and were barely visible. The only way a stranger might know something had happened was that she stayed at the far end of the lagoon for days and startled easily. She would no longer get within 10 feet of Cora.

In a strange way, Bernie seemed more affected. He wouldn't eat for two days. He stayed deep in the water for long periods of time, surfacing for air rarely. He didn't play with the others. When he did rise to the surface for a breath, his exhale seemed weighty and full.

Over the next few days, to someone who didn't know them, the dolphins would have looked happy, the permanent up-curl of their mouths, the way they chased each other and arced out of the water, immense and sleek.

But Cora saw how Mother stayed for hours near the chute, floating there with her beak open, tasting the water from the open sea. The incisions in her head were visible as bloodless slits.

On the other hand, Bernie ate less, sometimes mouthing a fish for a moment, then spitting it out. He spent a lot of time lying on the bottom of the lagoon, staring into the distance.

Kat and Junior seemed the least affected, tussling, eating and investigating. Kat continued to play with the bodies of the squid Cora gave her. One day Kat figured out she could grab the tentacles of a squid and, with a twist of her head, sling the body sideways through the air like a wobbly discus.

At first she could throw the body only a few feet, but she worked at the trick all that day, practicing with the different physics and center of gravity. There wasn't a lot else to do in the small lagoon. She got better quickly, first in terms of distance and then in terms of aim.

By the afternoon, her constant play had shredded every squid she had. The one she had left was grey and tattered. Who knew how long the body had been there, hidden on the bottom of the lagoon? She could sling it 30 feet through the air. A decomposing missile. The smell distinct.

The other dolphins stuck their heads out of the water and watched, a crowd of impressed bystanders. If any of them looked away for even a moment, Kat would peg that one in the face, *splat*. Furious, the dolphin would chase Kat for several minutes. Fleeing, she'd jump out of the water, head high, so pleased with herself.

7/2—Kat prefers to play with squid, rather than eat them.

* * *

Junior was playful also, curious about everything happening around him, from a sea slug crawling along the lagoon floor to Cora's detachable flippers.

One morning he imitated everything Cora did underwater, shadowing her. Swimming just beside her, looking in the direction she looked in, pausing where she paused, touching his fin to whatever she touched. Staring absorbed at the other dolphins as she did, then turning to her, his gaze wide with wonder, his head cocked at the exact same angle.

7/3—The dolphins at times appear to mimic humans, in posture and action.

* * *

Once, in tenth grade, her classroom visited a nearby museum. Cora, unable to hear what the teacher was saying in the echoing room, stared at a glass case full of household tools from the 1700s. One tool caught her eye. It looked like a leather belt laid out flat in the case, but it was different in three ways. It was too small to fit around even a child's waist; it had a metal lock and key instead of a buckle; and sticking up from the center of the belt was what looked like the bowl of a wooden spoon.

The card in front of it read: *The Branks—A punishment for women or slaves who talked too much, the branks was locked on around the head. The spoon in the mouth held the tongue down. The branks made speech impossible and could be locked on for as long as the master desired.*

She looked back at the belt. The bowl of the spoon was dark with wear.

Deafness had many layers. Because she had a hard time keeping up with a conversation, people tended to assume she wasn't smart. They did not ask her what she thought. If she offered out a novel idea, they would be startled. Rather than thinking her idea through, most people assumed she had misunderstood and re-explained the basics of the subject to her. She'd learned, over time, not to offer ideas.

At the museum, the teacher tapped her on the head to catch her attention and get her to follow the rest of the group.

She thought about the branks for a long time afterward. She imagined it locked around the head. With the spoon holding the tongue down, it would be impossible to eat or drink, or even swallow saliva. The woman or slave turned into a mute animal unable to plead, the dry weight of thirst building. Left on, it could kill within days from dehydration. Even an hour of wearing it would leave a physical memory in the mouth. One harsh look from someone in power and the thirst would return, the mute fear, the weight on the tongue.

At times, when she saw a teacher or boss or police officer stare, angry, eyebrows raised, at someone with less power, she noticed the reaction was shown frequently in the mouth. The person with less power closed the lips, moving the jaw from side to side, uncomfortable, and then just swallowed the saliva and the words, nodding at whatever the more powerful person had said. She wondered if a physical reaction, if fear, could be passed down from mother to child, if a mental branks could linger on the tongue for generations.

* * *

Each time Cora headed into the house/research center to visit the bathroom, she looked at the 12-foot-long glass tank in the main room, the narrow container Mother had been restrained in while they operated on her. It was fitted with foam cushions and straps to hold a dolphin motionless while the men worked. The tools lay on the table nearby, a strange combination of surgical and woodworking instruments. A scalpel, an awl, a hammer, forceps and some nails. Next to the tank was a large reel-to-reel tape recorder. Paper and notes spread everywhere.

Behind the tank were bookshelves, filled with leatherbound books with titles like *Experimental Psychology, Journal of Animal Cognition* and *Linguistic Epistemology*. On these shelves, there were more science books than in her whole high-school library, the books shared by just these three men. Here was their learning, their importance on display.

In school, unsure of what the teacher said during class, she passed the tests by reading and re-reading the textbooks. She tried never to speak any new word she learned from reading, because the word could turn out to be tricky phonetically. *Lethal. Choir. Colonel.* She'd pronounce the word the way it was written, and the listeners would pause, confused, then rock their heads back in a startled laugh.

Thus, her spoken vocabulary stayed close to that of an eight-year-old, her comprehension so much larger.

One day walking past the bookshelves, she spotted a book with Blum's name on the spine. Curious, she pulled it out. The photo on the back showed him younger and posed, his chin up and eyes focused on the distance, the type of photo found in an old-fashioned locket.

The book's cover had a drawing of a gorilla staring at the viewer. In the drawing, the top of its skull was removed, its brain floating like a wrinkled UFO above its head.

* * *

Arriving one morning, Cora walked around the left side of the house and discovered something new sitting on the lawn beside the building. It looked like an oversized bathtub, 8 feet long and 3 feet deep. A hard plastic liner in a partially built wooden frame.

She stopped and considered it.

For a dolphin to fit inside, it would have to curl up. On top of the tub, was a hinged lid that could swing closed. It would be as dark inside as a coffin.

A hose lay nearby, ready to fill the tub with water.

She walked by, uneasy.

* * *

Mother was floating by the sluice, her mouth open a fraction, tasting the water from the open sea. She'd been floating here for a long time, her eyes closed.

Interested, Cora snorkeled nearby, watching. After a minute, Mother opened her eyes and slid her chin onto the ledge of the sluice. She twisted her head from one side to the other, examining the concrete. From that angle, she couldn't see the beach 30 feet away or the sea. She must, however, have been able to hear the surf.

Mother slid her whole head onto the ledge, then, with some effort, humped up onto it, until the first third of her body was on the sluice, her flippers pressed down and balancing her there.

Cora watched, not breathing.

The depth of the stream was only 6 inches, Mother's head and back out of the water. Her whole body weighed at least 350 pounds. Out of water like this, when she breathed, it sounded a little labored. She strained, arcing upward. Perhaps between the rocks she was able to glimpse the sea and the waves.

After a long moment balanced there, she slid back into the lagoon.

* * *

Each time Cora tossed a new squid to Kat, she would hide it at the bottom of the lagoon somewhere, perhaps under a rock. Later that day, when the other dolphins had forgotten about the squid, she'd fetch one and fling it at another dolphin. A practical joker who didn't know when to quit.

One afternoon when Cora stood up out of the water and pulled off her mask, a decomposing squid smacked her in the face.

Surprised, Cora fell backward into the lagoon, inhaling water. Coughing hard, she stood up and, with some difficulty, tugged the squid out of her hair.

Kat was so pleased with herself. She flailed backward, waving her flippers, a perfect imitation of Cora's fall. The other dolphins peered out of the water, heads tilted and watching.

Furious, Cora stopped giving Kat anymore squid.

* * *

That afternoon after lunch, the men brought out paperwork and talked on the veranda, cigarettes bobbing in the corners of their mouths, comparing charts and discussing data. They refilled their glasses from a pitcher. At first Cora assumed this liquid was water, then saw Blum fishing an olive out of his glass with his fingers.

She had to go to the bathroom. Her hair was dry enough for her to wrap a towel around her head and pull on her hearing glasses.

Almost at the top of the stairs, she heard Tibbet say something about *ability*, his voice irritated, every consonant sharply hit. Looking at the men sitting there, she saw the tension, no one moving, the expressions locked down and staring.

Eh was facing her, so she could lipread as he said—When do we need results by?

Blum turned to look at her. He said—I told them one year.

She passed by the table. Swinging open the glass door to the house, she caught the reflection of Blum and Eh glancing at her in the bathing suit.

* * *

Early that morning, before the men were up and moving, Mother balanced the front of her body on the sluice and managed to shimmy 2 feet further up it.

She stopped there, her body balanced, halfway onto the chute, halfway off. Perhaps past this point, it would be harder to back up. Dolphins were not made for slithering along on rough concrete, mostly out of water. They were not intended for terrestrial gravity. It was 30 feet from here to the water and the surf there was very shallow. She could get beached. Mother paused and lifted her head as high as she could, looking up the chute, focused. This much out of water, her breath was labored. The surf beating on the beach, the deeper blue of the ocean beyond. She remained there, a long moment, looking. Cora could see the incisions on the right side of her head, just in front of her blowhole.

She looked behind her at the other dolphins, at Junior.

Then she blew all the air in her lungs out, a slow heavy exhale. She rolled backward to splash back into the lagoon.

* * *

That afternoon when Cora stepped out of the water, Blum was sitting in a chair reading her notebook. He watched her as she wrapped a towel around her body, tucking it in around her.

He said something.

She didn't have her hearing glasses on, and there was a little water in her good ear. She didn't hear anything he said.

She hit the side of her head, trying to get the water out of her good ear as she asked a stalling question.—What do you mean?

Junior surfaced 20 feet away. Blum jerked his chin at him. He seemed to be making a suggestion.

She pointed to her ears and held her hands palm up.

Irritated, he picked up her hearing glasses and handed them to her.

She shook her head.—My hair is wet. It'll short the circuits.

He said something.

She nodded.—It's a problem.

His eyes brightened. Later on, she'd learn this was the sign that he'd had one of his sideways ideas.

He said something fast that she didn't hear.

—What?

He held up a finger for her to wait, then strode off into the house. He was the man in power who didn't edit, who said whatever flashed through his mind and watched how others would react. He had little experience with holding back words, the mental weight of an awkward moment on his tongue, the branks of powerlessness buckled round his head. He came back in a moment carrying his electric shaver plugged into a long extension cord. With her watching, he mimed shaving the hair on his head off, then offered the shaver to her, his eyebrows raised in a question.

(The current fashion for women was to have hair long enough to wrap it several times around a foam sponge and pin the now impressively large bun on top of the head. Or, alternately, they could tease their locks up in a beehive several inches above their skull and spray it in place. The purpose, either way, was to showcase the volume and length.

Men, on the other hand, cut their hair short and greased it down, trying to make it as small and obedient as possible. Although some young men had begun to grow their hair past the bottom of their ears, this made the adults suspicious of them as true males.)

If she shaved her hair, she would be able to wear her hearing glasses more since her hair would dry quickly, but she would look different. Unfeminine. Deviant. And the strangely thick arms of her glasses would be visible, her defect revealed.

Surely, she thought, this would stop Eh and Blum from staring at her. She'd be able to work with the dolphins without being bothered.

And so, impulsively she nodded.

His face lit up. He admired unusual choices.

He held out the attachments for the shaver for her to choose from. Not knowing what any of them did, she tapped the nearest one and he snapped it onto the front of the shaver.

He gestured to a chair and she sat down. He flicked the machine on, its busy mechanical hum, and cupped the side of her head against his belly to hold it still. He paused, waiting for her to jerk back, to change her mind.

She didn't move, so he placed the shaver against her forehead and ran it slowly up into her hair. It buzzed up along the top of her head and down the back, a vibrating massage. Her hair fell to the ground in a sheet, as though it had been waiting to let go. He paused, staring at what must be the fuzzy stripe of her scalp. She could feel the admiration off him like a heat. Then he began the second pass of the shaver, and the third.

The wind against her skull was surprising, like skinny-dipping, the revealed neurons so awake. Her head lighter.

He was finished within a few minutes. By then the other two men were standing on the veranda, holding onto the railing, watching. She stood up and shook her head, ran her hands over the bristly egg of her skull. The stubble perhaps a quarter inch long. Such a different feel, like a soldier's head or a nun's. Her bare neck seemed longer. Her head free and unencumbered. At her feet was the nest of hair out of which she had been hatched.

She put her glasses back on, revealed and honest. She looked at Blum's expression, then Eh's. So hungry to see their discomfort or perhaps even disgust, to see their interest erased.

Instead they stared. Gaped, really.

(Later on when she looked in the mirror, she'd see the buzz-cut revealed the shape of her skull, a delicate egg on a narrow neck. With just a fuzz of hair, her eyes seemed bigger. This masculine cut, by comparison, made her body seem more feminine and surprising.

And perhaps, most of all, her haircut made her deeply aberrant. Like a woman wearing a dog collar and holding a whip, her hair was testimony that normal rules did not pertain to her, that with her, anything was possible.)

The focus in their eyes much worse.

She held her short towel around her, feeling naked under their gaze.

Blum ran his hand over the stubble on her head. His touch now slightly possessive, as though he'd formed her somehow.—You look good this way. Sleek.

His hand lingered. Another touch to tally.

THIRTEEN
July 9–13, 1965

The next day, when she waded out of the water, Blum was sitting on the dock waiting for her. She toweled her head off and put on her glasses immediately. A benefit of her new haircut.

Grinding his cigarette out, he considered her new look, his head cocked.—The back of your neck is much paler than your face.

She was able to hear better now with her buzzcut. Perhaps the rustling of her hair had confused her, or maybe it had reduced the connection between the amplifier and her skull. Mostly now she could hear most everything except *S*'s and soft *C*'s.

She ran her hand over the back of her neck.—It hasn't been in the sun until now.

—You can certainly tan.

—I'm part Seminole.

He went still at this information, head tilted.—You're an Indian?

A small part—she said.

He looked at her as though she'd changed in some way.—Maybe that's why you're good with animals.

She blinked and moved past this.—What did you do to Mother?

—Who?

—The dolphin you brought into the building the other day, that you operated on.

He said—Mother.

—I named her that because she acts like the mom of the smallest dolphin. What did you do to her?

—Brain research.

—What do you mean?

—We attempted operant conditioning.

—What?

Blum enjoyed lecturing others.—We inserted electrodes, ran a small amount of electricity into her brain and moved the electrodes around, while we watched how she reacted. We're looking for the pain and pleasure centers.

—Why?

—If I can stimulate the pain and pleasure centers, I can motivate them to learn.

—What will you teach them?

—How to talk.

Her eyes flicked left, then right. She risked the question— *English*?

He nodded, proud of his plan.—Dolphins have big brains.

When the dolphins vocalized, unlike most other animals, they didn't open their mouths. Underwater, it was hard to trace where the sound came from: which animal had made it, much less what part of the body. However, she'd begun to suspect the sounds they emitted didn't come from their mouths or throats. Hearing the dolphins squeal and call above the surface, even with her reduced hearing, she was gradually able to determine that the noises came from their backs, not their mouths.

A few times, she'd seen the blowhole tighten or loosen while the sound was being made. Underneath the blowhole, whatever organs were creating the noise, there were no teeth or lips or tongue involved. Asking a dolphin to pronounce English words through a blowhole would be like asking a horse to sing.

She imagined wires trailing from the dolphins' skulls to a car battery in Blum's hands, him yelling nursery rhymes at them, shocking their brains each time they didn't repeat his words.

She asked—How do you get the electrodes in the brain?

—Small holes in the skull.

—How do you make the holes?

—A knife.

—In the skull? You make those with a knife?

—Oh, no. To get through the skull, we have a hammer and a nail.

Her expression changed.

Blum added—The brain and skull have no pain neurons. The dolphin feels only the first cut.

* * *

Mother didn't play, not since the operation on her. However, she also didn't act like Bernie, lying near the bottom of the lagoon and coming to the surface only to exhale, slow and sad. Instead she cruised the lagoon, systematically examining every inch of its sides and bottom, beaming sound at it as though asking it to open. At times she tried digging her beak into the sand, determined, wiggling her beak between the rocks as far as she could. Then she'd pull back, a few scrapes on her beak, to move onto the next section.

After a while, she'd return to the chute to rest there, her mouth a little open to taste the water from the sea.

* * *

One early morning when Cora arrived, her hearing glasses on, she saw a crow in one of the trees cawing enraged at the lagoon. Kat had her head out of the water, watching the crow.

After each caw, there was a loud echo. Cora looked around, trying to figure out what the sound was echoing off. The building? The water? Wherever it came from, the echo seemed to make the crow angrier. It hopped forward on the branch, rocking with the strength of its open-mouthed call.

Even with Cora's hearing, she could tell there was something wrong with the echo. It wasn't a perfect mimic; instead it seemed a trifle high-pitched and muffled, the timing slightly off. This was when she noticed Kat was watching the crow with concentration, her head cocked. Each time there was an echo, her blowhole tightened.

The crow kept cocking its head, looking around confused.

* * *

While Blum was looking through Cora's notes, Bernie began to chase Kat. The two of them circled the lagoon at high speed. At one point, Bernie swam by just beneath the surface, upside down, his erect penis cutting through the water like a pencil. Blum seemed surprised.

He looked to see Cora's reaction.—How often does that happen?

She kept her eyes away from the dolphins.—Several times a day.

—I don't see it in your notes.

She said nothing. She could feel a type of branks in her mouth, holding her tongue down.

—To help with the research, you can't be bashful.

She looked at him.

He said—Researchers observe everything. We take notes on what we see, no matter what the behavior.

—We?

We—He gestured from himself to her.

She was surprised, the idea that she could be helping with the actual research.

—Mating is a natural behavior for all animals.

He told her to note down each time the dolphins mated. He had her say mating ten times in front of him to get over the embarrassment. He didn't look away from her lips while she said the word. With each word, she could feel the branks loosening in her mouth.

* * *

Blum might have thought she was shy about observing or discussing sex. He did not understand she grew up on a farm. Much of her family's income came from the pigs they raised and brought to market. A large part of that work was controlling who mated with whom and when, animal husbandry.

On her dad's farm, the boar, Luther, weighed 700 pounds. He huffed just from standing, and his bleary eyes peered about for something to attack. He was too unpredictable to be allowed anywhere near the valuable sows, so her dad moved an old weight-lifting bench into one of the empty pens and wiped sow secretions on it. This was common practice among the farmers. Each farmer had a preferred type of mounting bench that they swore by. The one thing they all agreed on was that wood was not a good idea because of the possibility of splinters.

When a sow was in estrus, Luther was ushered into the pen. Instead of a sow, there was that bench which Luther would sniff, then mount and heave away on top of it, a frustrated inchworm, unable to get anywhere.

And her dad would kneel, just as the other farmers did, to reach underneath with both hands, one to help Luther finish, the other holding the bottle ready.

Cora did not talk about mating or sex in front of men, not

because she was innocent or bashful. No, branks always came from a lack of power. The reason she didn't talk about sex was because she did not want to encourage ideas. She did not want the men's eyes to get intent and for them to stand closer and try to touch her more. She would not have to show any interest; they would still try to get her alone with them. Her branks was out of self-defense.

* * *

One morning when Cora waded out of the water, she heard hammering. She walked around the building to find Eh working on the big bathtub that sat outside on the lawn. He was nailing wood panels into place.

She paused there, watching the hammer work. On this side of the building, each hit of the hammer echoed off the hillside, *Wha-WHACK Wha-WHACK*. She wondered how hard Blum had to hammer to get a nail through a dolphin's skull.

Tibbet had mentioned Eh had been a tennis champion at Harvard. Eh moved the way one would expect: head up, eyes bright, ready to return any serve. He stood tall, cognizant of his strength and station in life, wearing a crisp polo shirt and Madras shorts. In a crowd, he would be the one noticed, the one to whom the teacher would direct the difficult question. The person hired, the employee rewarded.

She, on the other hand, posed there in her bathing suit like some hopeful beauty queen, with her deviant haircut and her glasses for the handicapped, uncertain if she'd heard the words correctly. Few teachers would look her in the eye, much less ask her a question. Concepts would be explained to her using short sentences.

She asked—What's the bathtub for?

He looked up.—It's a tank for Blum.

—What's he going to do with it?

His eyes had drifted down to her hips, examining them. At times, men surveyed parts of her body with an almost strategic attention, like it was a cliff they'd been dared to climb.

He said—Blum wants to float in it. With the lid shut, you can't hear or see. The water is body temperature so you can't feel anything either. He wants to meditate in it, learn what a total lack of sensation does to the mind over time.

—So it's not for the dolphins.

—No.

She exhaled. Less worried now, she considered the bathtub for another moment, imagining floating in it, in the dark.—He's experimenting on himself?

—Yep. It used to be the way things were done. Before you performed research on another, you tried it out on yourself.

—Really? Like what?

—Well, Newton put a bodkin in his eye.

—A what?

—Bodkin. It's like a . . . I guess like a hatpin. He slipped it in between the eyeball and the eye socket and moved it around. Went deep. He wanted to learn if it would distort his vision.

She grimaced.

—That's nothing. Blum always talks about a teacher he had who wanted to understand the structure of skin, so he cut off his own foreskin . . .

She interrupted—His what?

He repeated—Foreskin. And examined it under a micro-scope, keeping notes as the cells died.

She wasn't sure what her expression showed, but her eyes were wide.

Eh reacted by rocking his head back in exasperation and throwing his hands out. She'd learned long ago that people tended to gesture with more energy when they felt some self-doubt.

He said—What? This type of action proves their dedication. Their own bodies on the line.

If men like Blum cut off their own foreskin, there would be no limits with the animals they researched.

* * *

The men used the net again to corral the dolphins into the shallow end and then dragged them up onto the beach.

This time Blum selected Kat. They shoved the other dolphins back into the water, hefted Kat onto the stretcher and carried her into the house.

The remaining dolphins zipped from side to side in the lagoon, frantic. Cora found she couldn't stay still. She toweled off her buzzcut and put on the hearing glasses, then began to pace, wider and wider circles, until she had enough courage to climb the stairs to the veranda.

She stood there next to the screen door, staring at the ground. Whatever the men were doing to Kat, the sound was reverberating inside the main room. She listened, but could not get herself to look inside yet.

A hammer. A *thunk-thunk-thunk*.

Kat was shrieking, a repetitive sound rising and falling like a siren, echoing in the tank. A child would understand what she was saying.

The men ignored this, talking back and forth over her noises, busy. Their words were hard to make out over the hammer, but the tone and pace was audible. Tibbet was saying something in a measured tone, probably recording notes for the reel-to-reel recorder. Blum asked Eh for something. Eh responded with a statement.

Then the hammer stopped, replaced by the clatter of

instruments. Easier to hear now. The men talking to each other, asking questions and offering answers, trying to figure something out.

Outside the door, Cora was rocking back and forth, her arms wrapped around herself.

Then Kat's sounds stopped, mid-squeal.

Cora froze, her eyes flicking left then right.

Kat exhaled, the loud hydraulic release of her breath.

There was a slow moment, a thoughtful pause, and Kat started making different noises. Deliberate ones. The sounds no longer shrieks, but low-pitched hums, well within human hearing range. *Hmmmm hum-a-humm, hm.* The volume and pitch rising and falling. The rhythm changing.

Of all the sounds Cora had heard the dolphins make, she'd never heard anything like this.

The men didn't seem to notice. Not having swam underwater with the dolphins, they weren't familiar with their sounds, didn't know what was unusual. Busy with their actions, they continued to talk, listening to each other, not the dolphin. Blum issued a command. Tibbet stated a fact. Eh asked a question.

Behind their voices, Kat hummed. Her sound accompanying their conversation, a background melody to the beat of their words.

Cora had spent years listening as hard as she could. Unable to hear every word, she squeezed all the information she could from whatever she could perceive: the pitch, the beat, the emotion. She focused, her forehead furrowed.

When she understood, her eyes opened wide.

She listened for another few seconds to make sure, her eyes staring at the flagstones of the veranda. Then she inhaled and yanked open the screen door to step into the room.

The men turned to her. Kat lay inside the narrow glass tank, foam restraints and straps holding her in place. Blum stood beside the tank, his gloves smeared with blood. He was snaking a thin wire down through the hole in her skull.

Eh was next to Blum, holding some cotton swabs. Tibbet was by the desk taking notes. On the table was the metal suitcase of the tape recorder, its reels spinning.

She spoke to Blum. He was the one who had asked her to say what she observed.—Do you hear it?

Blum asked—What?

She stepped over to the tape recorder, pressed the Stop button. With a clunk, the reels halted.

Hey—said Eh and started to move in her direction.

She rewound the tape, then hit Play.—Listen. Listen to her.

Eh was struggling to pull off his gloves to turn the recording back on. Meanwhile, the audio played: Tibbet stating an observation for the notes and Kat's voice following an instant behind, a string of short declarative *hmms*.

Cora said—She's mimicking you.

The men paused, listening.

On the recording now, Eh asked a question and Kat hummed the same number of syllables, her pitch rising at the end of the sentence. Blum asked for more nails and Kat rumbled his request, lowering her pitch to match his, duplicating the beat of his words as best she could through the kazoo of her blowhole.

Listening, Blum stood very still, head tilted, his eyes on the corner of the room, as though he'd seen something move there.

Tibbet listened, eyes unfocused.

When the tape reached its end, now playing just static, Eh stepped forward to rewind it further and hit Play again. Now they heard Blum stating a flat command and Eh answering. Kat kazooed along behind, imitating their speech.

Eh asked, his voice high—Why's she doing that?

Cora looked at him with surprise.—To tell you she exists, that she is smart. To get you to stop hurting her.

All three of the men blinked and looked at Kat.

Tibbet said slowly, each word considered—It could be coincidence.

Blum was considering Kat with interest, as though she'd just been introduced. He still held the wire, halfway inserted into her brain.

Kat's blowhole opened, the rush of breath, then the knuckled closing. She was silent, watching them from inside the restraining tank. Her brown eyes magnified by the water.

Blum pulled the wire out of her brain. He put it down on the table.

He said to Tibbet—Patch her up and get her back in the water.

He added, his eyes direct.—Be careful with her.

Tibbet moved to do so. From the speed with which he moved, it was clear he had wanted to stop the operation a while ago.

Cora sat down in a chair, her knees weak.

Blum turned to her. Those eyes focused on her now.—Where'd you go to school?

—Henry B. Plant High School, South Tampa.

Ahh—said Blum—No, I meant college.

—I never went.

Eh the post-doc turned to her.

She saw, for the first time, she was good at something.

While Blum's expression was pleased, the other men's were not.

* * *

Once Kat was carried back and slid off the stretcher into the lagoon, the four dolphins shot together to the other side, getting as far from humans as they could. There they twined around one another, taking solace, rubbing against each other, quieting slowly, until tuckered out from emotion, they fell asleep there, their beaks holding tight to each other's flipper or tail.

The big male, Bernie, did not eat for the rest of that day. Each time he surfaced and exhaled, Cora could hear the combination of his responsibility and helplessness.

FOURTEEN
July 14, 1965

T he next morning when Cora walked onto the property, heading down toward the lagoon, she came upon Blum sitting cross-legged on the grass, his hands palm upward on his knees, his eyes closed. A bony birdlike man. She watched for a second.

His breath was slow and deliberate. He blew air loudly out his mouth, almost as if he were snorkeling on dry land.

When she started to tiptoe past him, heading down toward the lagoon, his eyes opened.—Do you want to try?

She asked—Try what?

—Meditating.

—Medi-what?

—Meditating. It's a practice from the Orient. Conscious breathing. It clears the mind of the details of life.

Her eyes moved from left to right. She'd always thought the details of life were the point.

He said—Sit down. Try it out.

She sat down on the grass, making sure to leave a good 6 feet between her and him.

He said—Inhale slowly, through the nostrils. Concentrate on the breath. Fill your lungs.

She imitated the speed of his breath, tried to make her inhale as loud as his. She wasn't sure what she was supposed to pay attention to in terms of her breath. Aside from being slow, it seemed to be going fine.

He said—Exhale now, out the mouth. Push out all the air

inside of you. Focus on your breath. Still your mind. What happens when your mind is freed of all its frittering?

You fall asleep, she thought.

She asked—Is this connected with the experiment you want to do with the bathtub?

He looked at her confused.

She jerked her chin at the oversized tub on the lawn nearby, the one with the lid. The wood frame around it was complete. It looked ready to be used.

Ah, the isolation tank.—He stopped breathing deeply, straightened his legs out in front of him and began to stretch, attempting to touch his toes with his legs straight. It was clear he did not stretch a lot.—Yes. I'm going to float in it, try out sensory deprivation, observe what happens in my mind.

She imagined floating in warm water in the dark. It made her want to pee.

He added—Man has explored the planet and space and the body. Our remaining frontier is the mind.

He bent forward into his stretch again.—A few months ago I met this Harvard researcher studying the mind, its powers and capabilities. The implications are fascinating. In a few weeks, he'll come here and be my guide for a trip.

—Where you going?

He looked at her confused, then understood.—Ah. No, I meant a *mental* trip. We'll use guided imagery and psilocybin.

—Ilo-what?

—Psilocybin. A psychoactive compound found in certain mushrooms. Leary, the researcher, found it opens doors to the mind, allowing for experiences like temporal distortion and synesthesia.

Each time she talked to Blum, he used words she did not know. She wasn't sure if he was purposefully showing off or if he couldn't imagine she didn't know these words.

Blum changed the subject.—Look. I'm glad you're here. I

have a project for you. That dolphin that mimicked our speech yesterday . . .

—Kat?

—Can you teach her to do that on command? Mimic whatever we say?

—What? Why?

—It'll show progress to the funders.

She paused.—I thought your goal was to communicate with the dolphins.

—Yes.

—Mimicking isn't communication.

—True, but it'll be proof of concept, that dolphins can physically make the sounds, that they are smart enough to imitate.

—Why me?

—You have an aptitude for this. You're able to work with them, to intuit their actions. If you manage, I'll double your salary.

He watched her to see her reaction to this offer. Working here, she already had more money than ever before, more than she knew what to do with. However, money was a power that she could collect. Who knew when she might need it to get others to hear her?

She asked—Is there a time limit?

—Our main funder arrives in under a month.

She blinked.—Not much time.

He nodded.

She looked around, the bathtub, the lawn.—I'll try on two conditions.

—Yes.

—I can borrow some of the books in the house.

He nodded, surprised. Pleased.—Of course, of course. What's the second condition?

She inhaled, then said it.—You can't operate on them

meanwhile. If I succeed you can't operate on them for two months afterward. On any of them. Agreed?

She saw the way his eyes flickered, registering her request. Like a bird, there was a certain coldness to him, a part of the brain constantly calculating.

Agreed—he said, but she could see that now he knew her weakness.

LANGUAGE LESSONS

After the agreement with Blum, she walked down to the lagoon, pulled on her snorkel, mask and fins and frog-walked in. She stayed in the shallows, watching the dolphins through her mask. She needed to figure out how to get them to mimic human speech on command.

In the water she was awkward and heavy-breathing, a tug-boat laboring along. They, on the other hand, cut through the water with ease, curving up to within a few feet to study her, making their noises.

Marbles bouncing down wood stairs.

It was impossible to tell which dolphin made which noise since, underwater, all sound was immediate and tactile, resonating in her teeth and nasal cavities, in her lungs and gut and bones.

Balloons squeaking against each other.

After they each greeted her appropriately, they curved away.

In order to train them, she needed a way to reward them. It was time to see if they would take food from her hands. She swam back to the dock and retrieved a butterfish from the food bucket. Ducking back under the water, she kicked forward slowly, holding the fish out toward them.

A cougar roaring, sped up to sound like a cricket.

Kat was the first to approach, gliding forward, the incisions visible on her head.

Cora was surprised Kat would get near her the day after the

surgery, would get near any human ever again. Kat paused just above her, staring. The eyes of a dolphin aren't on the front of the face like a human, but on the sides of the head. Because of this, most of the time the dolphins could look at an object from only one eye at a time. However from above, as Kat was now, both eyes could look together. Probably the focus was better. Kat hovered there, examining Cora for a long moment.

Cora had no idea what Kat understood of the surgery. Perhaps she'd simply noticed that once Cora entered the room, the men had stopped hurting her and she'd been returned to the lagoon.

Kat curved down and gently took it. Holding it in her mouth, she swirled away, her flipper brushing Cora's hand.

Junior, the adolescent dolphin, was the next one to take a fish from Cora's hand, then Mother. Finally even Bernie did. His sides raked with old wounds, his fin clipped, his brown eyes. He took the fish so gently, like a breeze lifting it away.

Knowing now that she could reward each of the dolphins individually, she swam to the bucket of fish on the dock. Standing up, she toweled off her head and put on her hearing glasses to start the training.

She needed them to mimic speech above the water so she would know which dolphin made which sound, so she could reward the right one. She stood there, waiting until one of them, Junior, stuck his head out of the water.

Holding a butterfish in her hand, she said—Talk.

* * *

Midmorning, she thought all the men had gone into town. She was leaving the bathroom, when Eh stepped into the hall from his bedroom. His hair slicked back, his checkered shorts.

As she started to step to the left, around him, he began to

roll his arm through the air toward her. It was the start of a big motion, a coordinated sweep of his right arm as though he was returning a powerful serve.

Attempting to grab her.

Time slowed. Five inches taller, he must weigh 50 pounds more.

Through the door to his room, she could see his bed. She knew where this was going.

So she ducked. His large swing meant his arm was committed, continuing its powerful sweep just above her, while she bolted out the door. She sprinted down the stairs and dove into the lagoon. Among the dolphins, she was safe.

Surfacing, he was nowhere in sight. She exhaled. Holding up her hands, she could see her fingers trembling.

Treading water, she knew her speed of response would work only once. If Eh tried a second time, he would be more prepared, have both arms out, move forward slower, be ready to grab.

She also knew what would happen if she tried to tell Blum and Tibbet that Eh had attacked her. There would be looks exchanged, a certain disbelief. Eh? Did she mean Eh? Why would he do that? They would not have to mention that he was a good-looking Harvard student, that he could be with anyone he wanted. That she would be lucky if he were interested. If, in response, she described what had happened, him grabbing and her running, the men would raise their eyebrows in surprise. That's it? That's all? They would be genuinely confused. They'd ask if something else was going on? Had she been spurned? The jokes would follow.

Considering these reactions, she could feel a branks in her mouth, self-preservation holding down her tongue.

From this point on, she didn't go into the house unless there were at least two men inside. She figured they wouldn't try anything in front of each other. She made sure none of the men were ever between her and the exit. She much preferred to stay in the water, with the dolphins, away from the men. In the water this much, she was able to work more, teaching the dolphins.

* * *

For hour after hour that afternoon, she stood waist deep in the lagoon, holding out a fish, waiting. Junior and Kat had their heads out, watching her and the fish. She said—Talk.

She waited a moment and repeated—Talk.

She said—Talk.

Junior squeaked, impatient. At this sound, she immediately threw him a fish.

Then she said—Talk.

She waited a moment.—Talk.

She said—Talk.

Kat made a sound, gurgling, so she threw a fish to her.

Normally each of them ate sixty to a hundred fish a day. Since she needed them to focus, she didn't give them any food at all unless they made a noise right after she spoke. She wanted them hungry and motivated.

It wasn't their habit to vocalize a lot above water. Up until now, for their entire lives, food had never been contingent on any behavior except their ability to catch it. As the day went by and they got hungrier, they kept their heads out of the water for longer, bobbing there, looking at her. Each time one of them made a noise right after she said *Talk*, she threw that dolphin a fish.

This first day, they didn't seem to be getting the concept. That first day, each of them got fewer than 15 fish.

* * *

That afternoon, a small log drifted in along the sluice from the sea and bobbed lazily across the lagoon until it got stuck against the metal gate that ran across the exit stream.

Mother seemed interested in it. She floated near it, considering the log.

After a few minutes, Cora swam over, curious why Mother was interested. She couldn't see any fish hiding behind the log. The log itself was a few feet long, 8 inches in diameter, with the stumps of branches sticking out. Its bark was long gone and the wood grey from the sea. It bobbed and scraped against the metal gate. The gate was solid metal and lowered halfway down, so the water burbled underneath. Mother studied the log, clicking at it.

There were a few strands of seaweed caught on the log. As Mother and Cora watched, a leaf got tangled in that seaweed and then a twig.

Cora figured there wasn't all that much happening in the lagoon. This log might be the most exciting thing around. Dolphins' senses were different. Perhaps Mother was entertaining herself, watching the turbulent water flow around the log.

* * *

The next morning, up to her waist in the lagoon, Cora held out a fish and said—Talk.

She waited a moment for any reply sound from the dolphins and then said—Talk.

She waited again and then said—Talk.

When one of the dolphins happened to make a noise right after she spoke, she threw the fish to that dolphin immediately. The other dolphins turned to watch that one swallow the fish in a single bite. This was the second day and they were hungry.

She said—Talk.

—Talk.

They studied her, trying to understand why she wasn't feeding them.

She imagined it from their side. They'd never been trained before, didn't understand the concept of a reward, that her gift could be contingent on an action. Perhaps they were wondering why she would keep them hungry, why she kept repeating the same sound.

After this second day she noticed a slight divot, an indent in the fat, behind Bernie's blowhole. She didn't remember seeing the divot before. He had been eating less than the others for weeks. She didn't know if the indent could be from him losing weight or if it was from age. She didn't know what was too skinny for a dolphin. She still didn't feed him. To survive they needed to learn this. This could stop the operations for two months. Those months would give her time to figure out how to stop the operations for longer.

* * *

Mother was still fascinated with the log that bobbed against the metal gate of the exit stream. She plucked a piece of seaweed from the lagoon floor and released it near the log, watching it twirl through the water to become snagged on one of the branches.

Mother brought another piece of seaweed over and released it, watching. She repeated the action with a twig and then a leaf and then some more seaweed. She repeated this again and again, watching what happened each time. More and more debris stuck against the log.

Cora watched her, no idea of what she was doing or why.

* * *

When the men were inside during lunch, she stepped into

the house. With all three of them there, she figured it was safe. Still talking, they turned to watch her walk to the bookshelves. She scanned the shelves for a book to borrow. She knew these books contained the words and concepts she needed to know in order to work with the men. These books would help her understand the men and help the men hear her.

Her eyes landed on the book with Blum's name on the spine, the one with the cover showing a gorilla with its brain hanging in the air over its head. The title was *Biological Computers*. She pulled the book out and held it up for Blum, so he could approve her borrowing it. He nodded, a flicker of satisfaction on his face.

Over the next few nights, in her boarding room in town, she read the book. She more than read it. She studied it, trying to understand Blum's thinking and values, the ideas behind his research. In the center of the book were a few pages of photographs, Blum in surgical garb standing beside an operating table. On the table lay a gorilla, its body slack, its head shaved, metal instruments sticking out of its skull. The next photo showed the gorilla's brain lying all by itself on a board. This animal had been taken apart to find out what had made it so miraculously capable when alive.

She considered every word in the book. Each time she came upon a term she did not know, she flipped to the glossary at the back. She wrote out the definitions by hand, kept the list taped to the wall by her bed so she could study them each night before she fell asleep. She learned words like *axon* and *occipital*. She learned terms like *negative stimuli* and *avoidant behavior*.

Some of the words were common ones she knew, but they seemed to mean something different in this book. She looked for them in the glossary but they were not there. *Subject. Controls. Trials.* The meaning of these common words must be taken for granted as concepts any reader should know.

The other thing not explained was the general attitude behind the actions in the book. She tried to deduce it from the context.

When she finished the book, she returned it and selected another one.

SIXTEEN

Decades later, Cora read a book about dolphins and sound. Their hearing range was ten times wider than a human's, and they used sound in ways humans couldn't.

The creaking noise they made was how they kept in communication with others. The sound cut through the water and could be heard miles away. No one knew how much information was coded into this creaking. It was hard to break the code when humans had difficulty underwater determining even which dolphin had spoken.

The crinkling (the voice Saran Wrap would have if it could speak) was how the dolphins touched things from a distance. This sound could be tightly focused, with or without power. With this crinkling, a mother could caress her baby from 50 feet away or shove a shark.

The final kind of sound, the clicking, was sonar, a form of vision. The clicking bounced off objects, the reflected information processed in the same part of the brain as sight. Potentially, the dolphin could see temperature, pressure and currents.

Since other animals were composed primarily of water, the clicking reflected off the densities of their internal organs in different ways. The sound and vision were combined in the dolphin's brain to create a single three-dimensional image.

Despite understanding this concept intellectually, Cora had been unable to imagine how sound and vision could be combined, until the day she accompanied her daughter to a pregnancy check-up. The jelly was squirted on the belly and the wand pressed against the skin. Then the monitor suddenly displayed the curled creature inside sucking its tiny thumb.

She grunted with surprise, seeing her first grandchild with a dolphin's ears.

C ora watched how Tibbet did his research. At no point
did he just let himself sit still and observe the dolphins,
how they moved and interacted. He did not wonder
about their personalities or perceptions or let his mind hold
big questions. Instead he focused on one small aspect at a time
and tallied up the associated behaviors. Knowing the numbers
made him confident about what he'd seen.

When she asked him why he studied the animals this way,
he paused for a moment, thinking, then told her a science
paper was like a recipe.

(While he spoke, there was no wind and she was sitting
close to him with her glasses on, so she could hear more of his
words. However it was apparent that Tibbet was also speaking
in a different way. He leaned forward and enunciated each
word, facing her so she could read his lips. He wanted her to
understand. His love for science in his face.)

He said a recipe was a list of the ingredients and actions
needed to get a desired result. A science paper was like that,
except it also postulated why the recipe might have worked
out that way and what the implications might be.

He said other researchers could then try to duplicate the
recipe to confirm it. By confirming recipes and improving on
them, scientists gradually evolved a better and better understanding of the world. That, he said, is how you got to the truth.

The word he said that was the hardest for her to hear was
science. Partly it was because it had an *S*-sound at the beginning

and end of the word, a sound so hard for her ears to hear, but partly it was that when he said the word, his voice got more breathy, a little like the way her Aunt Etty talked about God.

Tibbet mentioned twice that the highest possible standard was something he called a *double-blind experiment.*

It could be she'd misheard this phrase. It didn't seem like being doubly blind would be helpful. Maybe he was saying *double-line* instead. That night, she looked up both versions of the term in the glossaries of the books and journals she'd borrowed, but couldn't find either. It might be one of those obvious terms all scientists were supposed to know. Unsure of its meaning, Cora pictured Tibbet as the kind of high-strung horse that had blinders on both sides of his bridle so he wouldn't get startled or distracted.

When he talked about science, she saw he was trying to help her, to teach her. He was not an unkind man.

She knew he'd used the analogy of a recipe because he thought this was a concept that, as a woman, she might understand.

* * *

The third day, trying to train the dolphins, Cora held out a butterfish, saying *Talk, talk.* Kat considered her for a moment, then dove under the water and came back, holding in her mouth a grey and bloated object. With a fast flick of her head, she threw it onto the dock beside the bucket.

It was a squid, with only one leg left. She'd clearly been saving it for a while. Probably it was her last one. Cora hadn't given her any since Kat had hit her in the face with one.

Kat looked at her.

Cora went to the outdoor fridge and came back with a bag of squid. She held up one where Kat could see it and said— Talk.

She waited.

—Talk.

Kat rose, peddling her tail back and forth, standing up in the water. In this dull lagoon, with nothing to do, she wanted the squid even more than she wanted to eat. She squealed with frustration.

At this sound, Cora threw her the squid.

Kat caught it. Overjoyed, she flipped it up in the air again and again, a pom-pom of flesh, a drum majorette in a butcher's parade.

Cora picked up another squid, held it out for Kat to see.

Kat paused, focusing.

Cora said—Talk.

Kat stared. Perhaps this was the moment when she understood the deal, the compact of trainer and trainee, the promise of reward for requested behavior. Or maybe she'd understood it from the start, but this was when she conceded.

Whatever went on in her head, she squealed a second time, even louder, the same key.

Cora threw her the squid. Kat caught it. Two squid in her mouth now, she rolled under the water to hide them at the bottom of the lagoon. A moment later she popped back up, eager.

Cora said—Talk.

Kat squawked, gurgling a little at the end.

The two of them repeated and repeated this command and reply, until Kat had squid tucked away in nooks and crannies all over the lagoon and Cora began holding up butterfish instead.

Each time Cora said *Talk*, Kat squealed the same note, catching the fish as they were thrown. She was so hungry, she swallowed them whole, repeating the trick thirty times in a row. The other dolphins watched this interaction with concentration: Cora saying *Talk*, then Kat making a noise and getting thrown a fish.

This was a concept that was new to them, having food be dependent on their ability to please a different species. Hunger, however, focuses the mind, shoving it toward innovation.

Once Kat was finally full, she stopped responding to Cora. Instead she circled the lagoon, her head out of the water, wearing a squid at a rakish angle like a fleshy Easter hat, pleased with herself.

With Kat no longer interested, Cora held up a fish and looked at the others instead. She said—Talk.

She waited a moment, then said—Talk.

Mother squeaked, hesitant, but willing to try.

Cora threw the fish to her. Mother swallowed it and then opened her mouth to bellow out lots of noises, her mouth open and hungry. Within an hour, even Bernie at times responded to the command.

* * *

The next day as soon as the dolphins saw Cora pull out the fish, they all squealed and clicked and trilled as loudly as they could, like opera stars warming up.

The men filed down to the lagoon. Standing nearby, each of them watched with a different expression.

In the silence right after she threw a fish, Tibbet spoke. He was facing her, close enough for her to hear.

He said—Maybe they do better with a woman's touch.

Don't we all—answered Blum.

* * *

Cora picked up a fish.

The dolphins, out of excitement, began making many sounds. Kat was beeping like a Martian spaceship landing.

No, no. Wait . . . —Cora said. She did not give them the fish. She had to teach them to wait until she said *Talk*.

Junior made a clicking like a stick running across fence posts.

Wait. Wait . . . —When they were silent for a second, she said—Talk.

Mother was the fastest, blatting out a baby's cries, filled with want and impatience, so Cora threw the fish to her.

Each time she waited until they were silent, then asked them to talk, rewarding the one who made the first noise after she said Talk.

Sometimes after she said *Talk*, one of them would bob there, motionless and concentrated, watching her. She knew well what people looked like when they were making sounds she couldn't hear. After a moment, she would be able to hear the dolphin's voice at the edge of her range, as high pitched as a dog whistle, more air than sound. Only once she could hear it clearly, did she throw the food.

Yes, someone else might have heard the sound sooner, but this did not bother her. She would teach the dolphins to speak as clearly as she wished all humans did.

Bit by bit, the dolphins and Cora worked at this together, defining through action what she meant by the word *Talk*.

* * *

One day while she sat on the dock, working with the dolphins, she was hit in the back with something cold. Jerking around, she saw Eh galloping down the veranda stairs two at a time. He vaulted over the railing to squirt her again with the water gun, this time from behind the cover of a lawn chair.

The terrifying thing was the easy grin he wore. That grin made it clear he didn't understand she might have been scared when he'd tried to grab her by force in the hallway the other day. Or perhaps it was worse than that. It seemed possible (from the *pchoo-pchoo* sound effects that she could see his mouth making as he worked the water gun's trigger) that he was so unable to imagine her point of view, he didn't know that she might find attempted rape unattractive.

She felt a shimmer of true fear inside her and rolled into the water among the dolphins, where Eh would never follow.

She might have a hard time perceiving sound, but some men had a similar difficulty with emotions (their own and others'). These men could range from the inconsiderate to the truly dangerous.

She swam 20 feet from the shore, then stuck her head out of the water to check he was leaving. She noticed Mother was watching him walk away. These days Mother seemed to have her head out of the water a lot, bobbing there, looking at the humans. Her gaze focused and unreadable, her eyes following the people as they moved around the lagoon. She considered their actions, studying their routines.

* * *

Six months before, when Cora had worked at the Tampa club in the bunny costume, there'd been a court case in all the newspapers. The case concerned two military men who'd been at a bar when a young woman collapsed on the dance floor. The men assumed she was drunk and carried her to their car to return her to her home. On the way, since she was unconscious and wouldn't know any different, they each had sex with her. Only afterward, when she didn't wake up, did they get alarmed. The autopsy discovered she'd had a heart condition and likely died while dancing.

In the photo, the men were shown in their military uniforms, looking sad, each posed with their wife and children.

Cora had been fascinated with the story. At times at the club, a man would attempt to corner her. Mostly she couldn't hear what they were saying, but she'd known from their expressions what would happen if they managed to get her alone. It seemed to her that the men acted this way with her a little more than with most of the other women at the club. She assumed it was because they sensed she was different.

In the newspaper photo, the woman smiled brightly, her chin tilted up. If Cora could figure out what she and this woman shared, perhaps she could change it in herself, or hide it somehow.

In the court case that followed the woman's death, the jury decided it was impossible to rape a woman who was dead, since by definition she could not say no. The men were not convicted of any wrongdoing.

Wanting to reduce how much the men harassed her, Cora had studied the women who the men didn't bother as much, as well as those who they bothered more. So far as she could tell, the harassment didn't have to do with looks. No, the men acted the worst with Netty, the brunette with an apologetic slouch and a slight double chin.

* * *

The dolphins learned quickly. Within days, they stayed silent when she held up the fish, waiting for her to say *Talk* before they began bellowing for food. Once they'd learned this trick, she required them to do more. She began to throw food only to the dolphins who responded with one clear sound.

Once they knew to respond with one noise when she said *Talk*, she began to teach them to respond with two noises to the command, *Talk more*.

Kat got the idea within an hour, teaching the rest through example.

A few days later Cora added the command, *Talk three sounds.*

Kat again was the first to respond with three sounds. Perhaps she was more motivated or verbal or smarter. Perhaps she connected with Cora better. Whatever the reason, she got rewarded frequently, with food and squid. She helped train the others by showing them what to do. Perhaps they all learned faster because of her.

When there was no training going on, Kat played with all the squid she'd accumulated, slinging them around the lagoon, at the dolphins and the humans. Gradually her range improved. If the men had lunch on the veranda, they learned to hunch over their food, protecting it. The windows of the building became targets. From inside, there'd be the slap of a squid, a silhouetted fleshy Rorschach, then the slow puckered release of its fall. Each morning, squid bodies lay scattered on the veranda and table and chairs as though there'd been a light rain of cephalopods.

Stepping out onto the veranda one morning, holding his coffee, Tibbet's heel landed on one. It was slimy from decomposition. His foot slid out from under him. He fell, bringing down several chairs. The clatter and yelling.

Cora ran up the stairs to make sure he was ok. Before he even got to his feet, he was bellowing that the dolphins were not allowed more squid. With her hearing glasses on and his voice so loud, she heard these words clearly.

(She noticed that he did not say *Kat* was not allowed more squid, but instead *the dolphins.* It was possible he did not know that Kat was the perpetrator, that she was the only one who threw squid at the men and the house. The only time he focused on individual dolphins was when he tallied specific behaviors. For him, the dolphins might appear to be one indistinguishable streamlined body, one grinning fishlike face.)

Stepping out onto the veranda, Blum listened to Tibbet's demand, then shook his head.

Tibbet limped around the rest of the day, furious.

* * *

Each day Mother was still letting go of leaves and twigs and seaweed by the exit stream, watching them roll through the water and get caught on the log wedged there against the gate. The log was no longer recognizable as a log, looking now like a large mound of debris. The mound no longer bobbed in the water so much, having become wedged in the space, bit by bit blocking the exit stream. The water riffled over it, backed up a bit.

* * *

One day Kat managed to hurl a squid and hit a seagull flying low over the lagoon. The gull tumbled in the air, then recovered. It flapped its wings, hovering, shrieking all around, not quite sure what had happened.

Kat surfaced to fling another squid. It hit the gull with a smack, sideswiping the bird so it tumbled into the water, then flapped off terrified.

The dolphins turned to Kat, impressed.

* * *

Tibbet noticed today that the water in the lagoon was higher and walked over to the exit stream to see what was going on. He looked at the mound of debris with disgust and, rather than touch any of it with his hands, simply slid the gate up out of the cement dam, removing it from the mouth of the stream to lay it down on the ground. Released, the water gushed down the stream, sweeping the debris away in chunks. Soon, just the log was left, too large to bump over the lip of the cement. Tibbet nudged the log with his foot twice, trying to get it over the lip, then reached down and picked it up and tossed it onto the ground, wiping his hand on his shorts. With the exit stream clear and the water draining, he picked the gate up and slid it back into its notched channel in the cement dam. He lowered it to the desired height and pushed it back into a notch to hold it there.

Mother watched his actions closely, her head up so both her eyes could focus.

Tibbet considered the flow of the water for a minute, then rocked the gate with his foot so it fell to the next notch.

Mother blinked at this.

After he left, Mother examined the gate for a long time, watching how the water moved under the metal gate and down the exit stream without the debris there. She did not let more seaweed go to watch it roll down the stream, but simply stared at the gate itself.

* * *

Cora now knew the different dolphins, their bodies and voices. Even with her eyes closed, she could frequently tell which dolphin made which noise.

Bernie's voice was the lowest, and he liked to issue long vibrating raspberries from his blowhole.

Mother had a tightness, a sort of quivering intensity to her voice.

Kat had the greatest vocal range and could create the widest variety of sounds. By now she could imitate the doves cooing or the metallic ringing of the phone in the house.

The youngest one, Junior, tried to imitate the sounds of the other dolphins, but couldn't make the same variety of noises yet. Like any teenager, he didn't have the full vocabulary of an adult.

One day Cora bought them a toy at the market in town: a 10-inch punch ball. When she threw it in the lagoon, Junior investigated it first, clicking at it, then tentatively prodding it with his beak. (While the dolphins still would not touch any food or object the men put into the lagoon, they clearly no longer considered Cora a stranger, for they would accept anything she threw in.)

Within minutes Junior was throwing his body on top of the ball, trying to keep it balanced under him while he pushed it deep under the water, then rolled off it to have it rocket up into the air.

He used his beak to flick the ball to Mother, but she just watched it splash onto the water near her and then turned away, uninterested.

Junior retrieved the ball and looked around. With no other dolphin at the surface, he flipped the ball to Cora. Surprised, she missed the throw, so the ball bounced onto the dock and rolled to a stop against one of the posts.

He stared at it there, out of his reach, the solemn stillness of a child. Feeling badly for him, she fetched it and tossed it back.

He jumped for it, so happy, then bopped it back to her, but it flew wide and landed on the sand of the beach. He looked at it. She fetched it.

This was how they started to play catch—with the dolphin throwing the ball and the human retrieving it.

* * *

The next book she borrowed was a copy of the *Journal of Behavior*. She chose it because the cover had a photo of a dog in a cage. She thought the featured article might be about how to train animals.

Like many of the other scientific articles, she found the writing to be awkward and hard to parse. The only mention of the authors was their names under the title. The text was written as though the experiment had occurred on its own, the words assembling themselves on the page, as though nothing as imperfect as a human had ever been associated with this project.

The researchers had put two different groups of dogs in two different metal cages. They wired the cages so electric shocks could be delivered through the floor. With one group, the bell went off, and a moment later the dogs were shocked no matter what they did. After enough of these trials, these dogs just lay on the floor whining. The second group of dogs could escape the shock if they pressed a lever when the bell rang. At the sound of the bell, these dogs did not lie down whining but instead jumped to press the lever. The article concluded the first group of dogs had learned to be helpless.

The animals' suffering distilled to a chart of numbers. She wondered who could possibly need the obvious spelled out this way.

Tibbet saw her sitting by the lagoon reading the article, and he nodded in approval.—Great research. Huge discovery.

She looked at him, understanding.

In the morning, the dock in the lagoon seemed to have sunk a bit, the water further up its sides. After a moment of looking around, confused, Cora realized that the water in the lagoon was backed up again.

She swam over to the exit stream. The gate looked like it was lower than it had been last night when she left. She wondered if one of the men had decided to lower it, or if there'd been a big wind last night, large enough to shift the metal gate, to rock it off its notch.

Mother had her head out of the water, watching her.

After breakfast, Tibbet noticed and walked over to the exit stream. When he saw the position of the gate, he cocked his head and looked at it, then around at the lagoon, just like she had. He slid the gate back up three notches and pushed it into position, rocking it there to make sure it was firmly in the notch.

Mother floated in the water, watching this.

* * *

When Cora said, *Talk*, all the dolphins now responded with one noise.

When she said, *Talk more*, most of the dolphins responded with something close to two sounds. Their response a little like a barbershop quartet on helium.

When she said, *Talk three sounds*, their reactions were more confused. Generally it was just Kat who would call out three sounds.

Kat was always the best, the showoff, repeating the rhythm, teaching the rest what was required. Her noises were rich and varied, rumbles and pops and trills, a parrot experimenting. She played, bored and innovative.

Each time Cora tossed Kat a fish as a reward, she swallowed it and paused, her head cocked, to hear Cora call out her praise. Not much else to achieve in the lagoon.

* * *

Two mornings later, when Cora arrived at the lagoon, she noticed the water was higher again, almost lapping against the bottom of the dock. She was surprised and looked at the gate. It was all the way down, blocking the exit stream completely.

She swam over to look. Nothing appeared any different, except for the position of the gate. Perhaps Tibbet, rocking the gate in place, had actually jarred it loose by mistake. For once Mother wasn't nearby. She was over at the other end of the lagoon, by the chute to the sea. Cora moved over to her.

All four dolphins were here. Mother had her head resting on the chute, listening to the surf. Because of the lagoon being backed up, the water in the chute was maybe 2 inches deeper. When she turned round to greet Cora, Cora saw her beak had a cut on it that hadn't been there yesterday.

Mother turned back to the chute, studying the water flow, the water not yet deep enough.

Cora watched, waiting, not telling the men.

Throughout the day, the water rose ever so slowly.

* * *

Bored, Junior played with the punch ball for hours, bopping

it hard with his beak, then racing to get it, like a boy left in a room with nothing else to do. Like Kat with the squid, he quickly became increasingly accurate with the ball. He could knock it right into her hands. At times he instead squeezed it in his beak so it popped out and flew high into the air.

Cora found he loved playing catch so much, she could use it to get him to practice vocalizing. She would hold up the ball and say—Talk.

As soon as he made a noise back, she'd throw him the ball. He needed extra practice, because he was not as verbal as Kat or Mother. It didn't matter whether Cora threw the ball directly to him or in a long pass to the back corner of the lagoon. He jumped for it either way, with speed and pizzazz, so happy to play. She was beginning to think of him as a very smart dog who loved to chase balls.

One morning a few days ago, when she was snorkeling in the lagoon, he had swum up beside her clicking, corkscrewing lazily through the water. Without thinking, as she would with a dog, she had reached out to touch him, running her fingers along his neck and down his side.

She hadn't thought it would be a bad thing to do. The dolphins were constantly touching, seemed to need the contact, rubbing their bodies against each other, twining around one another or sliding a flipper along another's side. Being social creatures, the touch must give them comfort. Since they needed to be able to sense currents, it was possible their skin was very sensitive.

In this moment, Junior had felt for the first time the touch of an articulated hand, of the soft pads of fingers running over his side, the way they could conform to the contours of skin. He froze, his gaze inward, startled.

Worried that she had offended or hurt him or broken some type of social rule, she had pulled back, but he did not swim away. Instead he hung there, his eyes motionless. As though after a lifetime of eating raw fish, he had just tasted pesto.

So, she had reached out hesitantly and touched his side again. His eyes flickered. She had run one finger along a curve of muscle. His skin was like a baby's. He allowed himself to drift closer, his body very still. She drew gentle Zs across his shoulder with one finger.

He had floated there, his eyes frozen and staring, his mouth slightly open.

Then abruptly he'd broken away and swum fast to the far side of the lagoon to recover from the intensity.

After this, each morning when she got in the water, he zipped over to her, greeting her first thing and wove around her like a cat until she touched his side again. Each morning for a few minutes she'd run her fingers over his sides and back.

* * *

The next morning, when Tibbet stepped out of the house, the end of the dock was under a half inch of water. He appeared confused and looked to the left and then the right, as though wondering if he'd somehow ended up at the wrong lagoon.

The dolphins were swimming in circles by the chute. Cora wasn't sure what depth they would feel was enough, but she believed if the water rose maybe a half inch more, they could wiggle their way up the chute like G.I. Joes with flippers. Their bellies would be scraped up, but they could reach the sea.

Tibbet walked around the lagoon, staring at the water, trying to understand what had happened. The dolphins stuck their heads out, watching him.

When he got to the gate, he coughed in surprise and pulled it back up, notching it in place, the water beginning to drain away. He moved the gate up and down in its channel, pushing it into different notches and wiggling it around to see if it was loose at all, if the water or wind could knock it down.

This time, just to make sure, he slid a 30-pound rock under it to hold it up. His neck was corded as he shoved it into position.

Mother sank under the waves and lay on the bottom of the lagoon next to Bernie for the longest time, their flippers touching. When they rose to the surface and blew, their exhales were full and slow.

* * *

The next book Cora borrowed from the bookshelves was about predators. She chose it mostly because there were photos in it, the text not quite so dense. There was a whole chapter on how predators select potential prey, searching for an animal that looked sick or weak, one that would be easy to catch and pull down. There was a photo of a cheetah on a hill studying a herd of gazelles, its yellow eyes intent.

The book described how the gazelles, upon sighting the cheetah, would prong 10 feet straight up in the air, high above the level of the grass, muscular popcorn, displaying their health and impressive strength, each striving to not be the one selected. The cheetah would watch, judging minute differences, then disappear into the grass, slinking forward in the direction of the one who looked the weakest.

Returning the book the next morning, she stepped into the building at a point when she knew all three men were inside. Opening the screen door, she saw them sitting at the table, drinking coffee and examining computer printouts (in the background, the dot matrix printer zipped back and forth, hammering at the paper, the furious buzz of modern technology).

As she walked in, the book in her hand, the men turned to look at her. Something about Eh and Blum's gaze, intent and assessing, reminded her of the cheetah.

Sliding the book into place on the shelf, she remembered Netty, the waitress at the Tampa club who tended to get harassed the most by the men. Netty walked with a slight slouch and she startled easily. Not the best looking, but the most hesitant. The woman who looked the weakest.

Standing at the bookshelf, Cora glanced over her shoulder. Eh was staring at her.

For the first time, she wondered how he perceived her. Frequently she was uncertain what was being said and how to respond. She would look from face to face, confused.

So, she straightened her spine, widened her shoulders and pulled her chin up to see what effect it would have.

Eh cocked his head, his brow furrowed.

She set off toward the exit, doing her best to stride, to broadcast that she was tough and capable and not a gazelle.

Eh watched.

Over the next few days, she found the more she walked this way around him, the more perplexed he looked.

* * *

Above water, the dolphins made noise occasionally, but underwater they vocalized nearly constantly, the breadth and volume of the sounds so much more impressive and haunting. She thought the range of these noises was something the men should hear.

So, while the three of them were eating lunch on the balcony, she climbed the stairs. As she walked toward them, she worked to look tough. She imitated as best she could a man plowing through the world, someone with a sense of his own value, someone who would fight back hard if attacked. She moved with a firm step, her arms swinging, her head up. The men watched her, squinting, clearly noticing some difference.

She imagined she was one of them, a man with no branks in his mouth. She spoke in a clipped factual voice—The dolphins make different noises underwater than they do in the air.

Tibbet said—And . . . ?

She held her body tight, her back straight and regarded the men with a level stare.—Hearing them might help you learn about them.

How are we supposed to hear them?—Tibbet asked.

She said—Install a microphone.

(Into her mind came the memory of a cop who used to visit the Tampa club where she'd worked. One day when he reached for his wallet, she'd spotted his shoulder holster, but she had guessed his profession long before that from his short hair and the way he strode into a room, scanning the crowd, his eyes ready for anything. He was not a large man, but he was strung tight as a bow. She'd touched him once on the shoulder to hand him his drink and he jerked around, his face blank and cold, and very ready.

This man, she realized, was who she was imitating.)

She said in a clipped voice—Then you could record the sounds. Tally them and analyze them.

(Imitating the cop, she could move and talk in a different way. She could issue commands.)

From his expression, she could see Tibbet liked this idea.

(At the club, the cop would knock back drink after drink, watching the women in their costumes. The women stayed as far as they could from him.)

She added—Sometimes the sounds get really high-pitched, then disappear.

Blum asked Tibbet—What's their vocal range?

(When the cop twisted to look at someone, his head turned as smoothly and mechanically as a tank turret.)

She turned to look at Blum in the same way.

Each of the men reacted differently to this change in her

behavior. Blum seemed amused, an interested smile on his face. Tibbet seemed confused. Eh had his eyes narrowed, his cigarette motionless in his hand, nonplussed.

Tibbet said—I don't know their range.

Blum asked—Is there a microphone that can record high-pitched sounds?

Tibbet stated—You just play the sound back slower. Then you can hear it.

Blum nodded and told Eh to find some sort of underwater recording system. Tibbet and Eh didn't like that she was suggesting ideas for them to enact. They looked from her to Blum and then back.

The recording system would arrive within the week. The microphone needed a small cage to protect it from the dolphins. It would take a while for Eh to connect it with speakers in the house so they could hear the sounds as they were recorded. In the end, installed, it cost about the same as a used car.

From then on, each time she went into the building, she would hear the clicks and squeals of the dolphins, as though the animals were caught in the building somewhere, searching for a way out.

* * *

Within a day of the gate being propped up permanently with the large rock, Mother was moving around and eating again. She spent a lot of her time on the surface, playing with seaweed or some other prop, while she studied the humans as they moved around the lagoon. If any of them engaged in an action she found interesting, she'd cock her head at an angle where both her eyes could focus on the action, while she idly mouthed the seaweed. Her whole body concentrated. Years later, when Cora saw Steve McQueen in *The Great Escape*, playing with his baseball and watching the guards, she thought of Mother and her seaweed.

Bernie, however, was eating even less. He lay on the bottom of the lagoon, only rising to the surface to breathe. Cora dove down to try to feed him, holding the freshest fish out to him. He'd look at her, but not open his mouth. The other dolphins dove down frequently to rub against him.

B y now, in the morning when she began to snorkel around the lagoon, each of the dolphins came to greet her. Mother, floating by the chute, tasting the sea, would turn to Cora, scanning her insides with sound. Kat would nose by, full of mischief, a squid in her mouth. Junior would dash over to have her run her fingers over his sides. As soon as she touched him, he'd freeze in the water, his gaze introverted, mesmerized by the sensation. Bernie would rise in the water to her, gliding close solemn and gentle, before surfacing for a big breath and then descending.

Then the dolphins would return to their normal activities, circling the tiny lagoon, playing and fighting.

The one thing that would get their attention was if one of the men opened the shed beside the lagoon. Then all action in the water would stop. The dolphins would surface to look at the shed, watching the open doorway to see, when the man stepped out, if he held the net that could stretch across the lagoon.

Since Cora's deal with Blum about teaching the dolphins, each time one of the men stepped out, he held something else: the sprinkler or a hammer or a trestle.

Afterward the dolphins would watch for another moment, thinking whatever they were thinking, a small break in time before they returned to whatever they had been doing.

* * *

When Cora had worked at the Tampa club, the cop had stood out. Although he wasn't much taller than her, he somehow created the appearance of mass and power. It was the slow solid way he moved, like a force that could not be deterred. And he had the blank stare of someone who had seen horrors and could respond accordingly.

At the research center, she tried to keep her face blank like the cop had, her eyes still and cold. She imagined, with her haircut, she might resemble him a tiny bit. When she acted this way, it was easier for her to speak, to say what she thought.

Eh considered her, his eyebrows knit, taking in this change.

* * *

Each time one of the wives dropped by the research center, they appeared a little surprised to see Cora still there. After Cora's hair was shaved off, their surprise was increased.

The first time Blum's wife, Babs, spotted Cora and her buzzcut, her eyes blinked. Then her perky smile went up like a wall. She would not, however, let her children walk down from the veranda to the lagoon anymore without her.

When Tibbet's wife, Terry or Carrie (Cora was still not sure) saw her buzzcut, her head rocked back in surprise and she laughed and said—My God, girl, what happened to you?

After that, Terry/Carrie still came down occasionally to talk with her, but neither of the wives invited her up anymore for drinks on the veranda. When the women did talk to her, the conversation had more pauses.

* * *

When she got back to her room in town at the end of each day, she tugged off her bathing suit to shower the salt from her skin. She'd catch a glimpse of herself in the mirror, naked. Her limbs so tan now in comparison to the rest of her, it looked like she was wearing a white bathing suit.

* * *

Talk, she would say or, *Talk more* or *Talk three words* and most of the dolphins would respond with the correct number of sounds. However, with all four of them making sounds (*vocalizing* as Tibbet said) at the same time, it was getting more difficult to know which dolphins had answered correctly and, thus, which ones to reward.

At some point during the day, Blum would walk down to the lagoon, look through her notebook and talk with her about what had happened that day, checking on her the same way he did with Tibbet, a Harvard professor. She felt proud of this. On the other hand, Blum sat a little closer to her than he did to Tibbet and kept his voice low so she had to lean in. At times he touched her arm or knee as they talked.

Around him, she imitated the cop, but Blum didn't seem as put off by it, more amused.

Today he told her the dolphins were making great progress with vocalizing on command, but she needed to get them to do much more. He wanted them to be able to mimic any sentence a human said, its beat and pitch, to talk *humanoid* as Kat had when he had tried operating on her.

He said if she managed to get one of them to do that in front of the NASA funder, he would officially make her a researcher. She would be one of the first *women researchers* in the field.

The first what?—she asked, thinking she'd heard the term wrong.

Woman researcher—he said, watching her.

Although she was currently spending the whole of each day

with the dolphins, studying them and noting down what she saw, the idea of being an official researcher was something she'd never imagined. In her family, no one had a job where they studied something. And of the jobs her family had, the women had the worst ones: part-time and seasonal, squeezed in around childcare. Waitress, berry-picker, launderer, line worker.

Thus, this idea of *woman researcher* took her a moment to grasp. Her eyes moved from left to right, putting the words together.

Considering the concept (observing the dolphins for years, interacting with them, hearing their surreal sounds), she felt something jump inside her, the want in her throat. She knew this was what she was designed for, this was how she was meant to spend the rest of her life.

Blum saw this desire in her face and smiled. It wasn't a nice smile. Now he knew a second thing she wanted.

And watching him, something about the phrase itself began to bother her, *woman researcher*. It caught in her ear, sounding awkward.

She realized the phrase didn't use an adjective and a noun (*female* researcher). Instead Blum had put two nouns together (*woman* researcher). The term sounded unnatural this way and perhaps that was the point. A lizard-donkey, a dog-mosquito, a woman-researcher: some chimera that should never be.

She said—I'll do the best I can.

—You have a little over a week before the funder arrives.

She said—Not much time.

He nodded—If you fail and the guy is not impressed, then I'll have to give them other results quickly. I'll have to catch up on my brain research.

Her face reacted to this threat. There was a flicker of pleasure in his expression. Bit by bit, he was finding the right rewards and punishments to make her perform.

She said—Get me a second pool so I can work with one of the dolphins intensively.

* * *

The next morning, an above-ground pool was delivered, a hard plastic shell and diesel motor dropped off on the lawn by the side of the house. Blum had purchased a fairly small pool, just 15 feet wide and 3 feet deep. Perhaps he hadn't bothered to look at the actual measurements.

Tibbet and Eh began to rig a diesel motor and a hose to pump water from the sea into the pool. Tibbet seemed in a bad mood, slamming tools about like an angry child. He would not look at Cora when she spoke to him, wouldn't respond to any of her suggestions (as though he was the one who was deaf). Last week Blum had said no to Tibbet's request to build a wall in the lagoon to create a separate smaller lagoon as a second testing facility. He said Tibbet was going through his share of the research money faster than he was coming up with results and that he needed to change that ratio. Now Blum was buying equipment for her, for some girl who had never gone to college.

Once the men had the motor working and brought the hose up to fill the pool, she pointed out the pool might be better placed a few feet to the right where the ground was flatter and there was more shade. Tibbet and Eh ignored her.

To get them to move the pool onto level ground, she had to suggest the idea to Blum.

By the afternoon, the pool was filled and ready for use. Tibbet asked Blum which dolphin should be placed inside it.

Cora said—Kat is the smartest and most vocal. She's the one who imitated us before.

Tibbet continued to regard Blum, as though she had not spoken.

Blum looked from her to Tibbet and then back. It was clear he enjoyed this position. She felt pity for his children. He said—How about Kat?

Tibbet's mouth tightened and he walked down to the lagoon with Eh to get Kat.

As the three men lugged Kat in the stretcher up the stairs to the pool, it became abruptly clear just how small the pool was. Kat was 10 feet long from beak to tail. They slid her in and she twisted quickly in a tight circle, but still her shoulder and flipper thumped into the far wall. Even with the pool filled to the rim, her dorsal fin stuck out into the air. It was like a human in a very small prison cell, or perhaps more like an athlete locked in a closet.

Kat circled in the water, terrified, looking for any way out, searching for some way to get back to the other dolphins. The water sloshed about, spilling in sheets out of the pool, reducing the depth so she had even less room to maneuver and felt more panicked. She was making distress squeals (like terrified styrofoam). These sounds were loud enough that, even this high-pitched, Cora could hear them. Touching her fingers to the pool's side, she could also feel the vibrations.

The other dolphins called back to her from the lagoon below, the volume intense. They must have their heads out of the water to be this audible.

Please go inside—Cora said to the men.—I'll calm her down.

Blum ushered the men into the house and closed the door. She knelt by the pool and placed one hand in the water, murmuring—I'm here. I'm here. I'm here.

She talked to Kat without pause, kneeling there. Kat let her side brush up against Cora's hand again and again as she circled the pool. Perhaps she took comfort from the contact, or maybe there just wasn't enough room to avoid the touch. Over the next thirty minutes, Kat began to slow, making fewer distress calls and rubbing more purposefully with each rotation against Cora's hand.

However, if one of the men stepped out of the house, Kat would bolt forward in her tight circle, frantic again, squealing. Hearing her, the other dolphins would call back.

Cora stayed beside the pool, talking quietly with Kat. She left the hose in the water, the pump going. This kept the pool filled. Before dinner, she saw Kat poop, the substance squirting out from underneath, a watery cloud. Cora grabbed the pool skimmer and scooped out as much as she could, but much of it was too liquidy to catch. New seawater poured in all the time through the hose, but this tended to freshen only the water at the top. The thicker effluent sunk to the bottom.

At 9 P.M., Cora stood up to head back to her boarding house room in town to sleep. As she stepped away from the pool, Kat began to utter distress squeals again. Dolphins were social creatures, rarely alone. She was currently trapped in a small pool next to a house filled with men who, in the past, had forcibly hammered holes in her head. Cora continued to walk away, but the squeals echoed, following her up the driveway, high-pitched and terrified. Before Cora got to the road, she turned and came back to the pool.

She tried twice more to sneak away when she thought Kat was sleeping, but both times Kat woke and squealed with even greater emotion.

So at 10 P.M., Cora placed a lawn lounge chair beside the pool and lay down in the chair, a towel over her as a blanket. With the back of the chair propped up, she could let one hand trail in the pool. Kat lay next to her in the water, making burbling contented noises, the side of her head bumping into Cora's fingers. The water lapped in the pool. Each time Kat blew, it was like the hot exhale of a cat who'd just eaten a very rotten fish, the mist of that breath gently raining down on Cora's face.

At times Kat clicked at Cora's hand in the water. Cora could feel the clicks against her skin and in the bones of her hand. Tiny morse-code taps of affection.

She woke up at one point. Her hand in the pool had fallen asleep and her whole arm felt like a dead limb. She pulled her arm in against her, flapping her jellyfish hand around, trying to get circulation back into it. The only light was the pinpricks of stars above. There was the smell of seaweed and salt. Kat was cooing to herself and spitting water high into the air like a bored child in a bath. Cora settled her arm into her lap and fell back to sleep.

At dawn she woke, her face against the plastic straps of the lawn chair. She could tell she wouldn't be able to fall asleep again. So she got up to start the training, fetching from the outdoor fridge a bucket of cut-up butterfish, with a few squid as special treats.

Talk—said Cora, and Kat responded with one sound. Cora threw her a chunk of butterfish.

Talk more—said Cora. Kat responded with two sounds and got another chunk of fish.

Talk three sounds—Cora said. Kat made three sounds and earned a squid.

It was so much easier to hear her responses without the other dolphins squealing at the same time. Kat's eyes followed her everywhere she went, nothing else to pay attention to. That morning, Cora taught her to respond to four sounds and then five. Kat listened, head cocked, focused on the puzzle of what was being requested.

Once the day began to heat up, Cora cautiously dipped her legs into the pool to cool down. Kat didn't seem to mind, so Cora eased her way all the way in, standing up in the water. Kat brushed against her repeatedly. Perhaps she missed the touch of the other dolphins.

Partway through the afternoon, Cora noticed Kat's back

was a little pink. Normally the dolphins were far underwater, not exposed to the sun. She wondered if dolphins could get sunburns.

She asked Blum to have the men hang a sail over the pool from tree to tree to shade it entirely. They did so within an hour.

Tying the sail in place, Eh noticed the lawn chair next to the pool and asked—You sleep here last night?

The branks of fear in her mouth, she pretended she hadn't heard.

But that evening she saw him looking out the window several times, to see if she was sleeping there.

So she placed an inflatable mattress in the pool and slept on it with Kat as protection. Eh would never dare to step into a pool with a dolphin in it, or even to reach for her across the pool. Kat seemed to like Cora being on the mattress in the water. She bumped the mattress and hummed low pitched rumbles through the mattress. Even though she couldn't wear her hearing glasses in the pool, Cora could still feel the sound vibrate the mattress. Kat hummed and burbled, talking to Cora all night long. Cora wondered just how much dolphin activity they were missing at night. Was it possible dolphins were nocturnal?

Cora half-slept on her watery bed, waking frequently. She dreamed Kat was singing to her in Portuguese, and then in Greek. Unfortunately Cora didn't speak either language so didn't know what was being said.

* * *

Bored and isolated, with nothing else to do, within two days Kat was imitating Cora's speech, not just the number of syllables but also the sound of the vowels. She was beginning to kazoo the way she had when being operated on.

Cora would say, *Talk three words*, and Kat would repeat the sentence as best she could through her blowhole, *Ahh Eeee Ooo*.

Each time she managed, Cora showered her with food and squid and much attention.

So Cora started saying *Talk* and different short sentences.—Talk. See the ball.

Kat responded—Ahh, eee eh ahh.

The bottom of the pool was getting murky. Each time Cora saw Kat poop, she would grab a net and scoop out as much as she could. She assumed Kat peed in the water too, but the urine she could not see or filter out. Her legs, she noticed, began to itch from being in the water and Kat was blinking a lot. So she asked Blum for a second above-ground pool so they could have a clean pool to move her into. He considered her request, not saying yes immediately. She imagined how much Kat's eyes might hurt.

She touched him on the arm, stepped in closer and said please.

He ran his hand down her backbone, letting his fingers come to a rest on her hip. Giving the flesh there a light squeeze, he nodded yes.

Tibbet watched this with angry eyes and popped another Tums in his mouth.

When the new pool arrived, she had it filled within two hours and they moved Kat to it, then drained the other pool. The smell made the men cough as they cleaned its sides.

In the new pool, Kat scrubbed every part of her body off on the clean walls. She blinked less. She rubbed against Cora and worked even harder on the lessons.

* * *

In the pool, with nothing else to do, no other dolphins

around, Kat connected with Cora in a way she hadn't before. Without other dolphins around, she focused on the interaction, on the training. Bored and social, she learned faster than Cora could have imagined.

That fourth afternoon, Cora tried gently scratching Kat's sides and Kat stayed still for five minutes, nearly hypnotized by the sensation of mobile fingers scrubbing. Then abruptly she broke away and moved as far away as she could in the small pool. Looking dazed. After that, Cora sometimes rewarded her for an exceptional kazoo by scrubbing her skin for a few minutes, telling her how well she'd done. Each day they worked and worked.

I t seemed likely that Kat's sunburned back hurt, along with the dry cracked skin on her fin. She was tired of being in the tiny pool, in the less circulated water, with no other dolphins, barely able to move. So perhaps it wasn't a surprise that she began to cause trouble. She'd started to flick squid at the kitchen window, at the upstairs bathroom, at the men anytime they stepped outside. From this new vantage point next to the house, Kat was much closer to her targets. The smack of the squid against a window made everyone jump, like the building was under attack.

When the men opened the side door to step out, they learned to duck, jibing left or right, moving fast around the corner of the building. If they forgot, they'd get slapped in the face with a low-flying squid. Kat figured out that Eh tended to juke to the right, so when he came out the door, she began to be able to consistently peg him in the cheek or shoulder. After a few direct hits, he started faking right and then diving left.

One day Blum opened the screen door and automatically ducked and a squid flew in past him to knock over a lamp. The lamp broke with a loud crash. Kat peeked over the edge of the plastic pool, her eyes shining.

The men ate their meals outside on the veranda. This spot was protected from her squid projectiles by the corner of the building, but she could still hear them, so Kat began to imitate their laughs, especially Tibbet's. He had a tight-throated *ack-ack-ack* that sounded a bit like he was choking. Each time he laughed, Kat would repeat the sound, the inflection and tone of it. This eerie *ack-ack* echo from around the corner. It would stop him mid-laugh. All of them listening, eyes down.

Tibbet said it didn't sound like him at all. Not at all. But when he was outside, he didn't laugh as much.

* * *

Each day Kat improved at kazooing, not just in the number of sounds she could repeat, but also in the emphasis. So Cora began to recite nursery rhymes. Stylized and exaggerated in beat and tone, the rhymes were easy for Kat to hear, easier for Cora to recognize when Kat had imitated her well.

Cora would say—MA-ree had a LI-ttle lamb, LI-ttle lamb, LI-ttle lamb.

Kat would answer—ah IH-eh ah IH-eh ah, H-eh ah IH-eh ah.

Standing above Kat in the wading pool, Cora could lay her fingers on the skin around the blowhole to ensure she was counting Kat's syllables correctly without her hearing glasses on. She could feel the sound in her fingertips. She noticed the blowhole didn't always have to open to make the sounds. In general, it moved very little, knuckling tighter or loosening slightly. The sound made somewhere inside.

When Kat exhaled that stench of rotten eggs and fish, Cora would peer inside. A short muscled tunnel down to a moist flap of skin that obscured what was below. However the sounds were created, there were no teeth involved, or tongue or mobile lips.

Even without hearing glasses, she could tell the vowels were increasingly accurate and clear. It sounded a little like a balloon learning to speak, a whistled squeaky enunciation. Perhaps there was a muscled orifice in there squeezing from one air sac to another. Consonants, so far, seemed impossible.

Tibbet hung a spare microphone from the tree over the wading pool. He recorded the training sessions between Kat and Cora, then printed out the oscillographic tracings so he could tally the results. He circled and counted the different components that Blum had discerned and created terms for: *sonic bursts*, *stimulus trains* and *matched responses*. Blum loved to invent terminology. They used other vocabulary too that Cora tried to memorize: *vocal stimuli, phonemes, waveforms, reinforcers* and *schwas*.

Even when Cora wasn't giving Kat lessons in talking, Kat at times continued to burble to herself. Bored and all alone, she played with the interesting new sounds. When she vocalized underwater, the noises echoed through the sides of the pool. Cora lay on the deck chair nearby, listening, her eyes closed. Out of the pool, she could put on her hearing glasses. Muffled through plastic and slightly distorted, it was still obvious that the noises each day became increasingly human, the beat and inflection. The voice of a toddler babbling nonsense to itself, mastering some language made of mostly vowels: Hawaiian perhaps or Finnish, a sense of umlauts. The sounds emerging from underwater.

When Cora stepped inside the building to get a new book, she could see two speakers set up, one on either side of the main room. Kat's babbling came from the left speaker. From the right came the squeals and clicks of the dolphins in the lagoon. The two sets of noises so different.

In the middle of the room sat Tibbet, his head cocked like a dog that had heard a whistle in the distance, listening with all his attention. He tallied the differences between the sounds again and again. No matter how he counted them, it was clear something dramatic was happening.

He would glance at her, his gaze so very cold, unable to understand how she could be involved with this work.

* * *

In the wading pool, she was closer to the house. She worked in her bathing suit in the pool with Kat all day.

Once she caught sight of Blum in the upstairs bathroom, standing and watching her. His hands were down out of sight, somewhere in the area of his zipper.

He looked her in the eye, flushed the toilet, zipped up and stepped back.

* * *

One evening, Eh asked her if she wanted to get drinks. There was a bar down the road, he said. In his eyes was that coldness. He tried to cover it up by stretching his face in a smile.

She replied she was tired, no thanks.

Looking at his expression she remembered the learned helplessness experiment. Clearly it was not applicable to some men. Instead, Eh was getting angry.

* * *

Kat loved being gently scratched. At a certain point in the day, she would no longer work for food or squid or even to play catch with the ball. The only thing she'd work for was the treat of fingernails lightly running over her skin. If Cora touched her this way, moving her fingernails over Kat's skin, she would freeze, her gaze internal, her mouth slightly ajar. For as long as the rubbing continued, she would not breath, even if her blowhole was already at the surface. She'd just float there, holding her breath, feeling the miraculous sensation of fingers.

Every day, she learned so quickly, nothing else to do. When

Cora walked away to go the bathroom or get herself some food, Kat would squeal with distress until Cora came back. Then, watching Cora walking back, Kat would trill with joy in her tiny pool.

At times Kat wanted more than her back and body rubbed. During a massage, she'd open her mouth and stretch her face toward Cora, her jaws wide, a dental patient waiting for the first touch. It appeared she wanted her mouth touched, her gums and maybe her tongue massaged.

Cora would step back from all those razor-sharp teeth. She knew that Kat meant no harm, but she would not place her hands anywhere near her mouth. Kat would stretch her head forward, reaching and reaching, but Cora would back away.

The NASA official arrived at the research center. The men ushered him outside, clustered around him, eager and obsequious. She didn't know what they'd told him prior to this moment. He blinked at the sight of Cora, wearing her bathing suit and hearing glasses, with her deviant haircut, standing in the wading pool with a dolphin.

Nervous, she told Kat to talk, then without any introduction began to recite "Baa-baa Black Sheep."

Kat kazooed along, a fraction of a second behind. The official looked back and forth from Cora to the dolphin. She watched him gradually comprehend what he was seeing.

Cora recited "Itsy Bitsy Spider"; she spoke the words to "America the Beautiful"; she sang "Put your head on my shoulder."

Kat mimicked the rhythm and pitch of the phrases. She hummed the gist of the sounds, a kid in church mumbling the words of a hymn she didn't know. It was morning, and she was hungry.

Meanwhile Blum spoke quietly to the official. He explained dolphins were the closest thing on this planet to intelligent extraterrestrials. He said this dolphin had spontaneously performed the mimicking one day of its own accord. In response they had taught it to perform the action on command.

The official was a linguistics professor who had been hired by NASA; his specialty was in heuristics. He'd never seen anything like this. His forehead was furrowed. He didn't know how to react.

His first questions were about Cora.—Who's the woman? Why is she here?

(It seemed possible he found a woman involved with science more remarkable than a dolphin mimicking English. The whole time he was here, she did not say one word directly to him.)

Blum answered—Women plant the germ of language in all of us. They teach children how to speak. They are specialized for the work.

The official grunted at this explanation and returned his attention to the dolphin. After a moment, he ventured—Parrots are better at this.

Parrots—Blum blew air out his mouth dismissively.—Tiny little bird brains. Raw memorization. Years of repeated exposure. This dolphin has only heard English for three weeks. It's mimicking a novel pattern, the beat and pitch. This takes intelligence.

The official considered this.

Blum asked him—What are your three favorite bands?

—My favorite bands?

—Yes. The Drifters? The Coasters? What are they?

—What does that have to do with anything?

—Trust me.

—Well, The Drifters are great, and The Everly Brothers. Lately I've been listening to a British band called The Beatles.

Cora nodded and said to Kat.—Talk. The Drifters are great, and The Everly Brothers. Lately he's been listening to a British band called the Beatle.

Kat kazooed the rhythm, imitating the vowels.

Jesus—the official said.

Blum unrolled a printout of an oscillographic recording he'd brought along, pointing out the similarities in the timing and sounds between Kat and Cora. He circled the sonic bursts, discussing them in terms of frequency spectrums and pulsing rates, multivariate analysis and statistical significance.

At times like this, when the attention of others was on him, Blum seemed to grow larger. He took the stage, confident and gesturing, his voice booming. Cora watched the official listening, his eyes bigger and bigger.

Near the end of his explanation, Blum began to slow down, emphasizing each word.—Imagine returning a year from now.

Blum did not have a problem with pauses.—By then, will they be able to converse? To truly speak?

Blum ruminated—They have a brain bigger than ours.

He let his eyes drift toward the horizon.—Last night I woke up. Maybe two in the morning. A thought pulled me from sleep.

He said—What would be the first question I would ask them?

He whispered—Imagine all we can learn.

Jesus—the official said again and again.

* * *

When Blum returned from taking the official to lunch and then dropping him at the airport, he was a little drunk, smelling of cigars and alcohol. He strutted around, his chest out, a banty rooster.

A year, a year of funding—he said, pumping his fists in the air.

The men picked Kat up in the canvas stretcher and lugged her back to the lagoon. She slid off the stretcher, diving into the water, so eager. The dolphins reunited, rushed and rolled around the lagoon, jumping in unison, filled with joy. Cora stood by the lagoon, watching, the ball of worry in her chest loosening.

Then Blum told the men to get the net.

Cora turned, dumbfounded.—What?

Blum said—I'm on deadline here.

—*What?*

He said—Grant requirements from last year. Fifteen more cranial explorations.

She said—You can't do that.

The other men turned to watch her reaction. They had known this was coming. She saw their satisfaction.

She sat down hard on the ground, her legs weak.

The big male dolphin, Bernie, tried to scare the net, to scare the men, slapping his tail and snapping his teeth. But the men ignored him as they stretched the net across the lagoon and began to pull it toward the dolphins.

Kat stuck her head out of the water, imitating Tibbet's *ack-ack* laugh. Tibbet looked at Kat, fury in his eyes, and tugged the net through the water faster.

Within minutes, Tibbet and Eh had dragged the four dolphins out of the water onto the beach.

The men shoved Kat and Mother back in the water. Bernie was still snapping his teeth and thrashing his tail, so they just left him there, beached. Instead, they stepped over to Junior, carrying the canvas stretcher.

This was when Junior understood. He looked at Cora, his eyes wide. The men hefted him onto the stretcher and lugged him up the stairs. The whole way, Junior stared straight at Cora, squealing. They eased him into the house, and he disappeared.

Mother was jumping high in the lagoon, screaming.

Bernie remained on the beach, only half submerged, breathing heavy and sad. The skin on his back drying in the sun. Gravity pushing on his lungs.

She got to her feet and approached Bernie, holding out her hands. He lay there, the weight of his world on his shoulders.

With her, he did not snap his teeth. She knelt in front of him, put her hands on his sides, and when he did nothing but sigh, she wedged her right shoulder in under his chin, wrapped her arm around his head and began to push. Even skinny like he was now, he still must weigh over 400 pounds. She dug her toes and knees in, gritted her teeth and used her legs. He shifted his weight and twisted, trying to help, sliding slightly in the mud. Her cheek against his baby-smooth skin.

She grunted and shoved harder with her legs, using every muscle she had. He wiggled and together they slid him back down the slope and into the water.

Returned to the lagoon, Bernie shot through the water, throwing himself high into the air with Mother, again and again, 6 feet high, 7. Eight feet high. Jumping in hopes of spotting Junior.

Meanwhile the hammering had started. Cora ran up the veranda stairs. Her breath echoed in her ears. Slammed open the porch door. Inside the room, she realized her vision had floated up out of her body, so she could somehow see the back of her own head, the swirl of shaved hair.

Junior lay in the narrow glass tank, straps holding him still.

Blum was holding a nail against Junior's head, the hammer held high. He looked at her, satisfaction in his eyes. He was showing her who was boss.

She heard herself speak in the cop's voice. Using his voice, she had no branks.—If you continue this operation, I will leave.

He blinked.

She watched her body from above. It made no gestures to soften her statement but stood still and straight.—They won't accept food from you. They'll starve. They'll die.

She said—You can catch more dolphins, but you won't be able to train them or feed them. They'll die too. None of them will ever talk humanoid again.

From her viewpoint near the ceiling, she could see him so clearly. His eyes narrowed, but he did not back down, not yet. Not in front of the other men. He needed something, some face-saving idea.

She listened as her mouth spoke more words.—Stop this. Let him go, and I'll teach one of them to speak. I'll do it the way humans are taught.

He was listening.

She heard the words coming from her.—If you stop operating on the dolphins, all of them, I'll live with one of these dolphins like a mom does with her baby. I'll teach the baby morning and night.

He cocked his head. He liked this idea.—How? The little pool won't work.

She looked around the room, searching for the answer. Her mouth said—Build me an apartment, half flooded with water. The dolphin and I will live there together.

His eyes were bright now. He loved this. Still, he did not say yes.

She needed something more to make him agree. One last detail.

Words. He loved jargon, loved to make words up. *Humanoid, stimulus train.*

Her mouth said—The question is what to call the space where the dolphin and I would live. It would be a *home* that was also an *aquarium*. A home . . .

His forehead knit, he did not respond.

Her mouth tried again.—Goodness. A *home* that was also an *aquarium*. A home . . .

. . . arium—he called out, pleased with himself.

Her hands clapped as though delighted—Homearium! Homearium! That's brilliant!

Which dolphin?—he asked.

(How do any of us really understand our choices? We hear

a decision issue from our lips and having no idea how we arrived at that choice, we ascribe a plausible motive, one that illustrates the person we wish we were.

The facts: Kat had shown by far the greatest capacity, learned the fastest, was the most verbal. Potentially a genius at this. She was the one most likely to succeed, to be able to speak.

The facts: Junior was the youngest, the closest to a baby. He was the one currently lying on the table with a nail inserted partway into his skull.

The facts: Blum and others would believe more in the capability of a male, would hear the words more easily and with less doubt.

The facts: even decades later, thinking back on this time, she couldn't deny this possibility that deep in her heart, she thought a male was more valuable, worth protecting, worth listening to.)

Her chin pointed—Junior.

Her mouth added—Build me that homearium. I'll live with him day and night, teaching him, until he can speak English.

Blum asked—Where?

Looking outside, the first thing she saw was the stone floor of the veranda, three steps down from the house. Made of flagstone and cement, the stone floor of the veranda ran along the whole side of the house, 50 feet long.

She said—The veranda. We will build walls around it and flood it and put a roof on top.

They all turned to look at the veranda, mouths open.

She said—Think of the progress I've made in just a few days. Think of all I will manage within a year.

A smile appeared on Blum's mouth.

She said—You will be famous.

The smile widened.

She said—But you have to stop harming them. No more operations.

There was a pause. They all listened to it, waiting for Blum.

He said—Yes. You do this, and I'll stop operating on *these* dolphins.

The dolphins?—she repeated, understanding he meant only the four here. She was sliding back into her body, disoriented and slightly nauseous.

He nodded.

There was a whole ocean of other dolphins out there that he could capture and experiment on. Still, these four were the ones she cared about. In this moment, she would settle for saving them.

Yes—she said.

He put the hammer down.

What!—said Tibbet.—Whoa! You kidding me? We're going to have to drop everything to build that thing. We don't know if it will work.

Blum smiled—Jim, sometimes you gotta gamble. You gotta have balls.

Blum grabbed the front of his pants and, with his hand there, flicked his eyes at her.

Junior was returned to the lagoon, and she sat down to sketch out the homearium's plans.

C ora had never done well at school or work. Since she
was eight years old, people did not tend to listen to
her. Instead they talked at her in a loud voice using
small words. Here at the research center, it was different.
Her observations and thoughts were taken seriously. When
she talked now, Blum listened, tilting his head, the Harvard
professor. Tibbet and Eh watched him listen, and they narrowed their eyes. She was surprised by the depth of her
hunger for this.

Blum hired several men from town to do the digging and
construction of the homearium. The islanders dug a pit off the
end of the veranda to create a deeper part of the pool for
Junior. The dirt from the pit, they heaped up into a 3-foot-high
berm around the veranda and the deep end, creating the walls
of the pool. They slathered cement along the inside of the
berm, the floor of the veranda and the pit, then covered the
cement with waterproof paint.

The first time they flooded the pool, one of the walls collapsed, so they drained it, rebuilt it and flooded it again. This
time, the water stayed. The pool was 20 inches deep everywhere except the deep end. Living in the homearium, she
would wade everywhere, water almost to her knees, while
Junior would have just enough water to swim, his dorsal fin out
in the air, his tail slapping the pool's floor. The depth of the
water would be uncomfortable for both.

Over this pool, the men built the home part of the homearium. It covered a little more than half the pool. The walls and roof were made of plywood and framing, the construction as simple as an oversized doghouse with big windows. The rafters were the important part. From them, the furniture hung on chains: a bed, a chair and desk, a propane camp stove, a wood shelf that served as both counter and pantry. Off in the corner was the shower, its opaque dandelion shower curtain trailing in the water, crinkling in the current any time anyone walked by it. All in all, the room resembled some sort of modern-art installation, the furnishings of a home hanging in the air above a reflecting pool. When the wind blew, the furniture swayed, the chains clinking.

Up the stairs of the shallow end was a door to a dry room with the fridge, sink and toilet. The other end was a wall made of sliding glass doors. The sliding doors ended at the level of the water so Junior could swim underneath at any time to reach the deep end of the pool.

She designed this space for herself and Junior, thinking the details through. She told the islanders to redo the work whenever it wasn't right. When she gave the men directions, they obeyed only once Blum had agreed. He agreed each time, and so they did what she wanted. She felt high with this power.

Busy with the building (designing it, buying the materials, directing the construction), she spent less time with the dolphins.

* * *

During those weeks while the homearium was built, Tibbet was ready to move from observation to his first active experiment. Having tallied a variety of different behaviors by which the dolphins might communicate (such as touch, sound and body position), he now wanted to test if there was any communication actually happening.

As the first step of this research, he asked Cora to train them to identify matching geometric shapes. This would give the dolphins some information to communicate.

So she stapled three metal shapes onto the dock (a black circle, a white square and a striped triangle), at the water line where the dolphins could easily tap them. There was 3 feet of space between the shapes so it would be easy to tell which answer-shape a dolphin tapped.

She broke the training down into stages, starting with the simple. For the first day, she prompted them by blowing a whistle and holding up one of the matching shapes. She threw a fish to any dolphin who then swam closer to the dock. Within a few days she could blow a whistle and hold up a shape and they would all swim to the dock. Next, she began to reward them only if they touched the dock, then only if they touched one of the shapes stapled to the end of the dock. Finally, she only rewarded them if they tapped the shape that matched the question-shape she held.

The different steps of this took time because she kept getting called away to check on different details of the homearium's construction. By the second week, Tibbet got frustrated with the slow pace. He tried to train the dolphins himself. Standing on the dock, he would blow a whistle to get their attention and hold up one of the shapes.

From the half-constructed homearium, Cora could glance down to see what was happening. The dolphins stuck their heads out of the water and examined Tibbet. They were close to the dock, but none of them moved closer or touched the dock or the answer-shapes stapled there. Tibbet would blow the whistle again, impatient. He was holding up the question-shape, in this case the striped triangle, with a fish in his other hand as the potential reward. Kat watched him, her eyes at the surface like she was trying to imitate an alligator.

He could not always tell the difference between the individual dolphins, had not built a relationship with any of them. He didn't ask for cooperation. He acted as though they ought to cooperate, like dogs or robots.

He shook the striped triangle now, impatient, and they just stared at him. For him, they would not perform.

After a while he gave up, and Cora was the one who continued to train them.

* * *

Blum's isolation tank, the bathtub with a lid lying on the lawn, was ready to use. The idea was for him to float in the tank in the dark, nothing but warm water touching his body, the lack of physical sensation letting him explore the dimensions of his mind. However the first time he tried lying down in the tank, to keep his face above water, he had to paddle with his hands. Working like this to keep his head high enough to breathe meant his heels gradually sank until they rested on the bottom.

This combination of half-swimming and his feet touching the bottom of the tank didn't allow for the meditative state he wanted, so he connected a hose and air pump to one of his children's oversized punch balloons to create a homemade rubber diving helmet. He systematically stretched out the neck of the balloon until he could pull it on, over his head (rolling it down over his face the way a woman rolled on nylons). When he let go, it snapped into place around his neck. The air pump wheezed, inflating the balloon, creating a featureless swollen head with an umbilical breathing hose emerging from where the left ear should be. Cora, Tibbet and Eh watched, eyes wide. Blum stood there in his swim trunks, calm, apparently breathing.

The balloon was red and utterly opaque. Blum looked like

he was wearing a hastily made Halloween costume. A pencil with a bright red eraser? The main character from *The Red Balloon*?

Unable to see, he waved his hands around until he bumped into the tank. He climbed over the side and lay down in the water. His big balloon face on a skinny body. Within seconds, he sat up and yanked the balloon off, water pouring out. After catching his breath, he tried again, rolling it back on and, this time, tying a string around his neck to reduce the water infiltration (a nice additional touch for *The Red Balloon* costume). After a few minutes of fiddling and experimentation, Blum announced, muffled from inside the balloon, that he thought this would work. He could always thump on the sides of the tank for help if he needed it. He lay down in the water.

All three of them paused, unwilling to close the top of the tank. Tibbet and Eh had their faces slightly averted, as though this pained them. It was apparent how different Blum was from them. He floated on his side in the warm water, fetal position, a baby with a swollen rubber head. He seemed relaxed, his limbs loose. His rib cage of a plucked chicken, the bag of air around his head, the hissing of the hose.

In this moment, both his strength and fragility were vividly displayed. His body, like his ideas, was floating there risky and unlikely, tethered loosely to safety. At any moment there might be a puncture and his career could whistle away.

Eh lowered the cover on the tank. All three of them sat there for the twenty minutes, Eh chain-smoking, before Blum thumped on the side of the tank to get out. He was grinning, thrilled, with a few modifications to make to the apparatus.

The other Harvard researcher, Timothy Leary, would visit in a few days.

* * *

By the end of the second week, Cora could blow the whistle and hold up the circle, square or triangle and the dolphins would tap the matching shape stapled to the dock over 90 percent of the time. Each time they got it right, she threw them fish as a reward.

Now that the training was complete, Tibbet and Cora began the active part of the experiment. She set up a collapsible pen on the far side of the lagoon, stepped inside and called Junior into it. She rubbed his back to thank him for obeying and nodded to Tibbet that she was ready. He stood on the dock, above the shapes stapled to the end of it, the other dolphins watching him. This time, when he blew the whistle, he did not hold up any shape. Instead, Cora (inside the pen, her back to the others so they could not see) showed the black circle to Junior.

Junior, in the pen, could not get to the dock to tap the matching black circle. The other dolphins by the dock could not see the black circle to know which shape to tap. The point of the research was to find out if the dolphin in the pen could somehow communicate the correct answer to the dolphins across the lagoon.

Mother, Bernie and Kat bobbed there, confused, waiting for Tibbet to show them a shape. After a minute Tibbet recorded the result, then blew the whistle to signal a new attempt and Cora showed Junior a different shape. If the dolphins could communicate, it would take them a while to figure out what it was the humans wanted. Tibbet planned to run this experiment every day for three months so they would have time to figure it out. This way, he could amass enough proof.

The first day, they tried for half an hour, at times switching out which dolphin was in the pen. Still, none of the dolphins seemed to understand yet. As usual, Kat was the one to try hardest. She tried answering by tapping an answer-shape at random in hopes of getting a reward. Whenever she tapped one of the wrong shapes, Cora could see Tibbet's cheeks puff out as he coughed air from his mouth, dismissive. However, the few times Kat happened to tap the correct shape, he'd straighten up and look at Kat before he'd throw the fish to her. Then he'd blow the whistle to signal the start of a new round.

That first day, Kat got the answer right about a third of the time. This was to be expected since, with three possible answers, being correct a third of the time was at the level of random chance. The next day, when they ran the experiment again, all of the dolphins began tapping different answer shapes, trying to figure out what the humans wanted. Again, they managed to answer correctly about a third of the time.

On the third morning, Tibbet began to scoff at their ability. At this point, Bernie was the one in the pen with Cora. She was holding out the white square for him to see. Tibbet and Cora were waiting for the other dolphins to tap a shape, to see if it would be the matching white square.

Tibbet was 40 feet away, standing on the dock, and the wind was blowing. Whatever he was saying, she could hear only occasional words, *never* and *can't* and *animal*. Still, the intent of his words was clear. He didn't seem upset at the possible failure of his experiment. There was instead a certain exhilaration in his voice. In this moment, she understood his secret intention: to prove methodically and with numbers that dolphins could not communicate, that despite the physical size of their brains, they were not all that smart. He wanted to prove Blum wrong.

The dolphins bobbed in the water, listening.

* * *

Blum picked Leary up at the airport and brought him back. Leary was a handsome man, rugged jaw, solid body. Wearing a suit, he could have played the part of any executive of a large corporation. However instead he dressed as though he were a Mexican peasant: an embroidered shirt, loose white pants and a necklace of large wooden beads. This was clothing different from what Cora had seen any adult male ever wear.

Introduced to Cora, he took her hand. He did not look at her while he did so. It was possible he forgot he was holding her hand for he did not let go of it the whole time he spoke with her.

He said—You're young.

He spoke with his eyes still and averted. He acted like he wasn't standing next to her, but instead was talking on the phone. Perhaps the call was long distance, since there were long pauses between his words.

He added—Smart.

She didn't know if he was saying that she was smart or that it was smart to be young.

He said—Once you get over forty, you change . . . Less interested in questions . . . or your body, or joy.

She wasn't sure how she was supposed to respond to this, or even if she should. He didn't seem bothered by her silence.

He said—Over forty, you start instead to desire power . . . and metal things. Guns, handcuffs, prisons . . . You don't want to explore anymore . . . You want control.

He let go of her hand, looking straight at her. That word *control* hanging in the air.

In the bright sun like this, she could see a slight tracing of wrinkles at the corners of his eyes. She had no idea how old he was.

She stepped back.

The men went inside. At times she heard the bark of laughter or the clatter of glasses. She could smell cigarettes.

* * *

After dinner, Blum and Leary walked down to the lagoon. They were laughing and laughing; she wasn't sure at what. Once they got close, she saw their eyes looked different, the pupils big, a bottomless black. Cora watched them, worried.

Leary began to wade into the lagoon, holding out his hands and talking to the dolphins. He called them his spirit guides.

Blum stopped laughing and said—Hey man, I don't know that you should . . .

Blum's vocabulary around Leary had begun to change. She had heard him try out the words *groovy* and *blast*.

Bernie stuck his head out of the water and clapped his jaw loudly, showing his teeth. She was surprised from this angle how skinny his face looked. The outline of his skull was more visible, somewhat peanut-shaped.

Leary waded forward through the water, closer, talking to Bernie, holding his hands out, saying—Spirit guide, I'm listening.

Bernie with his clapping jaw was communicating with him, but Leary did not understand the message.

Bernie sank just under the surface and shot forward, moving so quickly a wave of water rolled in front of him, his fin cutting through the lagoon. He aimed straight at Leary. At the last second he turned, slapping his tail down on the surface with all his weight, 3 feet from Leary. The clap as loud as a gunshot.

This communication got through.

Leary lunged toward the beach, splashing, high-kneed and panicked. Once he reached the beach he continued to flee, up onto the balcony. Standing there wet and shivering with fear.

HOMEARIUM

Once the homearium was complete, she moved into it with Junior.

During the day, sunlight flooded the room, twinkling off the water, a brilliant sideways light as if it was underwater, with the hanging furniture swaying in the breeze.

The water came to just below her knees. Wading forward was difficult, slowing her down and making every action more difficult. Before that first morning was over, her thighs were aching.

There was also the difficulty of moving around Junior. When first released into the homearium, he appeared terrified, squealing with distress and rocketing around the space as fast as he could, looking for an exit and the other dolphins. After the fear began to wear off, he became needy, or maybe just bored. He followed her about, rubbing against her calves, investigating everything, dashing between her legs, knocking her off balance, a 300-pound puppy. He would not leave her alone.

Used to playing with the other dolphins, at times he also nipped at her ankles. Kat had never done this. His teeth were young and sharp, not yet worn down by fish and sand. The slightest touch of his teeth broke her skin. She'd yell and jump away. When she pulled her leg out of the water, the cuts were shallow, but they welled with blood.

She assumed he would stop this soon, once he got used to being here and wasn't so bored. Meanwhile she had to struggle forward through the water, moving so slowly, while he could glide and turn quickly. Even though she watched her feet, she occasionally stumbled over him, falling badly twice that first day, landing partly on him and partly in the water.

The situation was not ideal for him either. In water this shallow, he could move much faster than her, but at nothing close to his normal speed. His tail scraped against the bottom with every flick. He could not dive or corkscrew or jump.

In order to live together, the two of them had to occupy this liminal zone, both of them hobbled.

Of course, if needed, they could retreat. She could step up the stairs onto land, and he could move into the deep end of the pool just beyond the glass sliding doors. The space under the sliding doors was open, so he could swim under them into the deep end whenever he wanted. However, that whole first day he didn't. He would move up to the doors, gazing underneath at the water beyond. Perhaps, without other dolphins, he was uneasy about entering this larger space. At this edge, he would at times squeal loudly, she assumed for the others. Once in a while, she could faintly hear the dolphins down in the lagoon respond. For her to hear them inside like this, they must have been screaming.

Meanwhile, when she needed the bathroom, she'd slosh across the homearium to climb the stairs out of the water. Moving through air was so easy in comparison, her legs nearly floated forward. In the dry room, she'd close the door and peel off her bathing suit. Sitting on the toilet, she faced the humming fridge. When she finished, she'd tug the wet bathing suit back on, double-check the material was covering her appropriately, and then head back out to the pool, where she'd have to slog forward again.

This would be an endurance event, she realized, akin to camping out in an aquarium.

* * *

That first day, she started working with Junior, speaking with him, trying to teach him language. She pretended she was talking to a child.

—Junior, want to *catch?* Catch the ball. Play catch?

Catch was his favorite game. As soon as he heard the word, he'd pull his head out of the water, flippers spread, whistling with excitement, preparing like an outfielder to jump in any direction. By this point he could bop the ball right into her hands, and at times when he wanted attention, he would hit her in the back with the ball.

He already knew how to mimic the number of sounds she made, but the sounds he made tended to be clicks or whistles. Now, using his love of catch, she would try to teach him to speak only humanoid.

She said—Talk. Ball. *B-allll.*

She rewarded him for any noise that could be a vowel or consonant. Unfortunately, he didn't learn as quickly as Kat. He continued to make clicks and whistles and then to slap his tail in frustration when she didn't throw the ball to him. He didn't seem to understand she was asking for something different. Perhaps, a young male, he didn't have a love of school, preferring to move fast and play.

Another difficulty was her hearing. For the first few hours in the homearium, she tried wearing her hearing glasses, but she worried about the circuits getting wet and shorting out. She wrapped the hearing aid part of her glasses with plastic and taped the seams shut tightly, but what she heard then most clearly was the crinkling of the plastic, everything else muffled.

And even with her glasses wrapped up this tightly, they still were not completely safe. Wanting attention, Junior would sometimes splash her from the side or squirt water at her from his mouth, catching her off guard. And when she tripped over him, she'd jerk her head up and stiff-arm the bottom of the pool, doing all she could to keep her head and glasses above the surface. New glasses would probably take a month to be made, and they would cost several weeks of her salary.

So halfway through that first day, she gave up, taking off the glasses and putting them away on a shelf in the dry room. She'd have to live without them in the homearium, returning to being mostly deaf while she lived here. And interfering here, with her very limited hearing, was the constant background noise of splashing water and the echoes off the walls.

This made the language lessons with Junior more difficult. With him, she couldn't lipread, or even know when he was making noise, since the sounds were formed somewhere deep inside, exiting from his blowhole with little to no visible movement.

However, she simply decided she'd have high standards. Without her glasses, Junior had to enunciate very loudly and clearly to get a reward, enunciating the way she wished all humans did. And luckily vowels were easier for him to pronounce and for her to hear.

She would ask him to mimic.—Talk. Mary had a little lamb.

When she heard a response that sounded vaguely human (a groaning *aaaah* or rumbling *eeerrrr*), she would throw the ball for him. He was not a star pupil like Kat, and she graded accordingly.

—Good job, Junior. Yes! That was *great*.

She used the same high-pitched tone she'd use with a toddler. Rising and falling inflections, simple words, lots of excitement. Junior eyed her, his head cocked.

—You talked human, Junior. *Talked* human. Good job!

Blum insisted that along with mimicking language, she should also teach Junior the first few letters of the alphabet. The alphabet, he felt, was what a toddler should learn. His wife, he said, was always reciting it to the kids.

So when she got tired of asking for humanoid sounds, she'd

say—Junior, let's practice the alphabet. You want to? Let's try. Talk. A, B, C, *Dee*.

He would click and she would not throw him the ball.

He would chatter his teeth at her in irritation and make the sound of a tea kettle whistling.

She would just repeat—Talk. A, B, C, *Deeeeee*.

Sometimes he got frustrated, wanting the ball and not understanding why she wouldn't throw it. At these points, he'd bellow over her voice, interrupting. This was breaking the basic rules of conversation.

—QUIET, Junior. QUIET.

He roared and squealed.

—Junior, wait til I've finished. *Quiet*.

The men watched from the kitchen and the central living room. They could see and hear through the screen door and the big picture windows while they made food and ate, while they read and wrote and worked. It seemed at least one of them was always visible, watching her argue with a dolphin. She felt ridiculous, ineffective. Incapable.

—Talk. A, B . . . Junior, QUIET! Stop interrupting! STOP.

He quieted down gradually.

—Good. Now talk. A, B, C, *Dee*.

Microphones hung from the ceiling, every noise she and Junior made was recorded. A computer traced the audio on a roll of paper. Tibbet changed the rolls every two hours, labelling each with the date and time. How long she'd lived in the homearium was visible in the increasing pile of paper spools on the table in the men's living room. Tibbet always seemed to be studying one of these spools, scribbling notations and frowning.

At least this reduced one of her worries: that Junior would start making human noises and she wouldn't hear them. If that happened, Tibbet would notice and tell her.

* * *

She missed snorkeling in the water with all four dolphins. Swimming underwater with them, she could watch them play and fight, their grace and speed. She could hear their underwater sounds, that eerie range. The breadth and wildness of these noises had made her feel she'd been living her whole life inside an insulated glass box and someone had just cracked open the lid, letting in the world.

Here, however, she lived with just Junior, who was unable to dance and play with any real speed in the shallow water. Here, she was constrained to working above the water, without her hearing glasses, all sound muffled and far away. And she couldn't let Junior make his natural sounds but had to restrict him to human ones. Both of them suffered with this narrow range of sound.

* * *

Since seawater was highly conductive, electricity was too dangerous to have anywhere near the pool. The only electricity in the homearium was in the microphones and spotlights, both of which were wired high up on the ceiling. For safety, the switches for both were inside the house, outside of her control.

At dusk, that first day, the spotlights clicked on abruptly, the bare kind of lighting associated with prison yards and guard towers. Looking over, she saw Blum in the living room, next to the switch, watching her.

By this point, her thighs were trembling from exhaustion, from wading all day through water. She had several bruises from tripping over Junior. She wanted a hot shower, followed by dry clothes, a big meal and then bed.

When she designed the homearium, she had thought it smart to put the shower inside the pool. Placed here, she could continue to talk with Junior, to work with him, even while showering. This arrangement, she believed, mimicked the way a mom worked with her baby, the two of them always together.

However what she hadn't imagined was how much she might want a shower at the end of the day, her skin itchy with salt. She hadn't imagined how brightly lit the homearium would be under the spotlights or that the men might be eating dinner just on the other side of picture windows or that they might have turned their chairs to watch the homearium like it was a large TV. Under these circumstances, she did not want to step behind a shower curtain, even if it was opaque.

So instead she started dinner. Within a minute, she learned how hard it was to cook on a propane stove hanging on chains from the ceiling. Anytime she flipped or moved the food, the stove twisted and began to swing. Objects sitting on the stove or counter would rock or fall over. While cooking, she had to hold the side of the stove with one hand to keep it still.

Twice, she realized she'd forgotten an ingredient. She waded across the homearium to the dry room to retrieve first the flour and then the milk. Her legs so tired, her hips aching.

After she finished eating, she eyed the shower again. If she waited until the men turned the spotlights off, she'd have to shower, dress herself and find her way to the bed in the dark with a dolphin winding around her feet.

The men had finished with dinner and were sitting in the living room cradling highballs and talking with each other, only glancing at the homearium occasionally. So, with determination, she stepped into the shower and yanked the curtain shut. She stood in a 3-foot circle with water to her knees. It took work to pull off her bathing suit and tug it off her feet in that small space. Belatedly she noticed her shadow on the curtain, her contorted undressing probably visible from the other side. When she cranked the water on, Junior got very curious, butting his way under the curtain, swimming around her feet, rucking up the curtain a few inches each time his dorsal fin went under it. She kept her feet spread for balance, trying not to trip on him and stumble out from behind the curtain.

Once she'd finished showering, drying off was awkward, the corner of the towel dipping in the water twice. She pulled the nightgown on over her head, then had to hold the hem up out of the water.

When she tugged back the curtain, all three men were sitting in the living room, heads up, watching.

Her arms wrapped across her chest, she walked to her bed. Designing the homearium, she'd made sure the bed was in the center of the water. This way, Eh couldn't reach her at night without wading through the water. He'd be too wary of Junior to do that.

Unfortunately, the bed being in the center of the room also meant it was in full view of the men in the house.

She pulled the plastic cover off the mattress and sat down, exhaling with relief. The bed rocked gently on its chains, an inch above the water. The end of a long day. Inside the building, Tibbet walked to the light switch and clicked the spotlights off: a kindness. At this, Eh and Blum looked at Tibbet, mouths tight. Now the men were the ones lit up for viewing, while she sat here in the dark. They rose and started to clear the dinner dishes.

She pulled her legs out of the water and lay down on clean dry sheets. Closing her eyes, she felt dizzy from exhaustion, the dappled water that she'd been staring at all day flickering across her eyelids.

However Junior was no longer able to reach her, and he began to squeal, distressed, loud enough for her to hear. He had never slept alone in his life, slept without other dolphins nearby, without holding Mother's flipper in his mouth.

He circled the bed, screaming and clicking, fear in his voice. Once she thought she heard a responding squeal in the distance, perhaps Mother responding from down in the lagoon. She tried to wait it out, figuring he'd quiet down.

Instead water hit her in the face. The blowhole of a dolphin can hold and squirt an impressive amount of water. She sat up fast, her pillow soaked.

Junior continued to squeal, a baby having a tantrum. He whacked his tail down on the water, splashing the mattress.

So she rolled her leg over the side of the bed to calm him, dangling a foot at the surface. He rubbed against her foot, circling it. She lay back awkwardly, keeping her foot in the water. All she wanted was sleep.

After a moment, she felt something close gently around her toes. Looking over the edge of the bed, she could see he had her foot in his mouth. She'd seen him hold Mother's flipper in his mouth while he napped, a habit he'd retained even into adolescence. She could feel his tongue against her toes, a rhythmic sucking pressure. He was nursing even as an adolescent.

She didn't pull her foot back. The sensation was strangely moving, the trust and intimacy. He began to quiet down, probably as exhausted as she was, the stress and fear of being separated from the other dolphins, the new location. Within minutes, he was asleep.

She tried a few times to ease her toes out of his mouth, but each time he would startle up and squeal, splashing water everywhere, soaking her and the bed. So she ended up sleeping that night with one foot in the water and her head on a wet pillow. This tired, it didn't matter that much.

She slept deeply, waking twice to hear him burbling at her. She felt, already, he was accepting her as his mother.

T wo days later, when she walked down to the lagoon to feed the other dolphins at 6:30 A.M., Bernie was lying still and sideways at the bottom of the lagoon.

The moment she saw him, she knew, but still she dove in fast, in her clothes, as though spotting a drowning swimmer. Under the water, the keening of the other dolphins filled her body, high-pitched and deafening, underwater banshees. He lay at the bottom, his fixed eyes and open mouth, his purple tongue, rocking gently in the current like some fleshy bath-toy.

The men had the vet's number jotted down by the phone. They did not seem surprised. She pulled Bernie into the shallows and they dragged the body onto the beach.

The vet arrived within an hour to perform the autopsy, a leather bag in hand. She was sitting there on the shore, blinking at the body. Somehow, she had not realized the dolphins could die. She had not understood.

The vet, whose name was Dr. Crantz, saw her expression and touched his fingertips to her forearm. It was a little like the way the dolphins touched each other, a momentary pressure.

He asked the men to move the body around the corner of the house for the autopsy, while he got his coveralls to do the work. She was grateful he wasn't cutting Bernie up where the other dolphins could see, where she could see. It was possible, of course, that he chose this spot simply because it was in the shade.

After an hour, he came back around the corner. He sat on the shore, scrubbing his face with the heels of his hands. There was no blood visible on him.

She sat down beside him. For the last few days she'd spent most of her day looking at Junior. Dr. Crantz's lack of a beak seemed surprising. At the moment, he appeared tired.

He looked up at her, saw her glasses with the thick arms and asked—Hearing aid?

Small teeth, his tongue moving neatly in his mouth, easy to lipread.

—Yes, I'm partially deaf.

Some people, when she told them this, shifted back a tiny bit, as though deafness might be contagious. He stayed where he was instead, examining her face.

—Can you hear me ok?

She nodded. Not having worn her hearing glasses much for a few days, she felt she could hear him remarkably well.— What happened to Bernie?

He said—The dolphin? No disease or problem I could find. No water in the lungs. He didn't drown.

—What killed him then?

He shrugged. She loved a gesture like this, so clear and grounding.—As far as I can tell, he took one last breath and didn't breathe again.

She waited.

—With dolphins, they need to will themselves to breathe. It's not automatic, like with us. If they don't breathe for long enough, they go unconscious. After that, of course, they can't will themselves to breathe.

The way he said these words, with a certain weight, she heard he was saying something more.

She asked tentatively—Could it be he was too skinny and just ran out of energy?

The vet shook his head no.—He wasn't that skinny.

She looked at the water.—Could it be that he just decided not to breathe anymore?

He inhaled and held up his hands.

She asked—Have you seen another dolphin die this way?

He nodded.

Here—she asked, a feeling in her gut.—At this center?

—Yes.

—They've had other dolphins?

He nodded—Oh yes.

She liked that he was not wordy.—Do captive dolphins die this way often?

—I asked Marine World. They said it happened sometimes at night when everyone is gone. A perfectly healthy animal. In the morning, it will just be there, dead.

She imagined the dolphin in the darkest part of the night, in a concrete pool, in captivity, deciding not to breathe anymore. Inhaling its last breath.

—It occurs mostly with dolphins who are left alone in their pools, without others.

They sat there quietly, thinking about this.

Kat surfaced near them, and the vet blinked at the incisions on Kat's head.

* * *

Without Bernie, there was such an emptiness. Mother and Kat were left in the lagoon, Junior in the homearium. Cora felt the weight of keeping the remaining ones alive.

She spent more time at night reading the men's books, learning their vocab. She worked harder with Junior, striving for progress, needing to impress Blum. She needed all the power she could get.

After Bernie's death, she made sure to spend at least an hour each morning with Kat and Mother in the lagoon, feeding them and playing with them and checking in on them. Tibbet noticed this and began to come down to the lagoon when she was there. He needed her help with his experiment about their ability to communicate about the matching shapes.

She was the only one the dolphins allowed in the water, and so she would wade out to the collapsible pen and call one of the dolphins inside it. Frequently Kat was the one who responded. She tended to follow Cora most places, curious. In the opaque pen, with her back to Mother, Cora would show Kat, for instance, the striped triangle, and Tibbet would watch by the dock to see if Mother then tapped the matching triangle.

Each time Cora helped Tibbet, she required that he step into the water just a little deeper than the day before. She wanted him at some point to be able to run this experiment on his own or with Eh. The first day he stood with just his feet in the water, and the dolphins did not clap their teeth at him for doing so. While he was in the water, he was generally busy taking notes. Focused on the work this way, he looked less threatening. He didn't move around a lot or stare at them for an extended period of time.

So each day, she had him move one step deeper into the water, until by the end of the week, he was in the water up to his thighs with them ignoring him.

* * *

Around six in the morning, Junior would wake her by splashing her and, first thing, she would walk to the shower, and tug the shower curtain shut around her. At this hour she hoped no one was awake in the dark of the house, watching her shadow through the opaque curtain as she undressed. Her skin was always so tight and sticky from salt water. A shower in fresh water made her feel a bit better.

Of course, within a few minutes of stepping out of the shower, clean and dressed in a dry bathing suit, Junior would splash her, soaking her again with salty water.

* * *

She tucked a plastic sheet over her mattress to stop it from getting wetter, but, in the heat, the plastic fogged up from the damp mattress. Within a few days there were black spots of mold all over the mattress. Each night, when she took the plastic off to sleep, Junior would splash her repeatedly, re-wetting it.

So she replaced the mattress with a 3-inch-thick roll of foam rubber. She tucked the plastic sheet in around the foam, then pulled fitted cotton sheets on over that. This way she didn't have to sleep directly on the plastic. However, with a plastic undersheet, the heat built up against her body, and each time she rolled over, the plastic crinkled. And whenever Junior splashed water at her, the water just puddled there, until she was sleeping in a tiny warm sea.

She took the plastic undersheet off and slept on the foam covered with a plain cotton sheet, all of it soaked. In the heat, the wet cotton was almost pleasant against her skin. This exhausted, she could fall asleep quickly. Every three days, she rinsed the foam out and hung it up in the sun. At the end of the day she'd bring it back, dry and warm, and put clean sheets on it. This way it didn't get moldy or crusty with salt.

She did, however, long for a dry pillow.

* * *

During the day, Junior continued occasionally to nip at her heels and calves. Each time, she'd yell and kick at him, but he would do it regardless. He nipped very lightly, like a sheepdog, but, given his teeth, her legs became laced with shallow scratches as though she was living with a pack of feral house cats.

Meanwhile, she was wading through the water that Junior defecated and peed in, in which bits of uneaten food floated. Clean water was constantly pumped in, and salt water was naturally antiseptic, but still grit and grime built up at the bottom. Some of her cuts became infected.

She used a pool vacuum to clean the bottom of the homearium, running the nozzle over every inch of the floor. She vacuumed each morning, like a dutiful housewife. She did it to protect both Junior and herself.

* * *

Blum believed that toddlers should have a daily routine, so she did her best to settle into one with Junior. After her early morning shower, she had breakfast. She fed Junior his breakfast at seven A.M., making him earn each fish through his lessons.

Although he was hungry, he was bored by the lessons and at times would ignore her. Instead he'd play with a toy, or sulk on the other side of the pool, or hump the life ring or inflatable raft. This humping action was so fast, it took her a little while to understand what he was doing. He'd slide on top of the ring or the raft and pump slightly, two or three times, and then slide off, done. Normally the dolphins mated with each other several times a day.

To get him to work on his lessons instead, she would call him over, holding up a butterfish and he'd ignore her as long as he could, playing with toys, bouncing the ball in the air, chewing on a pull toy. However, she was the only living being in the pool, and he was a bored and social animal. In the end he would swim over, sullen.

She would start the lesson saying—Talk. A, B, C, *Deee.*

He would copy the beat of her voice, but not try to imitate the actual sounds. Instead he would make dolphin noises, blatting or clicking.

—No, Junior. Talk *humanoid.* You can do it. Talk. A, B, C, *Deee.*

He'd whistle and squeak, making more dolphin noises.

She didn't know whether he was stubborn and didn't want to comply, or if he genuinely didn't understand what she wanted. She had to repeat the command again and again, before he would finally respond (perhaps accidentally) with a sound that sounded vaguely human, generally something like a vowel. She would call out praise and throw him food, but in response he would bellow out more dolphin sounds.

At 8 A.M., she would walk down to the lagoon to feed Kat and Mother and work with Tibbets on his experiments. By nine, she was back up in the homearium, vacuuming.

At ten, she made Junior practice humanoid again while she played ball with him. He seemed to have a lot more natural ability with catching and throwing the ball than with imitating human language. By this point, he was very accurate with the ball and could bop it right into her hands. Once when she was ignoring him, he hit her hard in the back of the head with it, and she yelled at him. Seeing how much he loved to catch, she used it as a reward and would not throw the ball back until he made some humanoid sound. Wanting the ball so badly, he would juke back and forth, squawking and blatting, until he finally uttered some noise that might have come from a human.

Lunch at noon was followed by quiet time. About 2 P.M., they had more lessons and then play time. At four, she wrote notes from the day and started on dinner at five. This was followed by free time and then bed at eight.

At times he didn't want more food or to play catch with the ball. So if she wanted him to talk humanoid, she'd offer to rub his back and sides. He loved this treat the most. While she rubbed his back, he leaned into her motion like a dog, sometimes angling his body to get at a different area. If she gently used her fingernails on his skin, he'd shiver. His eyes were unfocused, and he didn't breathe. She didn't know what this felt like to him, but it seemed intense. When he'd had enough, he would startle and scoot away, staying far from her for at least twenty minutes while he recovered.

Despite working for hours each day to get him to speak, for that first week, his language skills didn't seem to improve at all. She wondered about his capabilities. He was not like Kat, didn't focus, didn't seem to understand the point of the lessons. When she spoke words instead of the alphabet, most often he would just squawk or squeal back at her. He interrupted a lot, as males do.

She believed, since he was young, he would catch on.

* * *

Every day, Blum gestured her out of the homearium so she could give him a summary of the day's work. She would climb out of the pool to retrieve her hearing glasses and a towel and then walk onto the lawn for the conversation with him. It felt strange to move through the air. Behind her, she left a trail of water like a mermaid.

They would sit on the Adirondack chairs looking at the sea, out of Junior's range of splashing and the volume of his squeals. She would explain what he had managed that day.

Blum at least seemed impressed with the progress. He noted how Junior had accepted her as his mother. The bond, he said, was clearly there and growing. He was not worried about the language lessons. He told her they would see results soon.

* * *

Several times each night, Junior would wake, let go of her foot and squeal. If she didn't immediately respond, he'd splash her, freshly wetting the bed and pillow. Although she'd yell at him to shut up and stop that, he would keep squealing and splashing until she leaned over to rub his back while he calmed. Then she'd give him back her foot. Sucking on her toes, he'd fall back to sleep within a few minutes.

Evidently dolphins had more intermittent sleep than humans. Or at least adolescent dolphins did.

She woke each morning, groggy. At times, the simplest tasks seemed difficult, the sunlight sparkling on the water hurt her eyes.

* * *

By the fifth day, Junior still hadn't entered the deeper end of the pool, not once. This was strange, since he must have been tired of being in the very shallow water, unable to swim fast or flip or twirl or jump. It must be as frustrating as it would be for a human to live in a narrow underground tunnel, unable to stretch or stand or run.

It looked as if he did want to swim in the deeper water, for he would swim up to the edge of it, his beak (what she now knew was called a rostrum) just beneath the sliding glass doors, peering out at the water beyond. Still, he did not swim under the doors. He just looked, his eyes big, a little like a child afraid of the deep end of the pool.

So, she pulled on her mask and ducked down in the water next to him to examine the size of the opening. When designing the homearium, she'd measured his height from stomach to the tip of his dorsal fin to make sure she left enough room for him to fit. She eyeballed the height of the opening and his height to confirm she'd done this correctly. The gap was more than tall enough.

She modeled for him how to swim into the deep end, ducking underneath the doors, then swimming around on the far side and clicking at him underwater. Excited, he scooted back and forth on the other side, with his rostrum right underneath the doors, but he would not swim through the opening. He just clicked and crinkled and squealed, staring at her.

Perhaps his unwillingness to do this had something to do with why the dolphins would not jump over a net, not even to escape the men. It might have been that (accustomed to the wide-open sea and needing to return to the surface to breathe every few minutes) they had developed a strong physical aversion to any type of constrained space. They could not risk getting trapped anywhere, or caught on anything, for they could drown within minutes, in just a few inches of water.

Or maybe it was that their echolocation was confused by objects like rope nets and glass. Maybe that confusion made it difficult for them to see into the area beyond to know it was safe.

So she asked Blum to have the men remove the sliding doors, to take down that whole wall of them. The glass doors were her favorite part of the homearium and were by far the most expensive part. When she made this request of Blum, Tibbet jerked around to look at her. He muttered a sentence in which the only word she heard was *women*. Blum snorted, amused. He did, however, tell Tibbet and Eh to help her remove the doors.

When building the homearium, it had taken a half day to install the tracks for the doors. Removing the tracks and the doors, however, took only twenty minutes. She slid each door to the end of the track, and Tibbet and Eh unhitched them, one by one, piling them up on the lawn outside. Then they began to unscrew the lower track that the doors had rested on.

Junior watched all of this with attention, his head out of the water. Once the track was unscrewed, Eh picked up one end of it and began to walk it out onto the lawn, while Cora carried the other end through the water to the side of the pool. There, Tibbet took it from her, and the men carried it away.

With this thin track gone, Junior reacted as though a 10-foot-high wall had been removed. He shot into the deep end, without hesitation. In the deeper water, he swam at high speeds, twisted and turning. He threw himself high in the air and flipped onto his back. So happy.

She dove into the deep end with Junior. He shot over to her, chirping like a baby bird, so grateful. Underwater she kept her eyes closed, listening, the sounds clear and pure. *A radio being tuned. A metal flywheel clicking.* She soaked them up, this underwater sound so different from the distant muffled above-water sound.

Both of them stayed in the deep end, for a long time.

Each day Junior grew to depend on her more.

* * *

Junior was a young male dolphin. He got erections at different times for no apparent reason, while eating or playing with the ball or napping. It was understandable. In the pool with the other dolphins, he was used to having sex several times a day. Here he was alone, with no other dolphins. When he needed to, he got on top of the inflatable ring and rubbed against it. The action was quite fast; three fast pumps and he was done. Or he rubbed against the ball or the stairs.

She didn't think much about this. At Beach Ride Bobby's, the stallion, Mr. Pebbles, would sometimes get an erection while staring into the distance and chewing, or when walking through the field, or even while she tightened the saddle strap around his ribs.

* * *

Junior was used to being physical, to the thumping fast-paced play of dolphins. On the other hand, wading through the water, she was slow and fragile. It was like a tiger cub rooming with a lizard. No matter how gentle the cub was, the lizard got hurt.

Even though she yelled and kicked at him, he still sometimes tripped her or nipped on her heels. Her legs were covered with bruises and scratches.

By the time each evening arrived, she didn't have the energy to think of a meal she wanted to eat, especially not when she'd have to cook it on the swinging propane stove. So night after night she made the same meal, grabbing a butterfish from Junior's fridge and filleting it, then frying it in butter with a little salt. It was ready to eat in five minutes. For dessert, she ate a mango out of the skin, then washed her hands and face in the water to clean off. She ate for calories, not for fun. However, this hungry, even this plain and repetitive food popped in her mouth, the crispy fish, the sweet mango.

Through much of the day, she felt the gaze of the men who sat in the living room, taking notes on her progress, pointing and discussing. In front of them she felt like a fool, talking in a high-pitched babyish voice to an underwater creature with its big fixed grin *(Good job! Good boy!)*, trying to act like its mom.

* * *

On the sixth day in the homearium, she was particularly tired. Her head hurt from the interrupted sleep, and several of the cuts on her legs were infected, red and hot. Junior did not seem to be speaking humanoid with any greater frequency than he had that first day. When she asked him to talk, he still consistently started off by clicking or squealing. Mostly what he appeared to have learned so far in the homearium was how to bop the ball exactly where he wanted and how to weave around her feet to make her stumble.

So she climbed out of the water, put on her hearing glasses and walked out onto the lawn to try to muster the energy for another lesson. She sat on the grass, thinking she just needed to dry off for a moment, to hear normally, to be in the sun. In her gut, she knew this was a failed experiment, that she was making a fool of herself, that she should give up. Perhaps her thoughts were obvious from the way she sat there, staring at her hands.

Tibbet stepped out of the building to talk with her. He hardly ever came to talk to her, except when he needed her help running his experiment with Mother and Kat.

He sat down next to her on the ground. This was also surprising, since he preferred chairs. Still, he sat there, close enough that she could hear him. He was careful to face her so she could see his mouth. He spoke each word distinctly.

He said he had seen how difficult it was to live in the pool. They had all been impressed at what she was attempting, how hard she was working.

She nodded, touched by this unexpected sympathy.

Junior, jealous, squealed loudly at them from the homearium.

Tibbet said—If you need to take a break for a while, none of us would blame you. We'd understand.

She could feel how much she wanted this, to take a hot shower in a bathroom with a door that closed, to dry off and pull on real clothes, her skin clean and not sticky with salt, to wear her hearing glasses all the time and be able to hear again, to be with humans. To sleep on a dry bed and not be woken up, not once all night long. To walk around, not wading through water. To stop being observed all day long.

He said—None of us would think less of you.

Something about the way he worded this made her pause. She looked from his mouth to his eyes. He had his eyebrows knotted with sympathy, but the eyes themselves were cold.

He added—These conditions are not made for a woman.

She paused and her jaw moved sideways.—I'm staying.

* * *

That afternoon, she began to walk around holding a broom. Each time Junior got in the way of her feet or nipped at her, she jabbed him in the side with the broom's bristles. He didn't like the bristles on his sensitive skin and would jerk away.

Encouraged by this success, she began to raise the broom whenever he veered toward her. Seeing her ready, he would turn away before touching her.

Within an hour, he was tripping her and nipping at her heels less often.

* * *

The next day was her seventh in the homearium, Sunday. She and Blum had agreed that Sundays were her day off. She could spend the full day as she pleased, out of the water, away from Junior, the men and the homearium.

Heading into town, it was so easy to move through the thin air. A clean dry dress swished around her legs. Her hearing glasses on, she concentrated on the sounds of the birds and the wind. Once she reached town, she reveled in the human voices. She wandered around town, examining people who were fully dressed, their hair dry. No one was watching her, taking notes. She sat in a restaurant for lunch, eating food that she didn't have to cook on a swinging stove. She gorged on chicken pot pie and green beans, followed by an ice cream sundae. The crust on the pot pie amazed her, so delicate and flaky. The green beans were crisp, the dessert so sweet. She closed her eyes to concentrate on the taste.

On the way back, she lay on a beach for two hours and slept. She wasn't woken up once by a dolphin splashing water on her face.

However, all day, there was also a rising awareness inside her of Junior, of him alone in the homearium, the men watching him. When she woke, she could feel Junior's fear in her gut.

So even though it was only 3 P.M., she began to walk back, moving faster as she went, feeling the urgency. Near the end, she started trotting.

Turning into the driveway, she heard something in the distance, a painful squeak, some tired piece of metal rasping and tortured. It took her a moment to understand this was Junior's voice; he must have been screaming all day. She began to run.

He must have heard or known in some way she was approaching, because as she rounded the corner of the house, he was rising in the water, standing up on his kicking tail in the deep end, calling, bellowing with all the strength of his failing voice. Yelling at her, as clearly as he could, again and again— Ayy, Eey, Eey, Eey.

So scared, so lonely.

Yelling—Ayy, Eey, Eey, Eey.

She dove right into the deep end in her clothes, and he shot over to her, rubbing himself round and round her body, yelling and yelling, even underwater, so relieved.—Ayy, Eey, Eey, Eey.

Pronouncing over and over again, as clearly as he could, the first four letters of the alphabet.

For an hour each morning she walked down to the lagoon, where she helped Tibbet test the dolphins' ability to communicate about the matching shapes.

Each day Cora asked Tibbet to take one step deeper into the water. This was a way to get Mother and Kat accustomed to him so, hopefully at some point, he could perform this research without her.

When he moved at this speed, stepping just a little deeper into the water each day, standing still while he tallied the results, Kat and Mother didn't seem to get alarmed. However, the morning he stepped in deep enough for the water to reach his gut, both Kat and Mother stopped what they were doing and turned toward him, moving in closer.

Tibbet said something, but Cora wasn't wearing her glasses so she couldn't hear it. He had his hands up and looked alarmed.

She asked—What's going on?

He gestured to the dolphins. They were facing him, intent.

She ducked her head under the water. The dolphins' sounds (clicking and crinkling) were intense. From this angle, with her eyes, she could see Tibbet's skinny pale legs and his bathing trunks and his slightly distended gut above. She had no idea why Mother and Kat were reacting this way, what it was they were sensing. They were not acting aggressive or upset, just intent, studying something.

From that day on, each time he got into the water, they clicked at his gut and were gentle with him.

* * *

The skin on Junior's underside had become pink and angry-looking, from being scraped against the floor of the pool as he swam around, so Cora added water to the pool one night. In the morning, the water was an inch deeper.

Walking to the bathroom, she found this single inch made a big difference. She had to lean her torso forward and sway from side to side. If she wanted to move faster than a walk, she had to surge forward with each step, yanking her knees high.

Still, Junior was able to swim more easily, without rubbing against the concrete with every movement of his tail. He appeared so happy with this extra inch of water. He shot through the water, round and round, then came back to rub against her. His teacher, his fellow prisoner, his prison guard.

* * *

On the eighth day in the homearium, Cora found what looked like several kernels of black rice on the stove. She was moving her hand toward the rice, about to sweep it off into the water, when she understood *feces* and jerked her hand back.

The rats on the island were fast moving and feral. At the restaurant she'd worked at, they left droppings in the cupboards and on the counters. After closing, she occasionally glimpsed the creatures moving along the rafters of the building. Their bodies undulated as they ran—furry water or snakes with feet.

The question was, how could a rat reach the stove, which hung in the air 2 feet above the water?

She figured it out by process of elimination. From the side: no rat could jump the 15 feet from the edge of the pool to the stove.

From below: no rat swimming in the water could jump 2 feet up onto the stove.

So, her eyes moved reluctantly up to the rafters above. It was so easy to imagine a rat climbing down the chains that the stove hung on.

She stared, unblinking, for a long moment. Then turned to her bed which also hung on chains from the rafters.

That day, she rigged an aluminum pie plate as a collar around each chain. She placed the pie plate halfway down. She hoped the rats wouldn't be able to climb around these wide metal barriers.

* * *

When the men went to bed, they shut off the lights. Sometimes they forgot to give her warning. She would be in the middle of the pool, and there would be a loud *clunk* that left her in darkness. She'd have to find her way to bed by feel.

* * *

She started getting rashes where the edges of the wet bathing suit chafed against the edges of her crotch. She tried putting ointment on the area, but it got washed off quickly in the water.

She experimented with different types of clothing. A short dress got soaked from the water, and, underneath, the underwear sagged and chafed worse than the bathing suit. A leotard, with its snaps in the crotch, irritated the rash also. So, in the end, she began wearing a bikini top and bike shorts.

The men considered each of these outfits with appreciation.

They sat inside the living room by the windows, eating meals or working while they watched, listening to the sounds she and Junior made, broadcast from the speakers.

It was rare that they stepped into the homearium to talk to her, and when they did, she couldn't hear much of what they said unless she got out of the water to put on her glasses. So she was left alone, primarily in silence, talking at a dolphin, her voice echoing in her head. Few other noises were loud enough to penetrate her hearing. Luckily, Junior naturally tended to be loud, or maybe he'd figured out that she needed the volume.

She would say—Talk. A, B, C, *Deeee*.

Since that first Sunday she'd spent in town, Junior worked much harder at the lessons. He would repeat back the letters as best he could. He managed to replicate the timing and emphasis better than the exact sounds—Ayy, Eey, Eey, *Eeyyyy*.

She tried nursery rhymes and simple phrases, using a sing-song voice, the way you would with a baby.

—Talk. MA-ry HAD a LI-ttle lamb. LI-ttle lamb. LI-ttle lamb.

Junior would answer with something close to the right beat, but the sounds that came out were very different from her words. At times the noises could have come from different instruments in an orchestra pit. A squeal. A blat. A whistle.

She would repeat the words, exaggerating the vowels and pitch.

—No Junior. Try again. Humanoid this time, O.K.? Listen. Talk. MAAA-reee. MAAA-ree.

When she slowed down the words this way, it seemed Junior's response was slightly more likely to include the vowels she'd used, the *aaaa*, the *eeee*, although not necessarily in the right order, and the humanoid sounds were interspersed with clicks and squawks. She might, however, just be wishing the vowels were similar. She knew Tibbet was recording these lessons and analyzing them in the house. She relied on him to double-check her perception, and to tell her if there were sounds she was missing, below her level of hearing.

This type of nonsensical vocalization, perhaps at the level of a pre-lingual toddler, was the majority of the language she heard each day. It left her hungry for real language. So when she wasn't working with Junior or cleaning up, she read. She borrowed a book or two a week from the men's library, devouring them during her scheduled quiet times. There wasn't much else to do. She learned about the men through these books, about their words and values and thinking.

She started with books on language acquisition, learning how hard it was. Language was a complex code transmitted at high speed. A word was a sound chunk. In English, there were hundreds of thousands of different sound chunks that could be used in different orders in any sentence. Some of these chunks sounded identical but meant different things. Others sounded different but meant the same thing. And then there were all those prefixes and suffixes and irregular conjugations. Without ever having experienced language, a baby had to first figure out these audio waves were some type of communication, and then become a cryptanalyst, systematically breaking each sentence down, parsing it into chunks and guessing at the meaning of each. The only way to learn it all was through deduction and raw memorization.

After reading about language for a while, it seemed surprising to Cora that any child could figure it out.

So she decided to help Junior break this code by teaching him a few specific nouns and adjectives. She had Blum buy a child's set of large three-dimensional plastic shapes; squares, circles and triangles in different colors. The first time she presented them to Junior, she held out three triangles (a red, yellow and blue one), while she said—Talk. Triangle, triangle.

Junior cocked his head and examined her and the triangles, gurgling dolphin sounds and occasional vowels out of his blowhole. It was possible that, with his senses, he could perceive very different qualities than the shape. He could be seeing the minute differences in the contours or inner seams, or in how the sound bounced inside.

After ten presentations of the triangles, stating the name each time, she repeated the process with the squares and then the circles. She spoke each word as clearly as she could, exaggerating the mouth movements and looking him in the eye.

Then she moved onto colors, holding up different red objects (triangle, square and circle) and saying—Talk. Red. Red. Junior, this is *red*. Talk. Red.

Junior burbled and watched her.

Of course, it was possible the dolphins were color-blind.

Finally she added verbs, hoping that, even if he couldn't repeat a word, he could demonstrate through action that he comprehended the meaning.

Throwing all the shapes in the water, she said—Junior. Bring square. Bring square.

Like any baby, at first he just slapped the shapes around with his tail, or carried one around in his mouth or on his belly.

She repeated, holding out her hand—Bring square. Square.

Instead he began teething on the yellow triangle, the satisfying crunch of plastic between his teeth.

—Bring *square*.

In the end, he would bop the white ball over to her. It was his favorite toy, and he'd hit it right into her hands, so very accurate. She didn't know if he didn't understand what she was asking. Perhaps instead he considered her sentence less of a command and more a part of a dialogue.

Each day, she practiced these lessons with him.

* * *

One of the books she read was an older one about phrenology

by a British anthropologist. She wasn't sure why the men had decided to bring such an outdated science book. Perhaps they thought it was funny what science used to believe, or perhaps one of them was secretly sympathetic to the concepts.

Each chapter described the typical measurements of the skull of a different race (Semite, Hamite, Negroid, etc.) and used these measurements to make statements about that race's propensities. Each race was compared to the typical Anglo-Saxon skull, the gold standard.

The third chapter was about the Eskimo race. The chapter was based on eight skulls in the Berlin Natural History Museum. There was a footnote mentioning that these specimens had come from two families who'd been persuaded to travel to Germany in the 1800s, where they had been exhibited in the Berlin zoo for a few months before dying from smallpox (no one having remembered to vaccinate them). The footnote stated the paucity of the sample size, just eight skulls, was somewhat compensated for by the samples covering the gamut of development from a fifty-year-old to a ten-month-old.

She stared at that footnote for a long time, absorbing it.

(With each book, she felt the words on the page were like following the path of some never-before-seen creature through the woods. For clues she had some broken twigs, and the footprints, maybe some scat. From these details, she had to imagine the animal that had made them, what kind of gait it had and how far it could see, what gave it sustenance and what frightened it, what destination the creature was aiming for and why.

The creature who had written that footnote terrified her.)

That night she dreamed of those two Eskimo families in the zoo. She was floating high above them, moving closer. She could see them, lit up in their enclosure, a large crowd watching from just outside the glass. The families appeared to be still healthy. She circled down, almost swimming through the air.

The audience, she noticed now, was wearing white lab coats and taking notes.

It was beginning to get dark, so one of these people stepped over to the wall to turn on the enclosure lights.

Just before the lights clicked on, the person turned to look at her. It was Blum.

Although it might not seem like it, this was a nightmare. She got it repeatedly. Each time, she woke up from it, breathing hard, her heart thumping. She blinked around at her bed and the homearium. She stared at this exhibit she had designed and the men had built and she had entered. The dark windows of the house facing her, the microphones above. She had an inkling of how the families had felt in their enclosure, waiting for what might happen next.

When she was a child, the family collie, Got-Fleas, used to try to hump her leg. She wasn't sure why he chose her. Perhaps because she was the one who fed him, or maybe, at the age of ten, she was the only nearby female close to his weight. Some days his desire seemed to get worse. On those days, anytime she stood still, he would try to wrap his leg around her knee. Even after she shook him off, his hips would continue to work wistfully back and forth, as though not yet willing to believe she had pushed him away.

Thus she wasn't that surprised when one afternoon, during a language lesson, Junior tried to rub against the back of her leg. After all, he'd humped nearly every object in the homearium (the inflatable raft, the ball, the base of the bed, the stairs of the pool).

At the point he did this, she was standing by the stove making breakfast. He rotated sideways to angle his lower belly against the back of her calf. With his first thrust, her knee gave way and she fell over, luckily missing the edge of the stove. Struggling to stand up in the water, she saw his erection and understood.

From then on, each time she saw him about to try this, she'd jab at his side with the broom's bristles. He moved so much faster than she did that generally by the time she had raised the broom a few inches, he had scooted 10 feet away. He continued, however, to watch her, clearly plotting his next attempt. She was the only other living being in the pool with him, and her calf was the easiest part of her to access.

* * *

It was difficult in the homearium. She slept each night on a wet roll of foam. Her salty skin was itchy all the time. She took showers in the pre-dawn, pulling the shower, curtain tightly shut while Junior wove around her legs, watching everything she did. She rinsed the dirty outfit in the shower, and when she and the clothes were clean, she turned off the water, dried herself as best as she could and pulled on a clean pair of bike shorts and a bikini top. Yesterday's outfit she spread on the cement beside the pool to dry.

At the research center, she had transformed, was now the color of café au lait, wet all day and nearly bald. She had become like Junior, smooth curves and practical muscle. She felt sexless, exhausted and not completely human. She didn't want to wear the chafing clothing but did so because of the men.

Food was just fuel. She ate the same type of fish Junior did, fried, bolting it down with a few pieces of fruit on the side, everything slightly soggy. She wanted to earn the right to be that *woman researcher*, to show the men she could do this, to live with the dolphins, studying them for the rest of her life. She struggled to prove herself.

At this point, she thought of Junior as a large underwater Labrador retriever, a puppy who got in the way and nipped at her heels but was still her loyal companion. He slept when she slept, floating beside her in the water, sucking on her foot. He woke when she woke. He went where she went, his side against hers. And like a dog, he studied her emotions with his large brown eyes.

One night in bed, feeling tired and overwhelmed and so

alone, perhaps a bit pre-menstrual, she put an arm over her eyes and cried, her breath catching. Her breath came unevenly, her ribs shuddering, *huh-ah-ah-hahh*.

Junior, asleep with his head under the water, somehow sensed this and awoke. He let go of her toe and pulled back a bit. From the corner of her eye, she could see him focusing on her.

She looked over. His blowhole was winking open and closed, repeatedly.

Worried, she leaned over to place her fingers on his blowhole to feel what was going on.

Breathy exhales. *Huh-ah-ah-hahh.*

Surprised, she looked him in the eye.

Creatures designed for living underwater, dolphins would never express sadness through breathing. Yet here was Junior imitating her sounds with an urgency in his breath. *Huh-ah-ah-hahh.* How do you read the emotion of an animal with a fixed grin?

He dipped his face in and out of the water, making the sounds. An uneven inhaling and exhaling, a pained wet huffing. *Huh-ah-ah-hahh.*

Watching him, she forgot to cry. He took one of her toes very gently in his mouth and sucked on it, a comforting touch. They were here together.

* * *

Each day she stepped out of the homearium, onto the lawn, to report on her progress to Blum.

These days, he wore his shirts unbuttoned. Before he left, Leary had given him a wood bead necklace, as well as a bottle of pills. The pills, he said, were for research, and the one time she saw them, she was surprised at how tiny they were. How could taking those tiny pills make him act so differently? Blum wore the necklace every day, the beads clinking on his skinny chest. He tended to stand closer to Cora than before, and while they talked, he would touch her at times, on the shoulder, the waist or hip. If she shifted back, he'd look surprised.

He said—You're uptight. Get with the times.

His language had changed. At times, he used words like *downer* or *fab* or *bummer*.

She'd adjust the position of her glasses, trying to hear better.

Biology—he said, patting her hip.—We're all just animals.

She thought of Bernie. He used to treat the female dolphins the same way, touching and tapping, sonaring and bumping, seeing how far he could get.

* * *

One afternoon, Blum stepped from the living room into the homearium, laughing so hard he bowed over with the power of it, wiping his sleeve across his eyes. She asked what he was laughing about, but in the pool without her glasses, she couldn't hear his response; wasn't sure with his face pointed down like that, if he made one.

He took a step closer to her, looked and stopped his laugh with something close to a click. He was staring at her now as though he'd never seen her before, as though he'd never seen a human being before. His eyes were open wide and very dark, all pupils. The pills.

After a long moment, he turned and lurched out the side door. In his hand, he carried the gasketed handmade diving balloon. He was heading for the isolation tank.

Behind him, in the window, Tibbet and Eh stood watching, as he connected the hose, turned on the air pump, rolled the balloon down over his face and clambered into the tank.

* * *

The next afternoon, Tibbet lugged a 25-pound bag of salt across the lawn to the isolation tank. Cora waded to the end of the pool to watch him pour the whole bag into the tank and stir it until it was absorbed. He was making it salty like the Dead Sea, so Blum could float in the water without a breathing apparatus. She thought probably this was Tibbet's idea. If Blum drowned, the research center would close.

* * *

She talked to Junior like a mother, emphasizing the rise and fall of her voice, talking in a high pitch closer to his, baby talk, vacuuming up his poo, putting away his toys, watching how much he ate and slept, making sure he was healthy, teaching him colors and shapes and the alphabet. She worked and worked, striving to get him to talk, knowing that progress was all that would keep him and Mother and Kat safe from Blum, that would let her stay here with them, protecting them.

Each morning, she went down to the lagoon to feed Mother and Kat, and to help Tibbet test Mother and Kat's ability to communicate about the matching shapes. Each morning she was relieved to see no new surgical incisions on their heads. Both of them looked healthy and strong. And each time Tibbet walked into the water, up to his waist, they would click at his gut and be gentle with him.

Both Junior and she were trapped together the rest of the day, every day, struggling through water that was too high for her and too low for him, no one else here but the other. Their tempers fraying.

And Junior would thump against her, wanting to play or trying to hump the back of her leg, rough in the way of the dolphins. He was a teenager, so much stronger and faster than her, weighing almost three times more. She was bruised and scratched up. She jabbed at him with the broom's bristles when he was too rough. He would jerk away, not liking the feel of the bristles on his skin.

One morning, maybe six A.M., she was just getting out of bed and walking toward the shower, when he shoved her without warning from behind. Whether or not he meant to make her fall, she did, chin first, hitting the side of the pool, biting the corner of her tongue. A flash of pain, the copper taste of blood. Furious, she flailed upright. Raising the broom high above her head, she slammed, not the bristles, but the hard wood shaft down onto his side with all her strength. A *whack* even she could hear.

Shocked, he jumped forward, pumping away from her, following the curve of the pool, building up speed, moving faster now than she'd ever seen. (She understood in this moment how patient he was with her normally, how much he held back his power, puttering around all day like a speedboat in a bathtub.) At first she thought he was fleeing, then he reached the far end of the pool and turned. She had a single image of him cutting back through the water, spray arcing off his fin. Hurtling toward her with the power of a god.

She did not feel the impact.

She woke to find herself on the stairs of the pool in the shallow end, his body pressed against hers, holding her there, propping her face up against the cement wall so she could breathe. He held her there, so still, so careful.

Once she groaned and sat up, he backed away. He looked her in the face, his eyes wide. Her right hip was in pain. She touched the area gently. Nothing broken, but a spreading pain, deep in the muscle. The bruise bloomed that day, over 6 inches wide. Later, during the process of healing, the colors shifted through a fleshy sunset of surprising shades before fading.

The rest of the day he followed her, attentive and careful, never pushing or shoving, just watching her, worried.

She knew the attack was her fault. The two of them limping around the pool, tired and hurt. Hiding what had happened from the men. Their first fight.

S itting up in the morning, she saw something small and
furry paddling around in the water at the far end of the
homearium. A rat. She stood on the bed to get as far as
possible from the water and yelled at Junior to *get it, kill it, eat
it.* The rat must have fallen into the pool during the night and
could not get out.

Junior, who had been sleeping, jerked up and followed her
pointing finger (he was capable now of comprehending this
human gesture). He swam over to the rat but didn't swallow
it in one bite as he would a fish. Instead, he circled it, investigating. His presence panicked the rat. It twisted away from
him, its tail turning like a rudder. She didn't know how long it
had been swimming, but its head was low in the water. The
cement walls of the pool must be too high for it to scramble
out. Each time Junior got close, the rat jerked away in another
direction.

With Cora still yelling, *eat it, kill it,* Junior cut in close
on the right side. The rat jerked left, toward the shallow end
of the pool and then past that, toward the far side. Junior cut
in then on that side, turning it back toward the shallow end.
He continued this way, cutting back and forth as necessary,
not snapping at the rat, simply correcting its direction, herd-
ing the animal toward the shallows until it reached the stairs
there.

As soon as the creature felt the concrete under its feet, it
sprang up and out of the water. On the ground, it bolted away,

liquid motion, along the wall to the open end of the homearium and was gone.

Junior pulled his head out of the water to watch, intent, as
the rat escaped. Even after it was gone, he continued to stare
out the open end of the homearium for a long time.

Then he swam straight to the bottom of the deep end of the
pool. He spent the morning there alone, like Bernie used to, rising to the surface to breathe only when he had to. He wouldn't
interact with Cora at all.

* * *

Junior disliked it when any of the men entered the homearium. He would bark and blat and squeal, and spit and slap
water around with his tail. The man, unable to communicate
with her and getting soaked, would soon leave.

The men said he was a jealous baby wanting his mama's
attention.

One day she noticed that after Blum left, fleeing all the
noise and splashing, Junior swam a lap around the pool, flashy
and proud. The instant shift from temper tantrum to pride
made her suspicious.

So the next day, she watched closely when Tibbet came into
the homearium to inspect the microphones. While Tibbet
climbed the ladder to the microphones, Junior blew raspberries and shrieked and splashed him with water. He was performing the dolphin version of pounding his fists on the
ground and screaming. However, the moment Tibbet stepped
out of the homearium, Junior's fit just stopped, as though a
director had called out *Cut*.

She watched Junior, curious. Could he have noticed that
when he was loud and out of control like a baby, the men joked
and relaxed and left?

Either way, she began to play her supporting role. Each

time the men were in the homearium and Junior began shrieking, she told him to stop in a voice filled with dismay, while
waving her hands at him.

After the man left, Junior and she exchanged a look and
returned to normal.

Each day, the bond between them grew.

* * *

In the homearium, she hardly ever wore the hearing glasses.
Mostly, the only voice she heard was her own, echoing inside
her skull. Her brain began to crave words again.

One night, Eh was washing the dinner plates in the kitchen.
She could see him through the open window, scrubbing and
putting the plates on the sideboard to dry. The sound she
should have heard was the clatter of dishes. Instead she heard a
woman's voice.

The voice was young and very angry. It spoke in her ear—
Slit Slit Slit.

She could hear the woman's tongue tap the wet roof of the
mouth, blocking sound, then releasing it in a burst of air, making the *T*. The clarity of the sound was always what betrayed
her auditory hallucinations, the quality so much better than her
actual ears could discern.

She didn't have to look around to know there was no
woman nearby.

Anytime she was out of the pool, she put on the hearing
glasses. On Sundays, when she went into town, she listened
hard to every conversation she could, trying to fill her brain
with words.

She was glad Tibbet had the tape recorder on all the time,
taping the sounds in the homearium. This way she did not have
to rely solely on her own perceptions.

* * *

That afternoon she put on the hearing glasses and stepped into the main room of the research center to report to Blum her day's progress.

His wife had left the day before with the kids, to visit her parents for two weeks in Connecticut. Cora stood a few feet back from him.

He nodded, listening intently, as she talked about the incident with the rat. On the table in front of him was a book with the title *The Psychedelic Experience*. She noted with surprise the author's name was that of the researcher who had visited with Blum: Leary. Above his name was a drawing of a bare-chested shaman, head thrown back, an eagle rising behind him.

When she had finished explaining how Junior had herded the rat to the stairs, Blum pursed his lips and said maybe she understood the dolphins so well, was able to bond with them, because of her heritage.

She looked from left to right, confused, then asked— Because I grew up in Florida?

He said—No, because you're Indian. An ancient people, connected to nature. You're more able to feel what the animals feel.

An image of her granddad flashed into her mind. He was the one in the family who looked the most Seminole, having the widest cheekbones and the darkest skin (although, it must be said, as a fisherman, he was also the one most in the sun). She remembered how he would grab each netted fish, his fingers slipping inside the tender gills to pinch the head still, the fish gasping at the foreign air, its eyes bulging, then he'd jab the knife into the belly and twist the blade upward, disemboweling the creature in one fast motion. He'd repeat this with fish after fish with all the emotion with which one turned off the faucet.

At Blum's statement, she snorted out a sound that could

have been a laugh, then gripped the bridge of her nose, her eyes closed, waiting until the feeling passed.

She thought, if anything, her ability came from her gender and lack of hearing. Like a mouse in a field of grass, she had to pay attention to survive.

* * *

Junior seemed to sense her urgency with the language lessons. He concentrated on making human noises now, even practicing during the quiet times while she read. He'd float at the surface, experimenting with sound.

Perhaps self-conscious, he practiced at the far end of the homearium from her. If she looked at him directly, he would stop.

So she'd sit on the side of the pool with whatever book she was reading, wearing her hearing glasses, listening. He babbled vowels, *Ahh ah-ha eh-eh*, like a toddler.

She kept her head down, staring at the book, only glancing at him occasionally from the edge of her eyes.

* * *

After each language lesson with Junior, she rubbed his back to say thank you. She told him she loved him. She had begun to use that word a lot with him. After all, it was the word a mother would use. While she rubbed his back, his focus moved inward, and he got very still. After a few minutes, he would swim away suddenly to the far end of the pool to recover.

Each time she looked at him, she felt warmth. He was her Labrador puppy, her companion, her friend.

* * *

One early morning, before dawn, after using the toilet, she stepped out of the dry room, back into the homearium. And an arm reached out and grabbed her.

Eh had been hiding, pressed against the wall. He yanked her to his chest and began to drag her back into the dry room. She caught a glimpse of the living-room windows, empty. The other men not yet awake. Eh was saying something muffled in her ear, the smell of cigarettes. She could hear nothing but her own labored breathing. She twisted and flailed, struggling. It made not a bit of difference.

Then something flew through the air, hitting Eh smack in the nose. The ball. Junior.

Eh startled back, his grip loosened from surprise.

She jerked forward hard, twisting free, and dove into the pool. Surfacing, she looked back. Eh had stepped up to the edge of the pool, but Junior was in the water in front of him, 300 pounds of sleek muscle.

For a long moment, Eh stared at her and Junior, his eyes very still. All emotion was gone from his face (his easy grin, his tennis-player squint). Instead his eyes were just empty.

The hair prickled on the back of her neck.

For Eh's benefit, Junior clapped his mouth open and shut, showing off his many razor-sharp teeth.

Without a word, Eh turned away, leaving the homearium. She stayed in the water. She rubbed Junior's back and sides for the longest time, whispering *thank you*. Her fingers trembling.

From this point on, she tried to be in the pool as much as possible. She only stepped into the dry room to use the toilet when more than one of the men was in the living room. She locked the door while she was in there and exited as quickly as she could, glancing around the edge of the door before stepping out.

She left the safety of Junior's side for three reasons only: to give Blum her daily report on the lawn, to feed and work with the other dolphins (staying close to Tibbet the whole time), or to walk into town on her day off.

* * *

That Sunday, she wandered through town, wearing a clean dress. She had lived in the pool with Junior for one month, a grey dolphin, a blue pool. In town, she found herself staring at all the different colors: the shocking orange of flowering bougainvillea, a store display of bright limes, a stucco house painted fuchsia. Staring at the house, for a moment she imagined herself living there, the ground floor flooded with water, the deep end of the pool out back for Junior. Here, there would be no more need for Blum or the others. Scientists would travel from far and wide to visit, amazed at the dolphin speaking and the woman doing research. The work so extraordinary, no one could deny it. Perhaps Mother and Kat were here too, but she wasn't sure. Even in her imagination, the details were a little vague.

So instead she focused on the town's dry street, at all the objects that did not bob or float.

And the sound. Wearing her glasses, the sounds filled her head: the birds, the wind, people's voices.

Someone behind her spoke. She concentrated so hard on the clarity of the consonants, she didn't recognize the word as her name until the second time it was said. Turning, she saw the vet.

He looked so strange. A flat human face with no beak, and he had fur on his head. He labored his way across the ground, upright and clothed, gravity's captive.

He smiled at her as he walked past, a bag over his shoulder, doing Sunday errands.—Lost in thought?

His voice did not squeak or blat or squeal.

It took her a moment to find words. Her voice, she found, came out a little singsong like she was speaking a nursery rhyme to Junior.—No, thank you.

He slowed down. Unlike a dolphin's face, his was so strangely mobile.—You O.K.?

She nodded.

He asked—How often do you get out?

Again speech took her a moment.—Out?

—Out of the research center. Out of that pool.

—Oh. Once a week.

He was walking now at her pace, studying her. There was a furrow between his eyes, his head tilted. He asked more questions. How long had she been living with the dolphin? Had the men talked her into it?

She answered each question after a short processing delay, using few words.

His eyes were not brown like a dolphin's, but green. He kept making her talk. Had she been born on the island? Had she always worked with dolphins? He clearly remembered about her hearing, since he asked each question slowly, his face turned to her. He waited until she answered.

He told her she looked like she'd lost weight, and he brought her to a nearby cafe for sandwiches, making sure she ate every bite.

By the time he walked her back to the research center, her answers were coming to her more easily. As they approached the homearium, he said each week she needed to have a conversation with a human about something other than dolphins and research. Humans needed conversation. They need to be around other humans. He stated this in a quiet voice. He asked her if there was anyone she knew on the island she could talk with. She shook her head.

He said then he'd meet her for lunch next Sunday at noon at that same cafe.

A few feet from the pool, he waved goodbye and left. Junior was in the deep end. Kicking his tail, he rose in the water, standing up to watch the vet walk away.

TWENTY-NINE

Homearium, Week 5

Each day while she read, Junior would swim away from her to the far end to practice human sounds. She sat by the side of the pool with her hearing glasses on. She made sure not to look directly at him so he wouldn't think she was listening.

He'd float at the surface, gargling vowels out his blowhole, lengthening and changing the sounds, trying to add consonants. Exhaling a long *Aaaa*, he'd add an almost-Yiddish *Hhh* at the end of it, like an old man about to spit. Or he'd grunt out an *Uuu*, shifting the sound into a growling *Rrrr*. Other times, he'd force a short burst of air out some glottic flap inside him to make a plosive *Khh* sound. His expression internal, he concentrated, saying *Khh . . . khh . . . khh . . . .* Frustrated, he'd slap his tail against the water. None of these sounds were easy for him.

Then one morning, his noises began to sound watery and cut off, a little like he was drowning. She looked over alarmed. He was rolling from side to side like a canoe while he practiced, dipping his blowhole in and out of the water. Each time his blowhole dipped in, the sound he was making was cut off. When the blowhole came out, the sound started again.

He played with the water this way, rolling in and out of it, stopping and starting the vocalizations. This way he could make murmurs and smacks and pops. Moving his blowhole in and out of the water, the sounds were thick and indistinct, like someone mumbling during a nightmare, but occasionally he managed to puff out a wet *Puh* or *Bhh* noise or sometimes a *Mmll*. He worked at this, trying to use the water like lips to shape the sounds.

Within two days, using the water, he managed to say *Glrrt*. She looked up and met his gaze. He shot into the deep end and wouldn't practice anymore that day.

* * *

Each morning she went down to the lagoon to feed Mother and Kat. While she was there, Tibbet would appear. He still needed her help with his research, testing their ability to communicate. He'd wade into the water with his clipboard. Mother and Kat swam in close, clicking at his slightly distended gut, examining him. Around him, they moved gently.

She set up the collapsible pen on the far side of the lagoon and called one of them into it. Generally Kat was the one who came. Cora rubbed her side to reward her. Mother stayed with Tibbet, the two of them near the end of the dock. Cora could see the different geometric shapes stapled onto the dock, a few feet apart, near the water line. The white square, the black circle, the striped triangle. He blew the whistle to signal the start of what he called a "trial." At the whistle, she showed Kat the black circle, her back turned so Mother could not see which shape she held.

Meanwhile Tibbet stood there, watching Mother to see which shape she tapped, to see if she would select the black circle. When she chose the wrong answer, his head rocked back and he blew air out his mouth. Over the last few weeks, Cora had studied his reaction. It felt like satisfaction.

He then tallied Mother's response and blew the whistle to start a new trial. Cora selected a new shape to show Kat.

Mother didn't pay much attention to Cora or Kat. Instead she watched Tibbet, rolling her face through the water. How much of his emotion could she see? Each day she selected the correct matching shape less frequently. Each day Tibbet seemed happier with the results. He was systematically proving dolphins couldn't communicate.

* * *

Inside the research center, the men would sit near the windows to watch Cora and Junior, but the windows were also how Cora could watch the men.

When Tibbet's wife came by for lunch, she sat and drank with the men. Blum's wife and children were still away on vacation visiting her parents. With her gone, it seemed as though Blum touched Tibbet's wife on the hand and shoulder more frequently than before.

Once when Terry/Carrie was trying to reach something high up in the kitchen cabinet and the only other person in the room was Blum, he stepped in close and touched her hip. She startled back and stared at him.

Then he reached up over her head and handed down a glass with a smile.

* * *

During Cora's language lessons with Junior, she continued to use the plastic shapes, the children's toys. She would hold up three different shapes (a triangle, square and circle), all of them the same navy blue, and she'd say—Talk. Blue, blue.

He eyed her. It was possible he was wondering if the word *blue* described the order of the shapes (triangle, square, then circle), or the distance between them, or the expression on her face.

He'd tilt his head and repeat the sound as best he could.— Eww eww.

She showed him three squares (one red, one blue and one yellow) and said—Talk. Square, square.

He'd exhale—Ahh, ahh.

She'd say—You can say it better. Talk. Square, square.

—Ahhr, ahhrrr.

She threw a few shapes of different colors in the water and asked him to get her the blue square. He brought back a red circle, a yellow triangle and finally a green square. The green square, she felt, was good enough, and she threw him a fish as a reward.

She practiced this way with him for an hour. The one time he brought back the blue square itself, she screamed with victory and dove into the deep end with him to celebrate. It didn't matter if he'd picked this square out of luck or not, she still celebrated.

He saw her happiness and worked for it. After all he was a dolphin, a very social being, and she was the only creature in the pool with him, the one he played with all day and slept next to at night. She was his whole world.

* * *

A few times a day, he'd sneak up behind her to try to rub his penis against the back of her calf. His first shove generally knocked her leg out from under her. If she managed to catch her balance, she'd turn and jab him hard with the bristled end of the broom. This hurt his delicate skin. He'd flee to the far end of the pool and sulk there for a while.

* * *

Occasionally now he opened his mouth and stretched his face toward her, squeaking. He seemed to want her to rub his gums, the same way Kat had wanted this.

Perhaps their gums hurt all the time and needed massage.

Or maybe dolphins commonly sonared each other's mouth as a way of showing affection, their version of a hug. Whatever the reason, Cora wouldn't do it. She would not get her hands anywhere near his sharp young teeth.

Still he opened his mouth and stretched his face toward her, whistling. Yearning.

* * *

Each day, Cora stepped out onto the lawn to report on her progress to Blum. She would explain her current strategy, give stories of Junior's progress and say what she would work on next.

Once a week Tibbet reported with her, summarizing any statistical improvement in the recordings of Junior's responses. That first week that she had spent in the homearium with Junior, Tibbet arranged on the picnic table a few sample print-outs of the spectrograms. At the top of each was the tracing of her spoken prompt; below that was Junior's response. Tibbet brought the reel-to-reel recorder to play the accompanying audio and systematically discussed the differences between her prompt and Junior's response: the amplitude, pitch and timing, as well as the number of sonic bursts. He'd circled with a red pen every way in which Junior was failing to imitate her. He tried to sound objective.

The second week of her living in the homearium, she had pointed out that Junior was doing better with the alphabet. He could repeat the number of sounds she made and was beginning to echo the vowels. Tibbet confirmed that Junior seemed to have memorized that set of sounds, but that accomplishment wasn't much more impressive than a dog uttering a specific howl on command.

The third week, placing the spectrograms on the table, he admitted that, during the lessons, Junior was now narrowing his vocal range to be closer to that of a human. They could all see it in the spectrograms. Before the lesson started, Junior's audio tracing flew from the top to the bottom of the paper, as complex as a symphony. However once she said *talk*, his voice paused and then responded in a more narrow range, closer to hers.

The fourth week, Tibbet struggled with what to say. When he spoke, he looked at the spectrograms rather than at Blum or her. He said that while he could not make statements about Junior's intent, there was a statistically significant increase in the animal replicating the beat of her words, as well as at times some of the sounds themselves.

Each week, from then on, he stated the correlation associated with this replication, and every week that number rose. To her, there was nothing more satisfying than Tibbet's weekly summaries of her work.

* * *

She read a book on animal cognition. One of the experiments caught her attention. The researcher placed different species in a cage with a mirror to see how they would respond.

At the sight of their own reflection, birds and prairie dogs and almost every other species tested, began a display of aggression, alarmed by the foreign intruder peering at them through the frame of the mirror. Their display did not change over time, the animals never realizing the reflection was not an invader. The only species who calmed down quickly (figuring out this was their reflection) were great apes and elephants.

Curious, she tried the experiment with Junior. She tied a large hand mirror onto a rope, with a buoy at one end of the rope and a weight at the other. She threw the whole thing into the water at the deep end, the mirror twirling slowly about 3 feet from the surface, held between the buoy and the weight. She ducked into the water with her mask to watch as Junior swam over to investigate. The moment his face came abreast of the mirror, seeing his reflection, he reared back in surprise, snorting out a swarm of bubbles.

He squawked and began to swim back and forth in front of the mirror, his body curved into an almost S-shape with his head high and his tail low. Puffed up this way, he looked twice as big as normal, and he was screaming loud enough to be an army of enraged dolphins. Moving with power and speed, he continued to display for a solid minute before his reaction began to lose conviction and his squawking became confused.

Gradually, he came to a stop, eyeing the mirror. He circled behind it, clicking, searching for the invader. Tense and ready to bolt, he eased in toward the mirror, from the side, to look into his own eyes.

He paused there for a long moment, then tilted his head. Staring in the mirror, he rotated 180 degrees, then quickly reversed the rotation. He snapped his beak, flapped his flippers and moved his tail from left to right, watching to see if his reflection did the same.

Now he was curious, inspecting his own body, twisting this way and that to examine what he looked like from different angles, his back, his dorsal fin, his blowhole, the sides of his head. He opened his mouth wide and considered the inside of his mouth, twisting his tongue this way and that to see his teeth and the back of the throat.

Afterward, she wrote up extensive notes about this, but had no proof of the kind Tibbet preferred: no tallies, no recording of any kind.

So the next day she explained to Blum what had happened and asked him to have the men set up two cameras. Because the cameras couldn't go underwater, they had to film from above. She had them point one camera at where she sat on the side of the pool, the other looked down through the water to where the mirror was.

Eh and Tibbet turned the cameras on at the same moment and signaled to her.

She called Junior over. With him watching, she picked up a blue marker and drew on her forehead a somewhat sloppy circle. Junior watched, interested.

Then she called him closer and drew a triangle on his forehead just above and between his eyes. He went cross-eyed for a moment trying to see what she'd drawn on his forehead, then rolled into the water and beelined straight to the mirror so he could examine the marking.

This reaction, they got on film.

* * *

Back then, she had believed that it was easy to tell if someone was speaking English or not. She believed that spoken language was a yes-or-no condition, a straightforward fact as distinct as a room one could stand inside of, with a door that shut.

However, a few years after the end of this experiment, she watched her twins, Rachel and Ned, learning language. Ned, at twelve months, would burble *mmm, mmm* while looking at her. Did he mean *mom*? Rachel once said *uk* as a truck drove down the street, but then wouldn't repeat the word for weeks. Was the sound happenstance or communication? Ned did say *buh buh* occasionally when he wanted the ball, but he also made that sound when he was eating cereal. The difference between babbling and language was not black and white, but a gradation. It was similar to how Rachel learned to walk, a lengthy and uninspiring process that started with an inauspicious rocking on the hands and knees. After each progression in skill (rocking backward a few inches or pulling herself up on the side of the couch to stand for a moment), she would regress for days, seeming to unlearn all she had mastered. Watching Rachel rock on all fours, her chin wet with drool, one would never imagine the height of the handspring she'd master in high-school gymnastics, her body flying through the air.

When Cora tried to teach Junior to speak, she had not known about this back-and-forth process: a new skill, then a regression. She would begin to believe he was doing better, then that progress would disappear and she would convince herself she'd been wrong.

And as with any young student, there were long swaths of time when she couldn't get him to concentrate on learning. He'd want to play catch or swim upside down in the deep end while blowing strings of bubbles. Or he'd have an erection and, having already mounted the inflatable raft eight times that day, would try stubbornly to rub it against her calf.

One morning he wouldn't stop trying. She was asking him to say *fish*, holding the fish in one hand and the broom in the other, ready to react with either. He would burble different noises in the air, appearing to concentrate on trying to speak, while he let his body bit by bit drift around, moving so imperceptibly she wouldn't notice, until his lower belly was beside her calf. He'd thrust, she'd stumble and jab at his side with the broom's bristles and he'd bolt away. Within a few minutes, he'd return, acting as though he was ready to re-commit himself to the lesson.

For two hours straight, she kept working, trying to get him to speak. The back of her neck had a rash from the constant seawater and sun. It itched, and, although she tried not to, she'd find herself occasionally raking it with her fingers.

She said over and over again—Talk. Fish, fish.

Last night, he'd woken her up squirting water at her face, waking her up so many times she'd lost track. The pillow had become a squishy puddle of seawater. Right now, her head hurt from the interrupted sleep, and the sun on the water seemed very bright.

She said—Talk. Fish, fish.

He didn't nip at her as often these days, but on her left ankle was a scratch that had gotten infected, the pink of the infection beginning to radiate up her leg. All she wanted was to crawl into some dry bed in a dark room to sleep. She felt like a fool, asking a dolphin to speak.

She said—Talk. Fish, fish.

Still he wouldn't concentrate on the lesson, wouldn't speak clearly, would only work to look innocent while ever so slowly letting his penis drift closer to her calf. For two straight hours, he persistently tried to hump the back of her leg.

Fish—she said—Talk. Fish.

At around 11 A.M., she closed her eyes and stood there, slightly swaying. She was trying to find the will to stay here in this pool, to keep living with this brainless underwater dog, to try one more time to teach him to speak.

Of course, while she wasn't looking, he thrust against her leg, and her eyes snapped open as she caught her balance. She didn't jab him with the broom, because it didn't seem important. She knew what she was going to do next. She was going to march out of the pool. She was going to jog along the beach, somewhere far away from him and the homearium, to sleep in the sun for hours. Her hope was that with her skin dry and her headache gone, she might at some point find the strength to return, tomorrow maybe or the next day.

Meanwhile, it was clear the desire must have built up inside of Junior over the past few weeks, for with the second thrust, he arched his back, grunted deep in his guts and, in the moment of his release, he spoke.

He rolled his blowhole into the water to make the friction of the turbulent *ffff*, then twisted upright to let the rest of the word escape with the loud exhale of a soda can, *ishhh*.

Fff-ishhh.

Standing above him, she had the perfect viewpoint. This word spoken by the muscled anus of his blowhole. Magic. It was like seeing the bony pliers of a parrot's beak open and language emerge.

No, it was more than that. For regarding her was not a parrot's beady stare, but instead it was Junior, his brown eyes offering this word in thanks.

And inside her, there was this gut-level comprehension. Her skin tightened. It was as though someone had been standing in a darkened room with her this whole time and she'd just recognized the outline, understood she was not alone.

Yes, yes—she yelled in victory.—Yes! Yes! Yes!

She danced around the pool, throwing him fish after fish and whooping in joy.

And Tibbet stepped into the homearium, his eyes big. He did not enter the homearium because he had seen what Junior had done to the back of her calf. No. He stepped in to check she had not said the word *fish* in a high dolphin voice.

The other men laughed at him when he told them, said he was imagining it. Until Tibbet played the recording.

THIRTY
Homearium, Weeks 6–8

For the next few days, she tried to get Junior to speak again. She tried and tried, but heard nothing like a recognizable word from him. Just the same single syllables that he'd uttered before: *Ahh* and *ehhh* and sometimes *urr*.

On the fourth day, while she was reporting to Blum, Tibbet suggested the possibility that Junior saying *Fish* that one time was an accident. With the dolphin saying so many humanoid sounds, it was bound to happen sooner or later that those sounds would combine into an actual word, akin to a monkey slapping at a typewriter.

She was mad, of course, and marched back into the water. Holding up Junior's favorite punchball, she said *Talk, ball, ball,* while under the water she let Junior use her calf again.

The men, standing in the office, could not see.

And of course, he said *Bhh-all.*

* * *

Through the window, she and Junior watched the men each night, the living room a lit-up stage. Without her hearing glasses, outside of the building, she could not hear a word they said. Undistracted in this way, she observed all that was revealed.

She could tell each time Blum took more of Leary's pills. He would stare at things and people for a long time, his eyes a little glassy, and when he laughed, he threw his head back and let the sound roll from his mouth.

She saw other things. She saw the way Tibbet ate Tums all day long and rubbed his belly along the side, a little like a pregnant woman, as though it ached.

She saw, when no one was looking, the way Eh's eyes watched the others, his handsome tennis-player face as empty as a plate.

She noticed that week something had changed with Tibbet's wife. She came for dinner more frequently than normal. Her face seemed bright, almost lit from within, and she would look at anything in the room except Blum. When she was around, he also changed, talking more than normal, his chest puffed out like a bird.

One evening, when Eh was at the counter washing the dishes, Tibbet got up to pour himself a martini. While both of them were turned away, Tibbet's wife touched Blum's hand and they exchanged looks.

* * *

She and Junior developed an agreement. Once a day, she let him use her leg.

Junior was so very grateful. At night, he floated beside her bed, staring at her. He went to sleep sucking on her toe. He worked for hours each day by himself, at the shallow end of the homearium. She'd placed another mirror there at the surface, and he would practice in front of it, at an angle where he could watch his blowhole as he tried to make different sounds. He was actively trying to get better, to make the sounds she wanted him to speak.

Like any mom, she began to learn his particular version of language, how he pronounced different words (*lo'* meant yellow, *ehrrr* meant red). He had learned to speak loudly enough for her to hear.

Frequently the men did not understand what he was saying, and she, the partly deaf person, had to translate.

She would hold up the blue square and ask him—What's this?

He would eye her and the square, thinking. His attempts at language sounded a little like someone trying to play the piano for the first time. One sound, then a pause, then the next.— Kh . . . air.

She yelled in victory and threw him a fish.

Then she'd ask—Ok. Come on. Talk. It's a BLUE square. BLUE. Blueee.

He'd keep his face in front of her, while twisting his body to try to touch his lower belly to her leg. She stepped out of the way, holding up the square, waiting.

The *B* sound, for him, was difficult. He'd push air out of his blowhole under pressure. Sometimes he managed a *Puh* or *Buh* sound; other times, it came out more as a simple burst of air.

He said—Puh . . . ewww.

Yes, yes—she yelled in victory, gave him a fish and rubbed his side.

Several times a day, he'd open his mouth and stretch his face toward her, wanting her to touch the inside of his mouth. This, she wouldn't do. Those sharp teeth.

* * *

The more clearly Junior spoke, the more power she had with the men.

With each new word he mastered, she would ask for more things for herself or the dolphins, and the men would get them for her. She asked for more squid for Kat and more tarpon for Mother. She'd bring these treats down to the lagoon and throw them to the dolphins one after another. She felt guilty for neglecting the two of them. She also asked for more toys for Junior.

One of the toys the men brought back was a 3-foot-long

inflatable dolphin. When she first saw that toy, she hoped Junior might transfer his affections to it, but he clicked at it just once and understood it as a plastic bubble filled with air.

* * *

Blum and Tibbet disagreed about the extent of Junior's progress. Blum would make sweeping exaggerated statements about the results and the potential. Tibbet would respond that Blum's beliefs were not demonstrated in the data in a statistically significant way. Blum would look at Tibbet with his bright bird eyes and declare that Tibbet had all the intuition of a calculator.

One day, while Cora was on the lawn, reporting, the two men began to disagree about Junior's ability to pronounce sounds such as *Th* and *T* and *D*. Tibbet underestimated Junior's ability, while Blum overstated it. Their voices became tense, and neither of them backed down. It seemed possible that something else was underneath the disagreement. Tibbet pushed each word out with more energy than was necessary, his face a little flushed. Blum's chin was up, his eyes glittering. Tibbet's wife had not dropped by the research center for days.

Cora attempted to interrupt with phrases like *Excuse me* and *I've noticed*, but the men talked right over her. Angry, they were beginning to make more categorical statements, both moving further from the truth. They would not let her speak.

So she got mad. She was the one who'd been living twenty-four hours a day in a swimming pool with a dolphin for seven weeks now. She was the one scooping up his poo and being woken at night by water spat in her face. She was the one working to teach him to speak. She was the expert here.

She broke in loudly, using the men's vocabulary, talking in the cop's voice.—His fricatives are improving, but his occlusives are not clear.

Both men stopped, turned to her surprised. She explained what she had observed. She did not overstate. Both men listened.

After that, she used their jargon more often to explain Junior's progress. Tibbet responded by listening, his chin jutted out, but still he listened.

Blum seemed to hear what she said only enough to feel encouraged. His shirt unbuttoned, his wood necklace swinging on his skinny chest, he would describe the future, Junior's potential, the ability of the whole species. Each day these visions seemed to get more grandiose. He said once they had learned how best to teach Junior to speak, they would teach a whole group of dolphins and then release them into the sea, where they could teach others. He had an image of this, all the dolphins free to come and go as they wished, conversing and interacting with the people at the research center. The exchange of information, the enrichment of both species.

Think of all the dolphins will teach us—he said.

When he talked like this, Cora would wonder if she could be mishearing his words. From where she stood on the lawn, she could see the corner of the dolphin surgical tank in the living room with its restraints. She knew the hammer and nail and other equipment were still laid out beside it. She wondered if he understood what he was doing to the dolphins, that if they were released, they would never return.

When Blum spoke like this, Tibbet and Cora were careful not to look at one another. They looked at Blum, keeping their faces blank.

* * *

Junior wanted to play catch with her for hours each day. He'd pop the ball over to her and then start to squeal, insistent. She would demand he talk before she threw the ball back.

She'd say—Junior, I have one ball here. Can you say that? Talk. One. One.

He'd squeal and blat, impatient, until finally he'd exhale and say—Nnn.

She'd throw him the ball right away and tell him that was great.

This game of catch was a way to get him to talk even when he wasn't hungry for fish. The way he now seemed to prefer to return the ball was by pinching it with his beak until it popped out of his mouth and through the air.

It might be that this action was hard on his jaws, because over time he couldn't seem to pop it into the air as far. At the beginning of the week, he could easily send it 12 feet through the air to her, but with each day that passed that distance decreased. To catch the ball she'd have to move a little closer. By the end of the week, they stood 6 feet apart while playing.

Still he insisted on the game. She assumed if his jaw really hurt, he would stop.

* * *

Junior continued to practice language by himself each day after lunch, on the far end of the pool, wanting privacy. He'd float in front of the mirror, angled so he could see his blowhole while he worked, rolling it in and out of the water, practicing and practicing, trying to enunciate.

Watching him stare at his own blowhole while he tried to talk, she wondered if it would help him to see more clearly how she formed the words with her mouth. So one morning, she covered her face with a very pale face powder, making her skin white as a doll's. Then she applied the darkest lipstick she could find, a color called *Plumtastic*. Whether or not he was colorblind, this difference in contrast would help him see the exact motions her lips were making.

She bent down, leaning in close, where his eyes could focus on her mouth. She spoke slowly.—Talk. Square. Squu-are.

She looked a little like a geisha, her face painted for him. She said—Talk. Squu-aaaare. Squu-aaare.

She leaned in close, as though she was about to kiss his beak, moving her glistening lips in exaggerated motions.

He stared at her, tilting his head this way and that, trying to understand.

She said—Talk. Squuu-aaaare.

Of course he learned. This was what she wanted. His language did improve each day. By the end of the week, he could say—Ssss khh-arrre.

He could pronounce the *S* loudly and clearly enough that even she could hear it. However, some of what he learned was different than what she had intended. In the morning when she said the word *talk*, he began to get an erection.

* * *

On Sundays when she went into town for her day off, the vet met her for lunch.

These lunches were like visiting a foreign country, such different customs. In town, she had to wear more clothing and sit with her legs crossed. She could not bolt down food like she did in the homearium, wordless and hunched.

Aching to hear spoken language, she asked about the vet's life. He had a deep voice that was easier to hear. He faced her and spoke clearly. He'd grown up in St. Thomas, had a mother and four sisters. He never mentioned the father, and she assumed she should not ask. As a child, he was always bringing sick wild animals home to try to nurse them back to health. Bats, toads, baby birds, a mongoose, a fawn and a feral donkey. One day when he was nine, his mother opened the hall closet and found an owl glaring at her from the clothes rod.

After that, he wasn't allowed to bring the animals into the house anymore.

The vet answered Cora's questions, but unlike many of the men she'd been around, he always returned the conversation to her, asking questions about the dolphins, about living in the pool, the research center and the men there.

When she spoke, he would not interrupt, but listened, attentive. The corners of his mouth, a little tight.

After lunch, he walked her back to the research center and said goodbye at the entrance to the homearium. Junior and the men in the building would examine him. Waving goodbye, he'd remind her to meet him next week at the same cafe.

The thought crossed her mind that he might be trying to care for her, might consider her similar to one of his hurt animals.

* * *

Junior's progress continued. By the eighth week, during her daily report to Blum, she barely had to say a word. Eh would step into the room also, while Tibbet played the best examples of Junior speaking. The men stood there listening, their eyes pointed in different directions, each thinking their own thoughts.

One day Blum ushered a man and his child into the homearium. He introduced the man as Professor Fred Curry from Clark University, and this was his three-year-old, Greg. He said they were vacationing here, but since Fred's wife felt sick today, the two of them had decided to visit to see the work with Junior.

During these introductions, Cora noticed each of them was focused on different things.

Blum watched Fred.

Fred stared at scantily clad Cora with her buzzcut standing in the middle of a pool, the furniture hanging from the ceiling, a dolphin at her side.

The child spotted Junior, squealed and ran to the edge of the pool.

And Junior beelined to the child, popping his head out of the water, a foot away, to examine the tiny human. It was clear he'd never seen a child before.

It took her some time for her to persuade Junior to turn away from the child and focus on the lesson instead. Meanwhile Blum and Fred started discussing a conference they'd both attended last year. From the way Blum did most of the talking and Fred kept nodding at everything he said, it was clear who was the Harvard professor. Neither of them paid attention to Junior. The child, however, never looked away from him.

When Junior finally spoke, saying *fff-ishh*, there was a skip in time.

Fred turned, almost as though his name had been called. He looked at Junior, then around the homearium. Perhaps searching for Allen Funt of *Candid Camera*, for everyone to burst out laughing at the joke.

Blum, on the other hand, looked as satisfied as a well-fed cat.

Seeing Fred's surprise, Junior refused to say another word in front of him, no matter how Cora pleaded over the next few minutes, nor how many fish she held up as bribes.

So Blum led Fred into the research center to have lunch instead. She watched them through the window. The men gave Fred a mixed drink and a large meal, then a second drink, while they talked and talked. Tibbet brought over some spec- trograms for Fred to examine and pressed play on the reel-to- reel recorder. While the recording played, the men watched the ceiling with their lips pursed, as though this was classical music.

Meanwhile it was assumed, of course, that she'd look after the child. The two of them sat by the pool and played catch with Junior. The three-year-old had no assumptions about dol- phins and their abilities. When Junior had said *fffishh* earlier, the child had simply squealed, delighted.

The child held the ball up for Junior to see. The child said something, his small high-pitched voice hard for her to hear.

Junior, however, seemed to hear it fine. Nearly vibrating with excitement, he responded in his much louder voice— Bh . . . all.

Rather than throwing the ball, the child pulled it closer and raised his chin, stating a one-word demand.

Junior considered this.

So the boy repeated the word in a louder lower voice, imi- tating a parent—*Please*.

So Junior mimicked the word as best he could—Eee-sss.

The child threw the ball. The squeals of the child and the dolphin were close to the same pitch. They played and played.

After lunch, Fred stepped back into the homearium to listen some more. His gestures were looser, his eyes half-lidded. Junior turned to examine him for one long moment and would not speak again. Instead he swam round the pool, balancing the ball on his beak, acting like a dumb seal. After a few more minutes, the man called his child to leave.

His boy waved at Junior and called out.—Bye bye.

* * *

After this, more scientists visited. One would drop by every few days. Like Fred, these first visitors were on vacation with their families. Probably Blum, Tibbet and Eh were telling others about the research, about the results. The scientists would call up, asking if they could drop by. Arriving, each of them seemed already convinced whether this was real or not. Their predetermined attitude surprised Cora, seeming unscientific.

Although their families might walk down to the lagoon to see Mother and Kat, the scientists didn't. They concentrated on Junior.

Each time one of these strangers stepped in the door of the homearium, Junior would examine him for a long moment and seemed somehow to sense what the man's attitude was toward the research. If the man walked in with his eyes wide and his voice excited, Junior would speak enough to make the man gasp, then swim away pleased. If instead the man walked in, staring at Junior from the edge of his eyes, his nostrils flared, Junior would only whistle like some brainless bird.

Having noticed Junior's preference to perform in front of those who were excited to be here, Cora asked that each visiting researcher first be brought into the research center to listen to the recordings and see the spectrograms, so she could have a few minutes to get Junior ready. This way, by the time the man stepped into the homearium, he would have a more open attitude. And seeing that attitude, Junior was more likely to perform.

* * *

One day, a German scientist arrived. After playing the recordings for him, the men ushered him in, flocking around him, eager and grinning. When Blum introduced him, Cora recognized his name from the men's bookshelf. A few days earlier, she'd borrowed one of his books, but hadn't yet started reading it. The back cover showed him, as a much younger man, bottle-feeding a young chimpanzee. The description said he'd worked with animals all over the world. In the flesh, he was surprisingly short, but his eyes were the same brown as Junior's, and they were filled with a quiet sadness.

At the surface, Junior rolled his face through the water for a long moment, considering the man. His blowhole opened once as he exhaled. Then he turned to Cora, ready.

In front of this man, Junior did not squawk or slap water around, the class buffoon. Instead, he was the serious student, enunciating every word with concentration.

He recited the start of the alphabet. He requested the ball. He counted to three.

The best, however, was when she held up the blue square and asked—Talk. What?

Junior replied—Kh-are. Ewww.

Even Cora was surprised. He'd never put an adjective and a noun together before.

The man did not appear surprised. Instead his face filled with pride, as though this was his child's recital, as though he had expected nothing less.

At the end of the presentation, the man inclined his head in respect. She didn't know if the nod was for her or Junior, but both of them watched him as he walked away.

B lum called the local St. Thomas newspaper.
The reporter arrived and spent a while in the research
center talking to the men. When he stepped into the
homearium, he held a glass of what looked like water and ice,
but maybe wasn't since he drank it by sucking it in through his
teeth with a lot of air. He walked around the pool for a while,
photographing her and Junior, and then left.

Blum showed her the newspaper the next day. In the
printed photo, her haircut had grown out enough to look sleek
and daring, her eyes large in her face. She was sitting on the
chair in the middle of the pool, looking at Junior, who had his
beak open (as though he spoke with his mouth). The text mentioned twice that Blum was from Harvard, and the only quotes
were from him.

The next day, a reporter from the *Miami Herald* called to
schedule a visit.

* * *

The famous researcher also sent visitors. Within a week,
two separate groups of scientists appeared, each staying for a
day. This time none of them brought their children or wives.
They flew in just to see this research. Cora knew they were
important people because, showing them around, Blum had
his shirt buttoned up.

The scientists started off inside the research center with

Tibbet showing them the spectrograms and playing the audio, while Blum explained the work. Cora could see Blum through the window, expounding on the work. By the time he led the scientists into the homearium, they all regarded Junior with wide eyes. In response, he performed well in front of them.

These men looked at her in a different way too. She was an under-dressed, under-educated female with a tan that was suspiciously dark, but these distinguished men, the university professors, stood by her pool to watch her work. They watched her with their brows furrowed, not as though she was stupid, but as though she was something they couldn't classify, some new type of life. Any questions they had, they did not ask her, but instead asked Blum, as though she were incapable of speech. She knew better than to answer for Blum, or to use her new vocab and concepts.

He was the researcher, the established scientist, the showman. By standing here and talking, he claimed all the credit. She and Junior were no longer active participants who had worked hard and achieved the results. They were the experiment.

* * *

Each morning Blum started the day by floating for an hour in the isolation tank, followed by yoga on the lawn. He was reading a series of books by Krishnamurti with titles that contained words like *Awakening* or *Freedom*.

At least once a week Blum's pupils seemed very dilated, and he would stare at a coffee cup or a fork or the wall for extended periods, his lips moving.

* * *

Junior mastered several new words each week now. He

learned shapes and colors: *ir-kuh* (circle), *i-guh* (triangle), and *g-een* (green) and *err-ed* (red). He could count to three: *ohn, eww, t-ee*. His effort was clear, the word spoken slowly, each syllable separate. Because she lived with him, observing him closely all day long, she could translate what he said when the men were not sure.

As a reward for his work, she gave him food and rubbed his back and played ball with him. And of course, once a day, she let him rub against the back of her calf. His rubbing was rougher now and took longer, and she had to brace herself against the pool wall. She didn't think anyone standing by the pool, looking down into the water, would know what was happening under- neath. It would look as though he was roughhousing, the exact movements indistinct. However she only allowed him to do this rubbing in the pre-dawn, when the men were not yet awake.

After Junior had finished, she'd lie on the inflatable ring in the deep end, watching the sun come up. Junior would float beside her, examining her human limbs hanging in the water. She'd feel him clicking at her arms and legs, the sonar pinging in her bones. He studied her fingers and toes with the greatest attention. They were so unlike a flipper. He seemed to find every part of her endlessly fascinating.

* * *

One afternoon he made a new humanoid sound.

She'd just finished scrubbing his back gently with her fin- gers. Normally at that point, he would swim to a distant corner of the pool and recover there from the intensity of the sensa- tion. This time, however, he turned and looked her in the eye as his blowhole said—*Khh*.

She wasn't sure why he made this noise, since she hadn't asked him to speak, and this didn't sound like any of the words she'd taught him.

That day, he said the word several more times, his pronunciation gradually changing. *Khh. K-ohh.*

He seemed to expect some sort of reaction, watching her each time he spoke.

Could this be a sound that was just fun to make? Or had he invented a new word? Or was he doing a very bad job of pronouncing one of the words she'd been trying to teach him?

She pointed to different objects around the homearium, the desk, the chair, the shower, and asked him—Khh? Koh?

He did not react when she pointed at any of these objects. He just kept repeating the word, using the same emphasis, waiting for her to understand.—Khh. Khhh-oh.

* * *

He continued to want to play catch with her. She would throw the ball to him, and he would return it by squeezing the ball in his mouth to pop it into the air. Each day, however, it flew a little less far, a bit less energy, so she had to step forward to catch it. The two of them were 4 feet apart, then 3.

So far as she could tell, he did not seem in pain and he still enjoyed this game, insisted on it. And this game was how she got him to practice speaking after he was no longer hungry for more fish. So she continued to play with him, throwing the ball and catching it, while watching him, worried. Animals sometimes acted healthy until they were quite sick.

* * *

K-hh—he said—K-oh. K-rrh.

Several days had passed, and he was impatient at her lack of understanding. He acted as though he was playing charades with someone who was a little slow.

Each time he said the word, she considered the situation.

So far as she could tell, the word was not linked to any particular action or object.

So she began to bring him objects from outside the homearium. She showed him an ear of corn and asked—Koh?

He tilted his head at her.

She showed him an apple core.—Krrh?

He exhaled, perhaps exasperated.

Whatever he was trying to say, he concentrated each time on the pronunciation. The muscles round his blowhole clenching. The word emerged, as visually surprising as a belly button speaking.—Kh-rrh. Kh—orr.

The only common thread she noticed about this word was that he used it when he was happy, when he woke up in the morning or when they were swimming together in the deep end.

She began to wonder if he could have made up this word. If it could be his word for *happiness* or *thank you*.

* * *

The largest town on the island was Charlotte Amalie. After the article in the local paper was published, the mayor of this town arrived one day with his wife and dachshund. Blum led them into the homearium, the dog in the wife's arms. None of them seemed to have considered the wisdom of bringing the dog. Perhaps this was understandable since the animal was plump and half dozing and didn't appear likely to do much aside from snore. Cora felt it was not her place to ask the mayor and the wife to take their pet out of the room.

At first everything seemed O.K. The dog did not appear to notice Junior. Cora showed Junior different shapes, and he said their names. He counted to three.

The problem came when she held up the ball and Junior said—B . . . all.

At that word, the dog's head came up, but she noticed too late, was already throwing the ball.

The dog vaulted out of the wife's arms, a surprisingly athletic move, a small meaty rocket splashing into the water. The wife and mayor screamed, terrified that Junior would eat their pet.

Surfacing, the dog looked quite surprised. It appeared to have limited experience with swimming. It kept throwing its front legs up on top of the water, as though the surface might be a ledge on which it could climb. Flailing this way, it began to sink. Cora waded toward it, but Junior got there faster.

He rose underneath the dog, so it lay on his head, a four-legged toupee. The dog rested there long enough to inhale one big breath, then kicked off, paddling more effectively now to the edge of the pool where the wife scooped it out.

Floating at the surface, Junior considered this next moment with great intensity. He watched the wife and her husband hustle out of the building. Carrying the dog, cooing at it protectively, they exited out the door through which he himself had been carried in three long months ago.

* * *

For the last few days, Tibbet had been analyzing the results of his experiment with Mother and Kat and the matched shapes. He and Cora had been testing them for weeks, Cora showing Kat a geometric shape on one side of the lagoon, and Mother, on the far side of the lagoon, unable to see the shape, asked to tap the matching shape. Watching Mother, Tibbet would snort at each wrong answer, so satisfied, and Mother rolled her face through the water, studying him. Normally the dolphins figured out what was wanted over time, improving gradually. Instead, as the weeks passed, Mother answered correctly less and less often.

Tibbet stepped into the homearium to show Cora the final

analysis of his experiment with Mother and Kat in the lagoon. He was waving the graph in his hand and smiling. Seeing him happy was unusual, so Cora grabbed her hearing glasses and walked with Tibbet onto the lawn to be able to talk without Junior splashing water at them and squawking.

He handed her the graph and announced—I've proved it. They can't do it. They can't communicate.

How do you know?—she asked.

—They answer correctly only 20 percent of the time.

—Sorry. Can you elaborate?

He sighed and said—They have to choose between three objects, right? A square, a triangle and a circle. By random chance, they should have picked the correct object a third of the time: 33 percent. Instead they got just 20 percent right. A coin flip would be more accurate.

Considering this, her eyes glanced up and to the right. She was hesitant.—The results are statistically significant?

—Very.

She spoke slowly, working through the thought.—If the results are significant and not the same as random chance, doesn't that mean something non-random is happening?

He looked so disappointed in her. A math teacher whose pupil had made a simple mistake.—Further research will determine why they are so bad at this. Whatever the reason, it's clear they can't communicate.

He took the graph back and changed the subject.—The *Miami Herald* reporter arrives tomorrow.

She asked—Why is another reporter visiting?

—Blum hopes publicity will create more funding, buy him more time.

—Buy him time? The research could stop?

—Of course. It has to stop sooner or later.

—What will happen then?

Considering this question, Tibbet began to look happy

again.—This place will be shut down. Me, I leave as soon as I can finish this experiment. With luck, I can publish it before the tenure committee meets.

She asked—What about them?

He looked confused.—The committee?

—The dolphins. What happens to them?

It seemed clear he'd never wondered about this before.—I don't know. NASA owns this center, probably the dolphins will be shipped to some other facility.

She was leaning forward, watching his mouth, working to hear exactly what he said.—What would happen to them there?

—They'd be part of whatever research was going on there.

By this point, she'd read through two straight years of the *Annals of Animal Research*. She knew well all that the word, *research*, could encompass. She went very still.

* * *

The *Miami Herald* reporter and photographer arrived and stayed forty minutes. The reporter sat in the research center talking to Blum. He never came into the homearium to look at Junior.

The photographer, however, stepped in the doorway and stopped. His eyes ran over the pool with the hanging furniture and the dolphin, and then he looked her up and down. He had a disbelieving smile.

For the photos, she assumed he'd want Junior to speak. However, he did not care about that. He wanted posed photos. He asked her to stand in the center of the pool and call Junior over, get his head out of the water.

He studied them through the camera, then asked her to jut out her hip. He said—Yah, that's it, honey. Real nice. Now you can do your trick thingie.

She blinked, the electricity of anger running through her veins.—I'll ask him for a palato-alveolar. He's good at that.

It was clear from the silence, the photographer did not know this word.

She said—Talk. Fish.

Ffff-ish—said Junior.

And she stared into the man's camera, her chin up.

In the published photo, it was the intensity of her gaze that caught the eye.

* * *

Junior still wanted to play catch, but with every day that passed, when he popped the ball back to her, it did not fly as far. She had to stand closer and closer in order to catch the ball.

She wasn't sure what was wrong. She ran her hands over his jaw each time before playing the game. So far as she could tell, his jaw was not swollen, and he didn't act as though the area was tender to the touch. And when she threw him the ball, he opened his mouth just as wide as he used to to catch it.

By the end of this week, they were just 2 feet apart, and in spite of this proximity, she had to crouch down to his level, holding out her hands so the ball traveled just a few inches. Over the twenty minutes they played, this distance decreased from 3 inches to 2 to 1. And even with the distance this short, it seemed to take him longer each time to pop the ball back. She waited like a catcher, her hands spread in front of his open mouth, watching him, worried, trying to figure out what was wrong.

And then he simply stopped sending it back, the ball remaining in his mouth.

After thirty seconds, worried his jaw had spasmed, she put her hands on the ball to tug on it. With her hands just starting to pull, she noticed his eyes. They were not narrowed with pain, but wide and focused.

In a flash, she understood. Her hands were between his open jaws. This was the action she had refused to do until now, out of fear of his sharp teeth. At the moment, her right thumb was touching the side of one of his incisors.

She coughed with surprise.

He had planned this. He had made it happen. He'd worked for weeks to get her to this point.

He had played catch with her, throwing the ball shorter and shorter distances, moving her closer and closer, until accustomed to this, she would do what she was doing right now, reach into his open mouth without fear. He'd realized she would feel safe, since she would know with the ball between his teeth, he could not close his mouth and bite her, not even by mistake.

She let go of the ball. She stepped away from him.

She felt a little scared. Unsure who was training whom.

Rubbing against the back of Cora's leg was not the same as having sex with another dolphin. As the novelty wore off, it became less satisfying and took Junior a little longer to finish off each day. Three seconds, four seconds, five. She leaned against the side of the pool to keep her balance, and even then, he sometimes shoved against her so hard she fell over. One day, she narrowly missed hitting her temple against the side of the pool.

So the next morning she tried instead sitting down on the pool stairs, her knees 18 inches under the surface of the water. Sitting, she couldn't be knocked over. He slid on top of her knees, his penis found the satisfying crevice under her bent knee, he rocked back and forth twice, and he was done.

* * *

Blum called her name from the doorway to get her attention.—Cora.

Junior squealed in excitement at this, then pronounced loudly and distinctly that mysterious word he'd been saying— Kh orhh!

The way Junior formed words took concentration. It reminded her of the Little Mermaid walking on land, a painful and technically difficult action. He was not one to waste words. Still he repeated this word with energy and import.— Kh orrh. Khh orrh!

A suspicion entered her mind. She ignored Blum to test out a theory. She pointed at Junior's ball floating in the water.

He said—Bh-all.

She pointed to the fish in her hand.

He raised his head out of the water. He knew where this was going.—Fff-ish.

Slowly she pointed to herself, touching her sternum with two fingers.

Kh orhh—he said, his impatience gone, such happiness, such joy.—Kh orh.

She'd never tried to teach him her name, was not even sure how often he'd heard her name, didn't know how he'd figured out this word referred to her.

He slapped his tail and flippers, so thrilled, water flying. Finally she'd understood. His blowhole winked open and closed.—Kh orrh! Kh orrh!

Blum observed all of this, his eyes bright with power.

* * *

Tibbet mentioned he was going to present the results of his experiment to Blum that afternoon. He seemed excited. She told him she hoped it went well. He said he was sure it would.

Later that day, she heard a loud voice. Looking up, she could see Tibbet standing in the main room next to the table, half yelling and gesturing. She couldn't see who he was addressing, so she rolled off the inflatable raft and stood up in the water. The side of Blum's head and upper body was visible through the window. Unlike Tibbet, he didn't look upset. Instead he was leaning back in a chair and seemed amused, tapping ash off a cigarette. When he spoke it must have been at a normal volume, because she couldn't hear any of it.

Tibbet's face was red and splotchy. He yelled back, baffled.

His mouth movements exaggerated enough for her to lip read; *20 percent!*

Blum said something. He was mostly faced away so she couldn't see the words. From the tilt of his head, it looked like a question. His expression was not unfriendly. His eyebrows raised, he waited for the answer.

In reaction, Tibbet's face tightened, almost in pain. He had no response.

Blum held his hands up, helpless in the face of this. He rose from the chair, said one short sentence, and left the room.

Tibbet stared after him, breathing.

Worried that he would turn and realize she had witnessed this scene, she ducked fast under the water.

* * *

Within two days, Tibbet had come up with a new version of his research into the dolphins' ability to communicate. Cora walked down to watch. There were a few crucial differences. He'd now permanently separated Kat and Mother with an opaque net that ran across the lagoon, keeping Mother on one side of the dock and Kat on the other. This way he felt sure they could not see which geometric shape the other was shown or which shape the other tapped. During the experiment, Tibbet no longer got in the water, but instead sat on the dock, hiding behind a blind so he could not give them unintentional clues about what he wanted. Finally, and perhaps most importantly, he did not give them any food all day long, except when they answered correctly. This way they would be strongly motivated to answer correctly.

Tibbet's wife, Terry/Carrie, didn't come to the research center anymore. Tibbet didn't say anything about this, but with every passing day, he looked more on edge. Before he could leave the research center, he needed to finish this version of the experiment. He needed to show that even when the dolphins were strongly motivated, and when they had no clues from him of what he wanted, they still performed badly on the test. These results would strengthen his research enough for him to publish it. His tenure review was this fall. He ate Tums and rubbed the side of his gut. His gut looked a little bigger than before.

Tibbet sat in the blind and threw the striped triangle on a string over onto Kat's side so only she could see it. Mother couldn't see which shape Kat had been shown or which shape she then tapped. She could see however when a fish was tossed to both of them as a reward.

Mother eyed the answer symbols stapled to the end of the dock and rolled her face through the water. Since this experiment was now the only way they received food, they would get increasingly hungry if they didn't answer right more often, if they didn't answer correctly at least as often as random chance.

Tibbet felt this version of the experiment would result in incontrovertible proof about their ability to communicate. For surely, if they could answer right, they would. Surely, they wouldn't willingly starve themselves.

Mother clapped her beak a few times, thinking. Then, staring at the blind where Tibbet sat, she tapped the white square, the wrong answer, with her fixed smile.

He didn't say how long the experiment would continue, how far he would push it, how hungry he would allow them to get.

* * *

During the Sunday lunches in town, she found herself staring in fascination at the vet's hands. He had fingers and fingernails. He had two legs and dry clothing and a face without a beak. She had been with the dolphins for so long that at night she dreamed of them and of flickering water much more often than she did of humans and dry land.

It was possible that the vet took this staring as interest, and perhaps it was. Either way, one afternoon as they walked back to the research center, he asked if he could kiss her. She was surprised, not that he wanted to, but that he'd asked. Other men, they just kissed, confusing their want with hers, never thinking they might need permission.

In his case, she did want to. He might not be the most handsome man, but he asked about her life. He listened to her and responded to what she'd said, not returning the subject immediately to himself.

So she answered his question by stepping in close and raising her face to his.

The act of kissing him quickly encompassed all her senses, all her attention. She had not been with anyone for so long. His body was lean and young. He didn't smell of cigarettes. She pressed herself against him, leaning into his warmth.

For months, she'd been watching the dolphins, how they touched and had sex. How they rubbed against each other and played. Perhaps this was why, standing on the dusty road in the late afternoon, kissing him, she began to sway gently, moving her torso against his. The feel of his ribs and hips and stomach. If it were up to her to choose, the two of them would take their time and rub every inch of their bodies together, the soles of their feet, the ends of their noses, the tender sides of their fingers. They would treat this moment like a sacred pursuit, the first bite in a fine meal. They would engage in a slow clothed tango. There was no rush. There were no rules. Her breath changing.

But he pulled away, his eyes wide. This was not normal.

His jaw moved around, uncomfortable, clearly a branks inside. Unable to speak about what was wrong with her behavior, he tried to demonstrate the way this was supposed to be done. He put his hand on her breast. There was no subtlety in his hand, no gentle enjoyment. If she had to name an emotion, as strange as it sounded, she'd have to say his hand was full of fear. She figured he was just nervous. Perhaps they could work this out over time.

* * *

Junior got better and better at speaking. He could form a *ppph* and sometimes even a *bbb* sound, spitting the noise out his blowhole with a burst of air. He could roll sideways in the water to burble a watery *mmm*, sounding a little like a sink gurgling the letter deep in its throat.

He still had difficulty with consonants such as N,T, X and K and the difference between the long and short vowels. Each sound tended to emerge with a pause between, a child practicing scales.

When she pointed to herself, Junior would respond—Kh orh.

When she instead pointed at Junior, he would whistle. She did not know if this whistle was his name for himself or if it was some other sound: an exclamation, a question, the dolphin equivalent of exasperation.

She'd lived with him for three months now, longer than she'd lived with anyone but her family. She knew his physical habits and preferences, the sound of him breathing in sleep and how he swallowed his food, the way in the early morning hours he twirled and jumped in the deep end. She fell asleep each night with him sucking on her toe.

She told him all the time she loved him. She felt this love rising in her throat a lot. It was not the love of an owner for a puppy, nor of a trainer for its star animal. She loved him now as a friend, as her roommate.

The two of them worked to keep each other happy in their constrained space, bonded together against the men.

* * *

They still played catch, a game that by now should have been renamed *Take*. She would crouch in front of him and hold the ball out on the flat of her palm. He'd pick it up from her hand with his beak and wait there for her to take it back. He'd hold the ball between his teeth, a guarantee that he could not bite her fingers.

She would place her hands on either side of the ball, letting her fingers brush his gums. He closed his eyes in pleasure. She understood touching the inside of the mouth as the dolphin version of intimacy. Was it some sign of affection or affiliation? A handshake, a hug? Blood brothers? Something more?

One day she dared to run one finger along his grey gums from one side of his mouth to the other, before she took the ball from his mouth. She knew this would make Junior happy. She thought of her vet while she did so, wishing he would comply with her.

Junior was overjoyed. His blowhole exhaled—Kh-orrh.

He shot over to the deep end and jumped and twirled in the air. He squealed and blatted and squawked.

The first sentence she wanted to teach him was—Set me free.

At the moment, what he said instead was—Kh-orrh. Kh-orrh.

One day, Junior took too long, the crevice behind her bent knees not as satisfying as another dolphin's body. Rocking on her knees, he seemed to have forgotten himself in the urgency of the moment. Although his body was mostly in the water, reducing the weight, he was still rocking back and forth. Her whole body was being knocked around, her kidneys slammed into the steps, her tailbone in real pain. Her butt scraped against the concrete.

Hey—she yelled, punching him in the side—Hey!

He continued, too focused to notice.

The image flashed through her mind of her family's farm, Luther the boar rocking away on the mounting bench, her dad crouched down and reaching underneath with his hand and the container.

So she reached down and helped Junior. Her human hand so adept. It took just two motions of her wrist.

Afterwards Junior stared at her surprised and clicked at her hand for some time, examining it. Afterward he recited the alphabet all the way to G.

* * *

Reporters and photographers continued to visit the center. At first they were from Florida newspapers—the *Miami Herald,* the *Orlando Sentinel,* the *Ledger*—but lately more regional magazines and even TV stations had started calling.

The reporters asked Cora questions about what it was like to live in a pool with a dolphin. They did not ask her about the work. They asked her what she made herself for dinner and if she missed spending time with friends and if she was ever scared of the dolphin. She would respond with simple sentences and small words.

Then Blum would step in front of her, and the reporters would ask him about the research. He had his shirt buttoned, his hair brushed, looking like a Harvard professor. He answered the questions, using his large scientific words. The reporters looked big-eyed. Each time he used a word they didn't know, they would assume it meant something important.

And as Blum had predicted, given all the news stories, foundations began to call, interested in the research. On the phone with the grant officers, he stood in the window of the office, glowing with satisfaction, looking out at Cora and Junior, his gestures large, his voice confident.

The grant applications began to arrive one by one in the mail. Eh sat at the typewriter for long hours each day, filling out the paperwork, pecking at the keys, a bottle of white-out next to him. Tibbet told Cora that within three to six months the money would start rolling in. Given the number of applications, Blum would have more money than he could imagine.

And that Tuesday morning, CBS news called. The camera crew would arrive in a week.

* * *

One day, sitting on the lawn beside the homearium, after she had finished reporting to Blum about the day's progress, he asked if she wanted to get high.

Given her hearing and how hard she had to concentrate on words, slang at times confused her. A familiar word but a different meaning. She looked around, searching perhaps for a ladder. Then she understood.—Oh. No, thanks.

Each time he took one of Leary's pills, his pupils got large, and he stared at things that were not there. He reminded her a bit of her grandma after the stroke.

He said—What about Junior? Would he like it?

—What?

—Would Junior like to get high?

She blinked at him in surprise.—Why would you even ask that?

He cocked his head.—It might help him learn faster. Help him break through.

She paused, collecting herself. There was a certain intensity in his face. He was very serious. She spoke in the clearest, shortest sentences she could.—He breathes air. He could get confused about what is air and drown. He could simply forget to breathe.

She said—Do not give him drugs.

She said—Do not do that.

* * *

Any time Tibbet got in the water, Mother and Kat would swim in close in order to sonar his gut. They moved around him, clicking at his belly, eyeing him. They seemed concentrated. They investigated him slowly and gently, not splashing him. This was so different from the way they treated Cora or the other men. It seemed to her that his gut had gotten a little bigger over the last few weeks.

He continued his experiment. From inside the blind, where they couldn't see him, he tossed the white square on the string over the blind on Kat's side so she could see it. Mother, unable to see the shape, was supposed to tap the matching white square on her side. If she did, both Mother and Kat were rewarded with ten fish.

They were given no food anymore other than what they earned through this experiment. Under these circumstances, it seemed logical Mother and Kat would try their best.

If they could select the matching shape at a rate higher than random chance, this would suggest that Kat was communicating the answer.

From behind him on the shore, Cora could watch Tibbet in the blind, running the experiment and recording the results. She saw his intensity from 40 feet away. His head went up at each wrong answer. He would pause, watching Mother for a moment through the observation slot in the blind, before he exhaled and noted the tally on the paper.

Mother raised her head, looking at the opaque blind that he hid behind. Did her sight work the same as human sight? What about her other senses? Could she hear his paused breath, his exhale? Could she smell his happiness at each wrong answer?

Whatever the reason was, her rate of correct answers continued to decline. There were only three choices. She should stumble on the right answer a third of the time. However her rate decreased each day: 16 percent, then 15 percent, then 12 percent. The two of them getting fed less and less. Each day, she got a little worse at the task.

Tibbet watched and noted each answer down. His neat row of tallies, his irrefutable proof. When he left the blind, he would whistle as he grabbed his equipment, his every movement satisfied. Although he was not sure why the correct response rate was so low, he was proving his point, proving Blum wrong. They could not communicate. They really really really could not communicate. The dolphins would bob at the surface, studying him as he walked away.

For several days now, Kat and Mother had been earning a fraction of their normal amount of food. However they didn't seem weak yet, both still played and jumped during the day.

He had not yet said how long his experiment would run, how far he would push this.

* * *

With the photographers, Cora would explain what the research was, so they would know what the photographs should show. One day, a photographer interrupted the point she was making, asking her to pout her lips a bit. She got angry and responded in the cop's voice, with vocabulary she'd learned from the science books. She used the terms *affricates* and *Tursiops* in the same sentence.

The man looked at her confused, wondering if he'd misheard or if she was making words up.

Blum happened to be nearby. He stepped in front, redirecting the men's attention to himself. He had started wearing a pair of sunglasses with large round lenses and white plastic frames. They made him look a little like an owl, wide-eyed and surprised at the world. The visitors would examine this Harvard professor with the sunglasses and wooden necklace. He'd smile, enjoying their reaction as he explained his experiment, rattling off the scientific jargon they expected from him.

At times, however, he'd drop in a different word or two, the kind of words that had been sneaking into his speech over the last few weeks. *Groovy, copasetic. Righteous.*

The reporters would look from him, to her, to Junior. They were not sure how to make sense of any of this.

* * *

She was sitting near the dock, with her hearing glasses, watching Tibbet getting ready to work with Mother and Kat.

She asked him—How long will you continue this experiment?

He said—However long it takes.

She said they needed more food.

Tibbet put another Tums in his mouth, rubbing the side of his gut. He said—They are the ones deciding how much they are fed, not me.

She asked—Have you seen a doctor about your stomachaches?

He turned to her, abruptly furious. Perhaps he was worried and her question scared him, that she had figured out his stomach hurt. Or maybe it was something else: that the reporters were not paying attention to him and his research. Or perhaps it was that his wife had not visited the center in at least two weeks (it was possible she wasn't even on the island anymore). Or maybe it was the tension between the three men who no longer made or ate meals together. Instead, each ate at his desk or in his bedroom with the door closed. These days, the few times Blum and Tibbet addressed each other, they stood far apart, their arms carefully loose at their sides. Their stance reminded her of gunslingers. The conversations were short.

Tibbet's face was flushed, his voice unnecessarily loud. He did not respond to her question about his stomach. He half-yelled—What the hell! Who do you think you are? My god. You aren't a researcher. You have no education or experience.

He said—The reporters come here because you look good in a bathing suit. The photos sell copies.

He said—You are an animal trainer. You should work at Marine World. If you were a man, no reporters would come here at all.

* * *

Then one of the articles, the *Savannah Morning News*, centered not on Blum, but on her. Tibbet was the one to spot the article, and he called her out onto the lawn to hand it to her.

She took it gingerly, uneasy at his expression. The title was "Woman and Dolphin Make Waves." It had a full-length photo and quotes from her. The article mentioned Blum only twice, describing him only as the Harvard scientist who had sponsored her work.

Tibbet drank in her reaction. Around the time she'd finished reading it, Blum walked out onto the lawn curious. Seeing the paper, he held out his hand.

She watched Blum scan the title and the photo, then search for his name in the text. Tibbet watched his reaction, showing his teeth in an almost shark smile.

* * *

Both Mother and Kat hadn't gotten fed much in almost a week. By now, they were moving with less energy, not playing much. They coasted through the water, keeping watch for any fish that might wander into the lagoon from the sluice.

Still when Tibbet came down to the lagoon for his research, they continued to select the wrong answers. The few times they selected the right answer, he'd inhale, then throw them both ten fish. After they gobbled up the fish, they'd return to selecting the wrong answer.

Each day their rate of correct answers decreased, 10 percent of the time, 8 percent. Behind the blind, Tibbet would rock with satisfaction, tallying every answer. The dolphins faced the blind: what could they sense, if anything, of his reaction? Could they hear his heart, his breath, or coughs of satisfaction?

Blum stepped out of the building. He walked over to sit by her on the hill. They were 50 feet from Tibbet, who was busy running the trials, watching the dolphins answer.

He asked in a quiet voice—Why are they answering wrong?

He was looking at her, his eyes focused on her face. His

pupils were not dilated, and he seemed to be genuinely interested in what she would say. So she answered honestly.

She said—You've seen that they show their intelligence
more in front of some of the visitors.

He waited.

She said—It's possible they sense what the visitor thinks. I
think they might show only as much intelligence as the person
believes they have.

Searching his expression, she noticed now how still his eyes
were. These days they tended to rest on an object for a long
time. In this case, on her face. Perhaps she had only wanted to
believe he was listening.

He said—I've been dreaming about them. The dolphins. In
the dream, I think at first they are swimming through black
water. Then I realize they are in outer space.

She was confused.—Outer space?

He nodded.—The two male dolphins.

—Bernie and Junior?

He nodded.—They are swimming around in space. They
move quickly, flying from star to star, so happy. I know in the
dream this is where they come from.

He looked at Junior, who was watching them from the deep
end. Junior did not like Blum. He did not like these daily conversations between Cora and Blum. Junior opened his jaws to
show Blum his sharp teeth while nodding his head vigorously.
She had seen the dolphins make this motion, showing their
teeth, before fighting with one another.

In response, Blum smiled and nodded back at Junior.—See?
They urge me to follow them. I struggle to keep up. I know they
are leading me toward wisdom. They are advanced spirits.

She asked—Advanced what?

Spirits—he said.

He said—I've had the dream for a while now. The dolphins
are leading me into the stars.

She interrupted, spoke clearly and with import. She needed him back on Earth.—Tibbet is not feeding Mother and Kat enough. He is not giving them enough food.

Blum did not respond to this. Instead he continued his parallel monologue.—I think the dolphins might be my spirit guides.

She said, enunciating every word, trying to break through—Tibbet is starving them.

How would we know—he asked—if the species were extraterrestrial in nature?

She continued—They will die.

He said—Open your imagination.

Instead she opened her eyes. She saw his hair was greasy and a little long. He was skinnier than before, his eyes still locked on Junior. She did not know what his eyes saw, only that it was different from what she saw.

She would not get help from him.

* * *

The CBS film crew was scheduled to arrive that afternoon.

So that morning she stepped into the building, the men working at their desks. She told them she would not ask Junior to talk while the CBS crew was here unless Mother and Kat were set free this morning, released into the sea.

Tibbet turned to her, his mouth open. Without Mother and Kat, he would not be able to finish his experiment. Months of his work would be wasted.

She said to Blum—Release them today or the only CBS footage will be of Junior squeaking like a dolphin. He will not say one word.

Tibbet started yelling, all sorts of things, so loud and fast, she could not follow them. She did not try to. He was yelling at Blum, not her.

She said to Blum—You don't need Mother and Kat.

Blum was watching Tibbet. In this moment she could almost see the pressure between the two men, the tension shimmering and electric. She wondered if this was like how the dolphins saw.

Blum did not care about Mother and Kat. He could always capture new dolphins. It was Junior who was the golden animal now. It was Junior in his dreams.

Blum said to her—O.K. Yes. Let's do it.

And in that moment afterward, Tibbet changed, his head went down, he stopped speaking. He turned and left the building. What scared her the most was that he did not move with anger, stamping his feet or slamming the door. No, he was quiet now and dangerous.

So Blum and Eh and Cora were the ones to drag the net through the lagoon to tug Kat onto the beach and then pick her up in the stretcher. With just three of them, they stumbled a bit with the weight, but they managed to lug her along the chute and across the beach into the surf, lowering her somewhat abruptly into the sea. She floated there, as they pulled the stretcher out from under her and stepped away. She eyed them, wondering if this was a trick. One extended moment. Then a wave splashed over her and she shot away, faster than any of them had ever seen her move. She was gone.

A few minutes later, they carried Mother down to the sea. She bolted sooner than Kat had, as soon as her belly touched the water. Her tail caught on the edge of the stretcher and yanked it out of their hands, up into the air. Then she was gone and the empty stretcher landed, with a splash in the waves.

For a long moment, they could not see either of the dolphins. Thirty seconds passed. A minute. Then in the distance, Mother and Kat jumped out of the water, again and again, 10 feet high, 15 feet high, a synchronized watery fireworks of joy.

The men left, but Cora sat there and watched, her mouth twisted, filled with so much.

The two dolphins jumped again and again, within sight of

the shore. Perhaps they were still leaping from joy, or maybe by this point they were jumping into the air to see if the men were carrying Junior down to the sea also. Over the next half an hour, they jumped higher and higher.

* * *

That afternoon in front of the CBS crew, she had Junior speak each of his twenty-three words, as well as recite the alphabet up to the letter G. Blum stood in front of her, expounding on his research.

* * *

The next morning she walked down to the beach. Standing there, she couldn't see Kat or Mother anywhere, but the moment she was in the water, her head submerged, she could hear them. Even at this distance, she recognized their voices. Calling and calling. For their families? For Junior? For her? She listened hard.

At one point she felt the pinging in her bones. One of them examining her. She spun, but could not spot the dolphin anywhere.

After twenty minutes in the water, she walked up the chute and climbed the stairs to the homearium, returning step by step to the pool there.

Over the past few months she had created her role, chosen it, actively built it.

Given her success, Blum would never let Junior go now. He was the miracle animal, Blum's golden ticket.

She waded forward through the pool to Junior. She could never abandon him. Both of them were prisoners now.

E ach Sunday when Cora met the vet in town, he'd watch her approach, his eyes a little helpless. He listened to her, was happy to be with her, brought her gifts, was impressed with what she'd managed with Junior. She'd never been with anyone who was so kind, who seemed to actually care what she thought.

There were just two things that bothered her. When other men were around, he acted insecure. He'd put his hand on her shoulder or hip and try to pull her close. This touch felt wrong. It wasn't about affection, and she would step away.

The second problem was that in bed he moved with a shamed intensity. Each time she tried to slow things down or be playful, to participate in any real way, he'd pull back. His expression was like the reporters' when she stood in the pool in her bikini top and used technical words. A lack of comprehension and a certain unease.

* * *

Junior had trained her to be less scared. He held the ball in his mouth as proof that he could not close his teeth on her hands, even by mistake. She would run her fingers along his gums. This touch seemed so clearly to be important to him.

Afterwards he looked her in the eye and said with labored pronunciation.—K-ohr.

* * *

Standing in the homearium, talking to some reporters from the *New York Post*, Blum stated Junior could pronounce twenty-three words.

Without thinking, she corrected him with the day's updated number.—Twenty-four.

Blum turned to her, his eyes sharp. She was contradicting him in front of the reporters.

She looked back at him. With Junior beside her, she knew her power. Blum could not replace her. Perhaps also, standing in this pool, she was angry. She was unable to abandon Junior, could not leave. Her gaze did not flinch.

Blum noted her reaction.

There was a creaking moment.

Then he smiled. He'd always liked a challenge.

* * *

On Sunday afternoons, walking back to the research center, the vet tended to get more physically affectionate the closer they got to the building. Perhaps it bothered him that she lived there with three other men. This Sunday, on a wide-open beach, a quarter mile from the center, he started kissing her in a serious way.

She did not want to lie down with him here. Someone could step onto the beach at any moment to see them. Also he probably didn't have any rubbers with him. Still she could tell he was feeling insecure and needed some physical declaration of her feelings. So she went for the best option and began to help him with her hands instead.

She concentrated, trying to make this quick. She imagined Blum or Eh appearing through the trees to see this, how they would treat her afterward.

Her vet breathed heavily, while he rocked against her. Perhaps, from among the trees, it would look as though he was only coughing or spasming and she was struggling to hold him up.

And, while her hands worked, she wondered what the definition of sex actually was. For the vet, his fingers tight on her shoulders, his eyes closed, this was clearly sex. For her, nervously surveying the beach and the forest, it was not. So was the act between the two of them sex or not? Perhaps it would depend on whether the person making the determination was looking at her expression or the vet's.

She thought of her dad and the boar. In that case, any witness would need only a moment to feel certain this was not sex, even if the person could see only the boar's expression. Her dad was a middle-aged heavy man hunched down in his faded overalls, his hands and the bottle under the boar. The boar rocked on the mounting bench, grunting, slobber hanging from his mouth. The radio in the barn droned on about the weather. Anyone glancing at this would know this was simply an unfortunate part of being a pig farmer. This was work.

Junior and she, however, would look different. She was young and slender, in a bikini top and bike shorts, her tan dark enough to make her look exotic. A sleek dolphin rocking on her knees, her hand reaching underneath. They wouldn't think of this as part of her job. They wouldn't think of her job at all. They'd stare at this scene surprised, unable to look away. In the flush of their reaction, they might miss her expression, or if they did see it, they would forget it a little more each time they thought of the scene, and they would think of the scene a lot, at the most inopportune times. Over time, their memory would give her a very different expression.

And standing here with her vet, him breathing in her ear, her hands working, trying to speed the process up, she understood what the difference was for herself, between doing this with Junior and doing this with the vet. With her vet, she wished he would do the same to her, not outside on a beach where others might see it, but instead in a room with a door that closed, where she could relax and enjoy it. That he would do it gently and with a certain teasing and ever so slowly.

She assumed there was something wrong with her and this was why she took so long in comparison to him. At times when the two of them were in a room with the door closed, him pumping on top of her in the way he liked, she would start to feel a heat in the distance, a hum moving toward her. But, before it could get closer, he would be finished.

Like now, panting hard, his eyes unfocused, moaning into her hair.

* * *

Since Blum had started taking Leary's pills, he had become more internal, busy thinking his own thoughts. Before he asked a question, he tended to have an answer picked out that he wanted to hear. If she gave a different answer, he had a hard time registering it. At times she would repeat her answer in several ways, trying to get him to understand.

After her next daily progress report, Blum brought up one of his ideas again. He said—With drugs, Junior might have a breakthrough.

She said, enunciating as clearly as she could, as though he was the one with the hearing problem—He might forget to breathe. He might drown.

She'd wondered if it would help if she wrote her words down and mailed them to him. Or perhaps she could try Morse code, or semaphore, or charades.

Blum said—It could open his mind. He might learn faster.

She spoke trying to break through.—If you give him drugs, I will tell the reporters.

His eyes blinked and cleared. This, he heard.

They stared at each other. They had reached a new stage, no longer on the same side.

* * *

She knew she could protect Junior for only so long. She spent time eyeing the distance between the homearium and the open sea. To free him, she'd have to carry him down the hill, the 50 feet or so to the lagoon, then along the chute to the sea. Junior weighed 300 pounds at least. She could not lift him on her own. She imagined a cart that would take his weight and length, but she'd have to heft him into it somehow. And she could not wheel such a cart across the rocks and beach to the sea.

So on Sunday she asked the vet to help her.

In response, he looked sad, as though she was a child asking to visit the moon. He said the center was funded by NASA. Junior was NASA property. It would be a federal crime.

* * *

Tibbet was still at the center. Unable to finish his original research without Kat and Mother, and desperately needing a publication from the summer's work for the tenure committee, he decided to test the limits of Junior's comprehension of language and publish on that.

To test Junior's comprehension, he would bring Cora twenty sentences a day, each a command made of simple words, a sentence Junior had never heard. *Put ball on stove. Carry towel around pool. Hold triangle in mouth.* At these sentences, Junior would regard her for a long moment, clearly wondering why she would ask him to perform such a task. Still, if she said *Please,* he'd generally perform some approximation. He'd pick up the ball, but not put it on the stove. He'd swim around the pool, but without the towel. She did not know if he didn't understand the full sentence or felt his action was good enough, or if, with Tibbet's narrowed eyes watching him, he just didn't want to do it.

Tibbet timed Junior's responses and tallied his actions, walking away taking notes. As soon as he had enough data to write the paper, he would return to the States. Although he still lived at the center, he did not speak to any of them unless he had to.

* * *

One of the new words Junior could say was *Love*. He pronounced it *Ufv*.

He had learned this word from her. She did not know if he understood what the word meant. Unlike the word *raft* or *ball*, she could not ask him to pick *love* up or carry it around the pool.

She dreamed at night he talked to her in long graceful sentences and she was the one who could not understand. Who could not speak back. Who was not smart enough.

* * *

It happened on a beautiful day, sitting on the lawn, the sun warming her back, the lagoon blue and sparkling below. How can one be scared under such circumstances? Why would one be careful?

She had just finished reporting to Blum on the day's progress.

Since she'd threatened to tell on Blum if he gave drugs to Junior, he'd been different with her. He wasn't in his head anymore, thinking his own thoughts. Instead he had become strangely attentive as he asked her questions and watched her reactions. He asked about Junior's health, his speed of learning, her thoughts about why. He seemed almost like he used to be, leaning in close behind his eyes, watching.

Today after asking a variety of questions, he took a sip of his coffee and jerked his chin at Junior in the deep end of the pool.—Poor guy. It must be uncomfortable for him to not get any sex for months.

The question was unexpected. Involuntarily, she coughed, amused.

He locked onto her reaction and asked—What?

Paying attention like this, he seemed able to hear, not just the words she said, but also what she did not say.

Ahh—he said—of course. He's masturbating.

She was silent.

He smiled at her expression.—Come on. It's a perfectly natural act.

He looked around the homearium and asked—What's he rubbing against? The inflatable raft?

He glanced at her to read the answer.

His voice was light, amused.—O.K., that's a yes. What else? The inflatable dolphin?

She could feel the danger, watch it walk closer. Her eyes open like a deer in the headlights, not even blinking.

His eyes considered her face. He could feel her panic and was curious.—Another yes. What about the ball?

She was so very still.

He absorbed this answer, then asked, his voice different— What about you?

A moment. Her world shifted. The before. The after.

Her expression.

He now stated it, no longer a question.—*You.*

His eyes were wide. Humor was gone. He was profoundly shocked.

In the silence afterward, desperate, she made the worst mistake possible. She quoted him.—It is a perfectly natural act.

She saw from his expression the depth of her misunderstanding.

The next morning, it was obvious that Blum had told Tibbet and Eh. She could see this through the window. Each time she glanced over, at least one of them was staring at her. Their expressions distant and flat.

None of them stepped into the homearium to talk to her during the day.

* * *

That afternoon, she walked into the building to try to explain, to tell them the exact action that Junior had been doing on her knees, but they looked horrified. Every word she said made it worse.

* * *

The next day, Tibbet and two reporters were sitting inside the house. The reporters were from the *Washington Post*, and their visit had been scheduled for a week. They sat at the table smoking, examining the spectrograms and looking through the window at her in the tank. The reporters were taking careful notes about everything Tibbet said.

Tibbet's stomach seemed more swollen now. He was in pain perhaps, maybe a bitter taste in his mouth. He was furious about everything here at the research center. He turned to her, his eyes cold, and then back at them, and she saw him say a short sentence.

The reporters' heads rocked, as though something small had hit them in the forehead. Their eyes wide.

They looked from Tibbet to her and back. After a pause, they began asking questions.

Always in the past, when the reporters looked at her, their expressions had been a little confused, trying to understand who she was and how she got to do this work. That confusion was gone now.

They did not take any more notes.

Blum walked through the room a few minutes later. His eyes glassy, his hair long. The sunglasses. His shirt unbuttoned. The reporters considered him.

They left soon afterward.

Tibbet had almost certainly sworn them to secrecy. No faster way to spread the information.

* * *

Over the next week, the reporters who had appointments called and cancelled them, one after the other. The phone rang, clanging and metal, less and less often.

The few times now they got a call from a reporter, Blum would take the call himself. Through the window, Cora could see the joy and hunger in his stance, his voice booming out confident as he answered the questions. Within a minute, however, his face would grow troubled. He'd tap ash off his cigarette while he listened. He'd speak maybe once or twice more, speaking sharply now. Then, he would bark something into the phone and slam the receiver down.

It was possible these reporters were asking different questions. It was possible they came from different magazines.

* * *

In response, the men became almost pre-verbal. They barely spoke to each other, or to her. Blum would only talk to her to demand greater speed from Junior, this creature who pronounced words through his blowhole. Blum wanted clear pronunciation. He wanted sentences.

She pointed out Junior was learning faster than any human baby. After less than six months of exposure to language, he could speak thirty words. From Tibbet's testing (*Put ball on tail, Push raft*), they knew he could comprehend at least 200.

Blum said it was not enough. Not anymore. Junior needed to learn a *lot* faster now.

It was apparent to all of them that the situation was her fault.

* * *

The men stopped answering the phone. She could hear it ringing through the speakers, could watch the men sitting, looking at it and then away.

Sometimes Eh picked it up just an inch, before slamming it down.

T wo long weeks after learning her secret, Blum called her over onto the lawn, outside of the homearium. He held two margaritas, one of which he gave to her. He said he wanted to apologize; he had lost perspective. They should toast their accomplishment.

He held up his glass, said—Together we have managed so much. We've taught a marine mammal to speak English. Astonishing.

They clinked glasses, and, since he drank, she did too. The afternoon was hot, the sun a weight on her back. The salty rim of the glass and the ice-cold drink was surprising. She could understand, in this moment, why the men seemed always to be holding a mixed drink. She took another sip.

He exhaled, looking at the homearium and Junior. He said—Clearly, however, things have changed now. We need to adjust. What is your advice?

So eager for this conversation, she did not study his face, did not let herself wonder at this sudden shift.

She spoke quickly—Once the research is published, it will speak for itself. We need to publish.

He asked—What if the journals have already heard the rumors and won't publish the paper?

She took another sip—We submit to another journal. If we need to, we expand the study. Add a second dolphin. A female. Add another researcher; someone with qualifications. I'll train the person how to do it. It will strengthen the results.

He listened, watching. She talked quickly, trying to persuade him, sketching out the protocols and methodology, the data that would result, how long the study would take and its impact. Since she knew he loved large ideas, she asked what would happen if, during the study, the second dolphin got pregnant. Would two talking dolphins teach the baby to speak? His eyes brightened at this, and she continued. She had never addressed him like this, this long, this impassioned. He did not interrupt, but he did ask occasional questions. He watched, one eyebrow slightly raised.

Near the end of the drink, she looked down, trying to come up with any other idea. There was a pause. She noticed a grass-blade near her foot shimmering. At first she assumed it had some moisture on it, a little water catching the light, but looking more closely, it seemed the whole blade of grass was slightly glowing, almost lit from within. She stared; the luminance had a slight pulse to it. Confused as to what it could be, she scanned the nearby grass. Another grass-blade was glowing a few feet away, and another a little further. She stood up and surveyed the lawn with attention. If she stood very still, she found she could see them everywhere, tiny glowing blades. Dozens of green pulsing stars in the lawn.

It took her a few seconds to understand. Turning back she could see Blum was smiling at her. She looked at the margarita and dropped it on the ground.

Her first fear was for Junior. She worried Blum might have somehow also slipped the drug to him. Junior was in the deep end. She jumped in and swam to him. It looked like he was breathing normally. He did not appear to be drugged. Perhaps she was no longer able to judge. She paused to watch the beauty of the dappled light on the bottom of the deep end.

By the time she got out, the sun was going down. The pool around Junior, she was surprised to see, was filled with writhing snakes. The snakes were talking. She couldn't hear their small breathy voices well enough to know if they were talking to her or to each other. Even in this hallucination, she did not have good hearing.

And while she was struggling to comprehend the snakes' words, time began to shift. It became something she could see. It flowed past her, muddy with moments.

She'd never realized before that time was a river. She suspected this was because its flow was so consistent and she lived deep under the surface, facing directly into the current. Under these circumstances, it was easy to miss the constant slide of it, the weight and press, the slow churn.

Until now, when it came to a gentle stop. The river stilled.

She turned. To the side, she could see the motionless current itself, the frozen turbulence. Turning further, she could see her past.

Curious, she kicked off, floating backward. She arrived at a day long before she was born, her parents courting, her dad clean-shaven and slender, her mom round-faced, nearly as young as she was. Her parents as almost-strangers, holding hands, walking along a dirt road, her mom looking at him from the corner of her eyes, luminous with hope.

So Cora dog-paddled forward, seeing their courtship, then the ramshackle farm. The births of her brothers. Then her.

She paused, watching that last night with her hearing intact, her feverish head on the kitchen table. How small she was, her eight-year-old shoulders, her jug ears, her mom singing at the sink.

She swam on, passing herself wearing the bunny suit in the loud club, weaving through the crowd, a tray of drinks on her shoulder, her expression confused.

Next she saw herself holding her mask and flippers, standing on the beach seeing the chute for the first time, then slowly walking down it to the research center, to the lagoon and the dolphins.

She lingered on this past summer, examining the dolphins, watching them fly through the water. She heard them sing, learned she loved them and this work, that she was good at this. This summer of a life she was meant for.

Once she reached the present, she could see Kat and Mother in the sea. They were in a pod of other dolphins, swimming fast through the dark deep water off the island, hunting fish, watching for sharks. As she approached, they turned to her, surprised. Calling out with joy, they scooted ahead. Of course they knew how to move through this kind of current.

Curious what the future held, she followed. Their sleek children appeared beside them now. Their grandchildren, cutting gracefully through the endless sea. She knew they were showing this future to her as a gift, as a thank-you. They surged on, wanting to show her more.

But unlike them, she was not a natural swimmer. She got tired. Time was tugging on her again, pulling her back to her original spot on the bottom of the river. Only at this point did she realize she hadn't seen Junior yet. She kicked as hard as she could in the direction of the homearium, but did not have enough energy to get there, to find him.

She was pulled back into her body. Back into time. It was dawn, and she was lying on the grass just outside the homearium. Blum was telling her to feel the bliss. Telling her it was a purple flame just above them. Telling her to touch it.

She could not see the purple flame. She could not see pretty much anything given the fact that he was on top of her, but she could hear him saying yes yes, she was touching the joy now. What she was touching was actually his chest, trying to push him off.

She knew Blum considered this sex.

Junior was in the water staring at them. She could feel how much Blum liked that part; his grunts were loud and long.

* * *

That day, Eh was the one to hand her the magazine. A men's magazine of a kind she'd never seen.

The front cover had a drawing of a naked woman arching with joy, her legs around the midsection of a grinning dolphin. The woman had Cora's haircut.

When she looked up from the magazine cover, Eh smiled. Perhaps he had made this happen. Perhaps Tibbet had. Perhaps it had happened on its own. Whatever the circumstances, she thought she would never be able to see a human smile again without thinking of the hatred on his face in this moment.

Thirty-eight

The older she got, the faster time seemed to go. Years, then decades, flew past. She'd lived long enough to time-travel into a new era. Push-button phones, then cordless ones, then everyone walking around with cell phones, talking into them. The speed of the travel tugging at her flesh, loosening the skin on her bones.

Each day Cora walked to the beach to snorkel. She now had hearing aids, remarkably small and powerful. It was strange to hear better now in her sixties than when she was young. Yet, before wading into the water, she'd take them out and leave them on her towel.

Standing in the waves, she pulled on her flippers and mask and dove in. She kicked forward, listening, as she had when she was young. She heard the roar of the waves, the clicks of rocks tumbling.

* * *

In the aftermath of the scandal, she'd married her vet. What else remained for her?

They had sex once a week, Sunday mornings before breakfast. It took fifteen minutes and involved primarily the missionary position. When she once asked if they could vary this a bit, he sat up in bed and looked away. His face held discomfort. Perhaps things could have been different, if not for that magazine cover. It haunted him. She'd tried once to tell him what had actually occurred, but he'd gotten very angry (one of the few times) and told her never to mention Junior or that summer again.

She felt fortunate he wanted to be with her at all. He was kind to her in other ways, listening to her about her day, smiling at her with his eyes helpless.

After the magazine cover, the research center was closed and put up for sale. In spite of the beach and the lagoon, no one wanted the infamous building. The price went lower and lower until her vet put a down payment on it, saying they might as well benefit in some way.

Before they moved in, he demolished the homearium using a sledgehammer and single-minded energy. The walls, the pool. Perhaps this demolition was his real reason for buying the place. He erased it all, filled in the deep end of the pool with dirt and rebuilt the flagstone deck. He said the building looked better this way.

After that, there was no sign she'd ever lived with a dolphin, ever taught him to speak.

They both hoped her pregnancy would bring them happiness.

* * *

She kicked forward, heading to the far end of the bay. There was a coral reef there where she liked to snorkel. She was still a strong swimmer. Her fins churned through the water. She listened to the hissing static of the ocean depths. There was the Martian ray gun *bweep-bweep* of a seal.

The seal appeared 30 feet below in the clear water, looking up at her with big cat eyes, then it shot away.

* * *

Seven months pregnant, she learned what had happened.

Tibbet had been the one to write to her. She didn't know if he'd done this out of kindness. He was undergoing chemotherapy at the time. Opening the envelope, she stopped for a moment to rub the side of her stomach, a little like he used to. When standing, she could no longer see her toes, and there seemed always to be movement churning inside her. At the birth, she'd find out she was carrying twins. Ned and Rachel.

She read the letter there in the hall. Three short sentences.

There was a kick in her gut. This life inside her was what kept her going.

She withdrew cash from the bank and boarded the next flight to Orlando, to the NASA research lab where it had happened. She did not tell her vet before she left.

What had she expected to learn?

She arrived in her maternity dress, at the lab's gate. The guard said she needed an appointment, a name. She was crying. She did not know the names of the researchers involved. She had not considered how to persuade anyone. She'd never imagined she might not have the right to see, to hear, to know.

She said she used to work with him, the dolphin who had died.

With these words, the guard jerked back, realizing who she was. For some reason, he seemed most alarmed by her belly, kept staring at it.

He didn't open the gate. He did not tell her what had happened, if Junior had suffered. He would not talk to her anymore.

* * *

In the deeper ocean, approaching the coral reef, the sounds changed. Crabs' claws scrambling, the alien whirr and pop of fish.

Once in a while, when swimming, she'd hear the clicking or

squealing of dolphins in the distance. She'd close her eyes and concentrate on the sound.

* * *

After Tibbet's letter, there was a month she preferred not to remember. She wasn't eating much, couldn't stop sleeping. Awoken, she would blink, wondering why she wasn't in the pool. Then it would all rush back. Her skin felt thin, the world removed, crystalline and unreal.

One morning, she spotted a short article in a magazine about Blum. Harvard had put him on a leave of absence, but the University of North Carolina had signed him as a guest lecturer.

The article called him controversial, but did not mention the scandal. Instead the piece stated he was performing valuable research with dolphins. She noted that preposition (research *with,* not research *on*). She imagined several Kats and Juniors in a small cement tank, circling and circling, waiting for their turn on the operating table.

Her fury saved her. Blum was given new dolphins to experiment on while she was left crying outside the gate, not allowed even to see where Junior had died. She drafted and redrafted a letter to Blum, twelve versions before she found the right argument. She hadn't been so awake in weeks. Her first paragraph started with formal scientific vocabulary, the type she had not used much with Blum. She pointed out the large furrowed cerebellum, the likely attendant intelligence and consciousness. Her concluding paragraph used his drug words. She said he was experimenting on his guardians without pain relief. He was killing his spirit guides. The letter was eloquent in a way that surprised her.

She copied the final version in her best hand and mailed it. Afterward she ate a triple-decker sandwich and two apples. She found she was famished.

She wrote a second letter to him the next week, and a third the week after. She drafted each letter for days before mailing the final version, one a week. Each letter a reasoned careful argument designed for him in particular, using both science and emotion. The letters gave her a purpose, a channel for her grief. In them, she said what she believed in the most persuasive way she could.

* * *

She could see the coral now in the distance, a multicolored hill rising out of the sand. Fish and fronds swaying. The water dappled and shadowy. Life congregated here. She could snorkel and dive, peering through the coral, glimpsing the fish.

* * *

Being hard of hearing made having twins more difficult. Several times each night, she would jerk out of sleep and run down the hall to the babies' room, wobbling with exhaustion, afraid they might have been crying and she hadn't heard. She imagined harm coming to them when she was not there.

So, by midnight, she'd end up on a quilt on the floor between their cribs, the babies in her arms. This was the only way she could sleep deeply, holding the babies, their solid weight on her chest, their warm exhales against her cheek. She knew this way they were safe.

Feeding them, burping them, rocking them to sleep again and again. Years of sleep deprivation.

She felt wordless and dumb, a heavy nursing cow staggering around, so tired. The auditory hallucinations returned.

The TV mumbling. A weatherman pointing to a map, his mouth moving.—Fff-ishhh.

The sink faucet squeaking on and saying—Kohr. Kohr.

At times, feeding the babies or walking them up and down

the driveway in the pram or lugging groceries into the house, she had what she thought of as a drug flashback. It was triggered most often when she smelled the sea. She did not have to be asleep.

The flashbacks were vivid. Sometimes, she would sit down fast, holding the babies close, scared she would get confused and drop them.

The visions were of that summer. They were not indistinct and confused like dreams. She could see and hear them. The sounds, especially, so intense and clear.

These dreams felt as though she was awake, as though she was happy. She carried that happiness inside of her for as long as she could through the day.

* * *

She dove and kicked forward, twisting around the coral, watching the seaweed sway, listening to the hoosh of the waves on the coral above. The strange chirping of unknown creatures.

A school of blue runners appeared, their silver bellies flickering, stretching out in a line and then bunching up into a ball, a single organism made of many shimmering bodies.

She came up for a breath, then dove again. She never knew what she might see.

* * *

Even during her sleep deprivation and hallucinations, she continued the weekly letters to Blum. She got books out of the library, about dolphins and cetaceans and brain research, about spirit guides and portals and meditation. She also read every one of his books, both his older science books and his newer spiritual ones. She used his ideas to leverage her message, to get him to stop hurting the dolphins. She checked each word for spelling and usage. Something good had to come from what had happened.

He never wrote back. She wasn't certain he even opened the letters.

Then, one day, in the third year of her letter writing, the librarian (who had seen her check out book after book on Blum), handed her the news story about him releasing his dolphins, by that point all fourteen of them, into the sea, setting them free. Of course he did it with publicity, with reporters there. The article was laudatory, and she soon found other stories and interviews, all of them writing about this kind, giving man. This gentle professor with diplomas and published books and brilliant ideas, this man who refused to do harm. He told them he would not experiment on these sentient beings anymore, these beings with consciousness. That it was time for the world to move past this cruelty. She xeroxed every story she could find and kept the clippings in an envelope in the laundry room where her vet would never find them. She read and reread them. They helped the grief recede.

* * *

Swimming always made her think about time, that fluid that her senses and her brain could not comprehend. She'd recently read a book by a physicist who called time an illusion, who stated that the past still existed, as solid as a ball that had floated out of reach. She knew this to be true, the different eras in her life, the people she'd loved, the times she'd been most alive, all of it drifting away. Her inability to perceive the past was a failure of her senses, a deafness to time, an inability to swim through the current.

She watched a nurse shark on the seafloor, finning lazily forward.

* * *

Her letters did not stop. She might not have fame, but Blum increasingly did.

His articles and books and speeches gradually changed. He talked more and more about the intelligence of dolphins and whales, their right to exist, the cruelty of human's experiments and hunting. In 1975, he released an album with music interlaced with the songs of dolphins and whales. He asked people to listen with their souls, to hear what was being said. The record was discussed on talk shows. Each year he grew a little skinnier and more birdlike. Turning the channel, she'd occasionally stumble upon him talking with a host, Blum slouching on a couch wearing sunglasses and a necklace. He gave talks around the world, in nation after nation. Bit by bit, he convinced people to stop hunting cetaceans. With all his weaknesses, he did this one great thing, working at it over decades.

The international moratorium on whale and dolphin hunting was passed in 1986. The killing of cetaceans worldwide cut dramatically. She read every article she could find.

She wrote one last letter, thanking him.

* * *

She was watching a cuttlefish pulse leisurely around the coral. Its big eyes spotted her, and it shot away, a fleshy bullet with legs.

Under the water she remembered the solidity of time, the way it was something she could move through if she could concentrate enough. She felt the past there, just out of reach. She could get there if she could only swim fast enough in the right direction.

As the cuttlefish disappeared into a crevice, she realized

she'd stayed underwater too long, forgetting to breathe. She looked around, dreamlike and lost. Her lungs straining. She kicked toward the surface.

* * *

With her kids grown up and her letters to Blum finished, she had more time, and so, at forty-three, she went to college, taking her classes by correspondence. She studied marine mammals, of course. It was a surprise to receive good grades.

Junior year, she heard about a scientist who chose not to study captive dolphins, but to instead observe them in the wild. Since no human could follow the dolphins, keeping up with them in the water, the scientist waited for them to come to her. She anchored her boat in the same shallow waters off Bermuda, day after day, every summer, waiting for the dolphins to visit. As soon as any were visible, she would slip into the water. She would not approach them or chase them, but instead would play with a toy in hopes of attracting them. It was their choice to spend time with her. She found that the most attractive toy was a simple scarf. Dragged through the water, it moved and rippled, could be played with in so many ways. The dolphins would approach and watch her playing. Once they trusted her, they would move close. Accepting her, they would go about their lives near her, letting her observe sometimes for hours.

The scientist made a series of important observations over the years, including about their social structure and methods of communication. She realized each dolphin had a key signature, a unique whistle that a dolphin used in its songs, that others would use when nearby. This whistle potentially was what some people would call a name.

For her college thesis, Cora applied for a month-long internship with the scientist. On the application, she used her married name and did not describe her past experience. Even decades later, dolphin researchers still talked about the scandal.

Her internship was in June. The scientist and her researchers, as well as five interns including Cora, boarded the ship. On this trip, the researchers were excited because they'd created an underwater keyboard that could play back the key signatures of the twenty dolphins who visited most frequently. The researchers would try the keyboard with the dolphins for the first time to see how they reacted.

They anchored the boat at the normal spot. A team of four was assigned to each watch. As soon as any of them saw dolphins cutting through the water, the team would grab the keyboard and some scarves and jump into the sea.

The first time Cora dove in, she felt such joy seeing the dolphins approach, at least thirty of them. She thought of Mother and Kat and their children and grandchildren, imagined them moving through the water like this, so curious and strong.

The dolphins had no fear of the researchers. They circled the main scientist, squealing with pleasure.

The first day, the researchers couldn't use the keyboard because the group of dolphins visiting did not include any of the twenty dolphins whose names were programmed into the keyboard. Each time a new group of dolphins came by, the team on watch dove in. It was eight days before one of the twenty dolphins visited, a male with a white-tipped dorsal fin. However, when they pressed the key to play his signature, no sound came from the device. Back on the boat, they took the keyboard apart and found it full of seawater. They installed new electronics but, a few days later, some of those circuits failed so they had to re-solder them. The device was clearly a prototype.

Each time she was given a turn in the water, Cora did not kick aggressively toward the dolphins like some of the interns did. Instead she simply played with a scarf. The dolphins would swim closer to her than the others, watching, would take the scarf from her when she held it out. The researchers noticed the dolphins' preference. They selected her to be on the dive team more often.

Thus, the day the keyboard worked, she happened to be in the water.

The dolphin, Snowflake, had a speckled beak and a divot in her right fluke. She had taken the offered scarf from Cora and was swimming away with it, moving quickly. This was the moment when the researcher with the keyboard pressed a key, playing Snowflake's name. The keyboard worked. They all heard it. A rising pitch with a trill.

Snowflake jerked around, so fast she skidded sideways through the water, staring at the humans, as startled as if a dog had spoken.

* * *

Cora was just a few feet from the surface now, kicking upward, her lungs straining.

Perhaps sometimes she stayed too long underwater, forgetting to breathe, a bit hypoxic, because she knew then she would feel the presence of those other eras, the solidity of the past. Under these circumstances, her ears ringing, lights flickering in the corners of her eyes, she could sense the past here with her.

Her hand almost at the surface now, she knew she could close her eyes and hold the twins close again, wrapped in the quilt on the floor, their warm baby bodies tight to her chest, their breath on her face.

She could close her eyes and see Junior in the pool, looking at her. Her looking at him. She could hear him, speaking to her. *Kohr.*

Love, eternal.

In 1965, a Young Woman Lived in Isolation with a Male Dolphin in the Name of Science. It Got Weird.
National Post, June 6, 2014

From outside it looked like another spacious Virgin Islands villa with a spiral staircase twisting up to a sunny balcony overlooking the Caribbean Sea. But Dolphin Point Laboratory on the island of St. Thomas was part of a unique Washington-funded research institute run by Dr. John C. Lilly, the wackiest and most polarizing figure in marine science history . . .

For ten weeks, from June to August 1965, the St. Thomas research centre became the site of Lilly's most notorious and highly criticized experiment, when his young assistant, Margaret Howe, volunteered to live in confinement with Peter, a bottlenose dolphin. The dolphin house was flooded with water and redesigned for a specific purpose: to allow the 23-year-old Howe and the dolphin to live, sleep, eat, wash and play intimately together. The objective of the experiment was to see whether a dolphin could be taught human speech—a hypothesis that Lilly, in 1960, predicted could be a reality "within a decade or two." . . .

Author's Note

Since childhood, I have been most awake when I'm around animals. When I write about them, my stories come alive. So over the years, I've learned to accept the subject I've been given.

In an attempt to make this obsession interesting to you, I make sure there is a strong plot, the possibility of violence and a touch of sex. I write every word with all the honesty I can muster.

I first read about Margaret Howe and the dolphin Peter in my teens. The story was riveting, but, even then, I noticed how much was missing and how little comment was made about the essential tragedy of it. This novel retells the basic events but with fictional characters. For instance, so far as I know, Margaret Howe is not hearing impaired, did not marry a vet and does not have any Seminole ancestors.

If you are curious about what actually happened, I recommend the Radiolab podcast, *Home Is Where Your Dolphin Is*, as well as some of John Lilly's books listed below.

The male characters in this book are not the nicest men. I made them this way to heighten the plot and Cora's isolation.

However, this is also how I remember many men acting in the 1960s and '70s. In the 50 years since then, much has changed—what a man can say to a woman on the street, at home or at the office. Through the work of so many people, the Overton window of acceptable behavior has shifted.

As much as I could, the actions of the dolphins in this book are accurate to the capabilities of the species. Below are some notes on that.

ACCURACIES ABOUT DOLPHINS:
- While John Lilly was operating on one of the dolphins, it imitated the sounds of the people speaking around it. This was what inspired Lilly to try to teach the dolphins to speak English.
- When Margaret Howe and the dolphin Peter lived together, he would nurse on her toes each night to go to sleep.
- The scene in this novel when Junior knocks Cora unconscious and then holds her head out of the water so she can breathe is based on an experience of Ric O'Barry's. He was the trainer of the four dolphins who portrayed Flipper in the television show. When working with the dolphins, he once punched one of them. The dolphin hit him back, knocking him unconscious, then pushed Ric onto the shore far enough to breathe until he woke up.
- Margaret was afraid of Peter's teeth. He trained her to get over that fear by playing catch and throwing the ball less and less far each time, until she had to put her hand in his mouth to take the ball away.
- Peter did learn to speak part of the alphabet and a recognizable version of Margaret's name. To make the sounds, he would roll his blowhole in and out of the water. He would practice the sounds for hours in front of a mirror, trying to

get the sounds right. Radiolab has an episode, *Home Is Where Your Dolphin Is*, with the recordings of Peter's vocalizations. It's amazing. He did not become quite as proficient at speaking as I show in this book.
* Unlike humans and almost all other animals, dolphins have voluntary breathing. In captivity, they will sometimes simply stop breathing and die. Some experts believe it is suicide.

INACCURACIES ABOUT DOLPHINS:
* So far as I know newly caught dolphins are not too polite to take fish from humans.
* Dolphins eat squid. It's one of their favorite foods. They don't just play with them.
* I don't know of any dolphin figuring out how to lower a gate, but dolphins in captivity have blocked pool filters to back up the water.
* The first researchers to publish that dolphins can recognize themselves in mirrors are Diana Reiss and Lori Marino in 2001, not Margaret Howe in the 1960s.
* Dr. Denise Herzing's research team did create a device to play the dolphin's key whistles back to them. Margaret Howe was not involved with this research. Dr. Herzing's research is still ongoing. She has a TED talk called "Could We Speak the Language of Dolphins?" She has a foundation, the *Wild Dolphin Project*, that funds this research. I am a monthly supporter.

PARTIAL BIBLIOGRAPHY
* *The Girl Who Talked to Dolphins*, BBC
* *John Lilly. So Far-*, John C. Lilly & Francis Jeffrey
* *Man and Dolphin*, John C. Lilly
* *The Center of the Cyclone*, John C. Lilly

- *Communication between Man and Dolphin*, John C. Lilly
- *Lilly on Dolphins*, John C. Lilly
- *Between Species: Celebrating the Dolphin-Human Bond*, Toni Frohoff & Brenda Peterson, editors
- *Behind the Dolphin Smile*, Richard O'Barry
- *Alex & Me*, Irene M. Pepperberg
- *The Wild Dolphin Project*, Denise L. Herzing
- *Dolphin Diaries*, Denise L. Herzing
- *Dolphin Communication and Cognition*, Denise L. Herzing & Christine Johnson, editors
- *The Dolphin in the Mirror*, Diana Reiss
- *Voices in the Ocean*, Susan Casey
- *Dolphin Mysteries*, Kathleen M. Dudzinski & Toni Frohoff
- *The Diary of Abraham Ulrikab*, Hartmut Lutz, head translator and editor
- *Sound*, Bella Bathus
- *Mean Little Deaf Queer*, Terry Galloway
- *Dark Pines*, Will Dean

Audrey Schulman is the author of five previous novels, including *Three Weeks in December* and the Neukom Literary Award- and Philip K. Dick Award-winning *Theory of Bastards*, both published by Europa Editions. Her work has been translated into eleven languages. Born in Montreal, Schulman lives in Cambridge, Massachusetts, where she co-runs a not-for-profit energy efficiency organization.